DISCO

DISCO

MIKE BARON

WISE WOLF
BOOKS

WISE WOLF BOOKS
An Imprint of Wolfpack Publishing
wisewolfbooks.com
1707 E. Diana Street
Tampa, FL 33610

Paperback ISBN 978-1-968733-28-5
eBook ISBN 978-1-968733-27-8

DISCO

CHAPTER ONE
NATE'S BAIT

DONNIE WAITS CROUCHED BY THE REAR BUMPER OF RALPH Speece's pickup, cradling a baggie of pot to his chest and listening to his mother and Ralph go at it through the open windows of their second-floor apartment. The four-unit apartment building sat on the outskirts of Gunderson, Wisconsin, a nowhere burg to which they'd moved three weeks ago when Kate got a job as executive secretary to Frank Werner, CEO of Werner's Meats. The redbrick building was plunked down at the edge of a cornfield across the street from a farm. Its nearest neighbor was a tire wholesaler a quarter mile toward town. Donnie wondered why a developer would build in such a spot.

"You don't tell me what to do!" Ralph was raging inside. He was a cut telephone lineman Kate had met at the gym, the latest in a long line of losers.

Donnie heard Kate talking low and intensely, the word "marijuana" rising in volume. Ralph had promised not to bring marijuana into the house or smoke anywhere around them lest Donnie find out. Too late for that. Ralph had offered Donnie a toke the first time they were alone.

Donnie felt bad about swiping the baggie from Ralph's truck, but Ralph should have listened to Kate. The argument escalated. A door slammed. Kate was giving Ralph the heave-ho, as she had so many others. Kate was destined to go through life being disappointed by men, and that included Donnie.

Donnie ran for the cornfield and had reached the back of the apartment building before Ralph emerged. He heard Ralph start the truck and peel out, with a rooster tail of gravel striking the dumpster. He'd be pissed when he found his reefer gone.

Donnie was seventeen, facing down the gun barrel of senior year at Gunderson High, the third high school he'd attended in as many years. Maybe this time Kate would like the job. Maybe this time they could settle down. Donnie whizzed through the corn stalks feeling the swish of silk and leaf on his cheeks and bare arms, smelling the rich, almost overpowering scent of ripe corn. It was a flawless hot blue day near the end of August. Next week he would undergo his annual ordeal, registering at a new school.

But today was his to get high and dream about becoming a millionaire rap star. Or maybe a country singer. He didn't really like rap, but it seemed like a pretty surefire way to fame and fortune. Just spittin' rhymes, and he'd always been good with words.

Or maybe he would draw comics.

Donnie burst through the far end of the field, where a sagging barbed wire fence separated the cornfield from Johnson's Creek, which meandered east-west through town. Donnie loved the creek. It was peaceful there, cool in the shade of ancient oak and cottonwood.

He sat on a flat rock by the sandy bank, pulled out the baggie and some Zig-Zag rolling papers. Someone told him Jesus had smoked pot and if he doubted it, all he had to do was look at the image on a package of Zig-Zags.

With nothing to roll on, he took off his Grendel T-shirt, stretched it flat across his knees and rolled on that to produce a fat doobie. He put his shirt back on and felt his pockets. Oh no. No lighter, no matches. How could he have been so stupid! He thought of sneaking back to the apartment, but Kate would be there seething and loaded for Cape buffalo.

The closest source of fire was Nate's Bait and Tackle, a ramshackle general store at Bateman's Landing where County Road HR ended. Nate was an amiable drunk who'd taken a liking to the young man, and taught him how to tie a fishing fly. Donnie had last encountered Nate passed out behind his own counter, TV blaring. It would have been the perfect opportunity to clean out the cash register and make off with several bottles of gin. Instead, Donnie had somehow manhandled Nate into his bed in the back room, closed the store and sat with him until he came around.

There was a black-and-white photo on Nate's wall of him and some Army buddies in Nam. Some of those kids looked as young as Donnie.

Nate's was on the other side of the creek through a pasture. Donnie found a spot where steppingstones allowed him to cross without getting wet. He gingerly climbed over the barbed wire separating the pasture from the creek and headed diagonally toward the bait shop. Maybe Nate would lend him his little aluminum skiff.

Donnie looked around. The pasture was empty, but

he stepped carefully to avoid the cow pies. He caught a hint of wood smoke, loving the day.

"Hey!" someone shouted. "Hey, kid!"

Donnie froze. Busted? By whom? For what? He turned and saw a man in a ball cap, overalls and a beard gesturing from fifty yards away at the fence.

The man pumped his arm. "Get the hell out of there!"

An explosive snort sounded from alder and gorse down by the creek. Donnie turned.

A black bull pawed the ground, staring at him with the gravity of a small planet.

Oh shit!

Donnie took off. He was quick enough to make the track team and poured every ounce of energy into the rush, feeling the squish of fresh cow pies beneath his feet as he pounded for the fence, the bull's hoofbeats sending shock waves through the ground. Donnie ran, limbs pumping, lungs wheezing as the beats got louder.

Donnie had no idea how he got over the fence. He had no memory of leaping, only landing and rolling, twigs digging into his flesh until he came up against a tree and looked back to where the bull had pulled up and was now peacefully cropping grass.

Groaning, he examined himself: ripped jeans, scraped elbows, a little blood. He swatted his pockets. Still had the baggie and the doobie. Donnie got to his feet and confronted the now sedate bull.

"You're a real asshole, you know that?"

The bull fixed him with one brown eye and slowly chewed. Donnie turned and made his way through the forest to Nate's Bait.

CHAPTER TWO
MEAT FROM THE SKY

NATE DIXON SAT ON HIS FRONT PORCH NEXT TO THE ICE cooler, feet up on the rail, bagged bourbon in hand.

"Look what the dog dragged in," he said as Donnie approached. "What happened to you? Fall out of a tree?"

Donnie gestured. "Hey, you know that farmer through the woods?"

"Hallahan? What about him?"

"He's got one pissed-off bull."

Nate laughed until he wheezed and coughed. "Yeah, old Andronicus don't take to trespassers." He proffered the bagged bottle. "Come on up here, youngblood. Have a snort."

Donnie climbed the three wooden steps and plonked down on a white plastic lawn chair. "No thanks, Nate. But I'll take a Coke if you can carry me till the end of the week."

"Help yourself."

Nate smelled of booze, body odor and cigarettes. He wore a Muddy Waters T-shirt and was the color of an old saddle, with a fringe of steel-gray hair around the back of his head. Inside the little shop Donnie opened the cooler, snagged a plastic bottle of Coke and went back on the porch. He sat in the chair and twisted off the cap, drinking deeply, Adam's apple bobbing. He smelled the creek, wood smoke, Nate and old leaves. Good to be alive.

"Whatchall doin' here?" Nate said. "Ain't it dinnertime?"

"Kate had a fight with her boyfriend. Ex-boyfriend, I hope. I decided to get away from the war zone."

Nate tipped the bottle to his lips. "I hear that. Fine lookin' as she is, yo mama shouldn't have to put up with lowlifes."

"She sure can pick 'em."

"Aw what the fuck do I know?" Nate growled. He had that smoker's rasp. "I been married three times."

They listened to the breeze through the trees. At 6:00 p.m. the sun was still high in the sky, casting a dappled pattern through the net of trees.

"The two most beautiful sights in the world are sun on trees and a woman's ass. Not necessarily in that order. You got a squeeze?"

Donnie made a guffaw face. "Jeez, Nate! I just got here."

"When I was your age I was hornier'n Bill Clinton. I stroked it so much, I got a merit badge. Lost my virginity to a high-class ho when I was seventeen, and by high-class I mean she dint have no scabies. You lookin' to get laid, we could always go into Milwaukee."

"I am not looking to get laid!" Donnie said, flushing. He only thought about it 90 percent of the time.

"You ain't queer, are ya?"

"Jesus, Nate! No! I'm seventeen!"

"Okay, I'm just sayin'. You need rubbers, advice, you

ask old Nate. I'll give it to you straight, y'know what I'm sayin'?"

He coughed into his fist. A fit of coughing descended on him like a summer squall. Donnie put a hand on his shoulder.

"You okay?"

"It's that damn Agent Orange! I got an appointment at the VA next month."

Donnie thought he saw a drop of blood on Nate's hand.

Nate wiped it on his jeans. "So what happened to your old man?"

"Never knew him. Took off before I was born."

"That's low class. A kid needs a father. Teach him how to be a gentleman. I got a girl by my first, Miss Florence, God damn her soul. Won't let me have a thing to do with her. Told her all sorts of lies."

"How old is she?"

"Must be twenty-fi' by now. Wish I knew then what I know now."

"What's that, Nate?"

"You got to believe in something outside yourself. A man takes care of his kids. A man don't whine."

"Can I borrow the skiff?"

"What for?"

"I want to smoke a joint."

"Well shit! Share that doobie and you can borrow the skiff."

Donnie pulled out the joint and passed it to Nate, who lit it with a bronze Zippo. Aromatic waves of marijuana wafted to the trees. It was the first time Donnie had been stoned in a week, and his head expanded like the Goodyear blimp. The canopy of leaves transformed into an insane moiré pattern that trailed off to infinity. His heart sounded like a kettle-drum in his ears.

Nate coughed and coughed. Finally he stopped. "Ho shit! Did I cop a buzz!"

Donnie had to pee. He remembered the skiff.

"Okay," he said, getting to his feet. "See ya."

Donnie went through the store and visited the head, then out the back door to where the skiff was tied to a wood pier that extended ten feet into the creek. Donnie walked out on the squeaking deck, pulled the boat close with his feet and got in, rocking uncertainly for a minute before he settled down. Whoa. Blitzed. He untied the line and used one of the two yellow plastic oars to shove off from the dock into the middle of the stream.

Fitting the oars into their sockets, he slowly rowed downstream toward town, dipping just enough for a little forward momentum. Bullfrogs chirped from beneath the loamy overhangs through which tree roots grew. Soon he was around the bend and out of sight of the bait shop or any other manmade structure. It was like being in Africa, he thought. Or South America. Maybe he should be an explorer like Christopher Columbus or Henry Morton Stanley.

What did you have to do to become an explorer? He could always join the armed forces and see the world. Problem. Hadn't everything already been explored? Weren't all the wild places used up, mapped out and accessible by guide? He would have to study anthropology, meteorology, geology. Fuck it. Too much work. It was enough to drift beneath the trees and imagine he was all alone in the middle of a dark continent. He wished he had an iPod. He'd been asking Kate for one. His birthday was coming up.

Whenever he asked for things, Kate said, "Get a job."

The only jobs paid minimum wage and were in town. He could always ride his bike, at least until the weather turned. Something to think about. He felt like a slug much of the time and knew he should do more to help Kate. She ragged on him to empty the garbage or put the dishes away. He wished he were a better son.

Maybe if he had a connection, he could make a little money selling weed. A fish plopped, and seconds later gentle ripples rocked the boat. Donnie stretched out on the flat bottom gazing up at the dazzling green lace of the canopy as the little boat drifted gently downriver. He had a vague uneasiness that Kate was looking for him. It was dinnertime, and although they seldom sat together as a family, she was militant about his dinner. He'd turn around in a little while and phone her from Nate's.

That's another thing he needed. A phone.

He closed his eyes and drifted, dreaming about girls, a new Alien Workshop skateboard, his rap career. A shadow crossed his face. He opened his eyes. He had come to a standstill beneath the Arliss Street bridge, a narrow two-lane on the outskirts of town. Faintly, almost subliminally, he heard the thud of bass, each beat louder than the last until NWA's "Gangsta" emerged fully formed from above.

The car had snarling glasspack mufflers that came nowhere near to drowning out the pounding bass as it screeched to a halt on the bridge directly overhead. He heard a car door open, followed by a grunt. Something fell off the bridge and landed in his skiff with a thump.

The car peeled out, tires screeching, bass booming.

Donnie sat up and stared. It was a dirty old pillowcase tied shut with a length of wire. It shifted as if it were alive, and a tiny whine came out. Donnie twisted off the wire, opened the bag, and out spilled a black puppy.

CHAPTER THREE
THE PUP WHO CAME TO DINNER

Donnie reached down and picked it up. The furball was black, short-haired, with a five-inch tail, bulging eyes and beagle ears, the unholy union of a Boston terrier and a woodchuck or a Maine coon cat. The pup shivered and whined, and Donnie brought it close, where it furiously began licking his face.

"Okay, pup. Okay! Jeez!" Laughing, Donnie set the pup in the bottom of the skiff, where it squatted and peed a shallow lake, causing Donnie to scramble backward to the bench at the rear.

Some sorry piece of human debris had tossed the dog into the creek to kill it. Sure enough, there was a brick in the pillowcase. Donnie wished whoever had done it would burn to death.

Well, fuck. Now what was he going to do? He couldn't very well set the pup ashore. It would hardly fare any better. He was stuck with it for the time being. Maybe Nate would take it. Realizing Kate would be frantic by now, he used an old rag to soak up the dog piss, washing it off in the creek. He resumed his position in the center of the skiff and rowed back toward Nate's.

Fighting the current, it took him a half hour, by which time it was seven thirty. He was up the creek now. Kate would be out driving around looking for him. He pulled the boat into Nate's landing, tied it up, grabbed the pup and trotted around to the front. No Nate. Tucking the dog under his arm, he went inside.

"Nate?"

He heard the sawmill from the back room. Somehow Nate had dragged himself inside onto the bed before passing out. It smelled like a distillery filled with dirty laundry. On the wall was a poster of Pam Grier as *Foxy Brown*. Donnie set the pup on the floor. It beelined for the filthy bathroom, standing on its hind legs trying to reach the toilet.

"Okay, okay!" Donnie said, going into the dish-encrusted kitchen, where he filled a plastic bowl with water and set it on the floor. The pup lapped the entire bowl.

Donnie thought about just leaving the dog there. Teach Nate not to pass out. But no, not a good idea. Nate was just as likely to turn the pup out as take care of it. There was no alternative but to take it home until he could give it to the county Humane Society. Or something.

He could always keep it.

The puppy raced around between his ankles, sitting to stare up at him with bulbous eyes, tail wagging.

"Aw fuck," he said, scooping it up. "You're coming with me."

He could hide it in the detached pole barn out back where the landlord kept farm equipment.

It was twilight by the time he emerged from the

cornfield behind the apartment building. The lights in their unit were on, Kate sneaking a cigarette on the balcony, pacing the floor, wondering where the hell he was. He couldn't very well take the dog upstairs. She'd freak.

Donnie let himself into the pole barn, redolent of hay, rubber and machine oil. Light shone dimly through a series of west-facing windows, illuminating a green-and-yellow tractor, a plow, a sit-down mower and stacks of enigmatic machinery. Donnie set the pup down and rummaged around looking for a container, the dog at his heels. He found a three-foot-by-two-foot empty cardboard box, threw in a pile of shop rags, put the puppy inside and set about looking for a bowl. He found an empty plastic food container that he filled from the big shop sink, and set it in with the pup.

He knelt and looked in the dog's big brown eyes. "You just hang for a while. I'll come back later with some food."

The dog plucked at the rags, made a little nest, circled three times and went to sleep. Donnie let himself out of the barn and entered the apartment complex through the back door. Kate could hear him coming up the stairs and was at the top with her arms crossed, mouth a slit.

"Where have you been? Do you know what time it is?"

"Sorry, Ma. I sorta lost track of the time. I was down by the creek."

"Didn't you hear me yelling? The whole neighborhood thinks I'm a fishwife."

"What neighborhood? It's just us, Tom Collins, Mrs. McGillicuddy and Charlie Chan."

"Don't call him that. His name is Mr. Lee. Doing what?"

"Huh?"

"Doing what down by the creek?"

"Nothin'. Is he gone?"

"You mean Ralph?"

"Yeah."

Some of the starch went out of Kate as she turned and headed back toward the apartment. "Yes. He's gone. Come on. I've been keeping your dinner in the oven."

Donnie followed his mother's slumped figure, feeling bad. Like she needed a puppy. She could barely handle him. Donnie wished there was something he could do for her, but he didn't know what. As long as he'd known her, save for rare occasions, Kate seemed disappointed, like a child who'd been promised a pony.

She stopped so abruptly, Donnie ran into her. She turned with fire in her eyes.

"Have you been smoking marijuana?"

Still stoned, Donnie went blotto. "Who? Me? No! Of course not!"

"Don't lie to me, young man! I can smell it on you! You smell awful. Where'd you get it? Did Ralph give it to you?"

"Of course not! I went to see Nate. Maybe he was smoking it."

"Empty your pockets."

"Ma!"

She used The Voice. *"Empty your pockets!"*

Busted. Looking away, Donnie pulled the baggie out of his pocket. Kate snatched it like an eagle.

"Where did you get this?" she hissed.

"I took it from Ralph's truck."

"So, you're not only a dopehead but a thief! Eat your damn dinner and go to your room. I don't want to see you until morning."

CHAPTER FOUR
BUSTED

DONNIE COULDN'T REMEMBER THE MEAL. MEATLOAF, HE thought. He lay belly down on his bed propped up on his elbows reading a *Badger* comic listening to the faint yelps emanating from the barn. He heard Kate tossing and turning in the next room, getting up, going back to bed, turning the TV off and on.

"What the hell is that noise?" she said in a voice verging on hysteria.

Donnie wished he could shrink to BB size and slip down the vent. It wasn't his fault she couldn't sustain a relationship, but he was far from ideal. He knew he caused her unnecessary grief.

The puppy yelped.

Finally, he went into the kitchen, parceled a lump of meatloaf onto a paper plate and was about to head out the door when Kate emerged at the end of the hallway bleary-eyed, clutching a terry cloth robe at the neck.

"What are you doing?"

"I'm going to see what's making that racket. Maybe it's some animal that's trapped in the barn."

"What are you hiding? Show me."

Reluctantly he showed her the paper plate.

"What exactly is going on?"

"It's a puppy, Ma! I found him wandering homeless in the woods. I'll take him to the Humane Society tomorrow."

Kate put her fists on her hips, and her pupils got scary small. "A dog? Are you out of your mind?" she hissed, trying to keep her voice low. "Where are we going to live if they kick us out of here?"

"He'll be gone in the morning. I swear! And I'm going to get a job."

Kate blasted him with withering contempt, but then her mouth softened and she pulled him to her. "I know it's been rough, kiddo. I'm sorry life has been such a mess lately. We're going to settle down here and make a go of it, okay? I'll try to get you that skateboard you want, but it would really help if you got a job."

Donnie was appalled to find himself getting a stiffie. His own mother! Blood flooded his face.

"I'll go into town tomorrow. I'll ride my bike. I'll get a job at the Piggly Wiggly."

"And you'll get rid of the puppy?"

"I swear!"

"It didn't bite you or anything? What if it has rabies?"

"Ma!"

The little dog yipped with metronomic regularity. With a sigh, Kate relinquished her only child and padded back to her room. Donnie shut the door quietly behind him and went down the back stairs. Old lady McGillicuddy's lights were on as he crunched across the gravel surface to the pole barn in the back.

He let himself into the barn and waited a minute for his eyes to adjust to the light. As he approached the cardboard box, the puppy stood on its hind legs, tail wagging, yipping happily.

Donnie got down on his knees. "Hey there, little fella. Brought you some dinner."

Before the plate had even touched bottom, the pup was on it, scarfing the food with stunning rapidity. Donnie reached down and lifted the puppy onto his lap, where it licked him furiously before wriggling free, going off a few paces and squatting to shit.

Donnie used a rag to pick up the crap and dumped it in a dumpster inside the barn, the pup at his heels. They returned to the box, where he sat Indian style, and the pup curled up in his lap and went to sleep. Reluctant to dislodge it, Donnie sat there for a half hour before placing the dog back in its rag nest.

Halfway between barn and block he realized no way was he going to give it up. He planned his defense as he mounted the stairs. It wasn't that Kate was against dogs per se; she just had too much on her plate at the moment. And she was right to fear that the burden of taking care of it would fall on her.

Donnie realized he had to step up. A man had to have a code. In the Middle Ages he would have been a father already. Only in modern America did puberty extend into one's forties. He'd seen it in Kate's boyfriends, man-boys. She went for the hunky blue-collar types and ended up lending them money to fix their cars, buy motorcycles, pay bail, pay off old credit card debts. It was a wonder Kate didn't end up on *Judge Judy*.

Of course Kate had too much class to make a fool of herself in front of millions. The one good thing to come out of this move was her job for Frank Werner. Frank Werner drove a Cadillac STS. He'd taken them out to dinner when they first came to town. Chef Louis' Steak House. It was the only game in town.

Frank was a snappy dresser who looked like an extra from *Goodfellas*. Frank was determined to drag his grandfather's antediluvian sausage factory into the twenty-first century. Kate had been hired in anticipation of a ramping up of Werner's media presence. For the past week her every waking moment had been consumed by meetings with media strategists at the Werner's factory on the other side of town.

Werner's Meats was having an end-of-summer picnic Sunday afternoon. Donnie was dreading it, as he dreaded all social functions, because he had no social skills. Pretty girls paralyzed him, and he never knew what to say to Kate's friends. There was only one item of interest. Werner had told him that his father, Frank Senior, had commissioned a Weenie Wagon from custom car designer George Barris, but it had been decommissioned in the '90s and now occupied a place on the back lot.

Donnie had difficulty envisioning the vehicle. He'd looked up Barris on Kate's computer and learned that Barris had designed the original Batmobile, which was cool. So maybe the Weenie Wagon had a 409 blown Chevy engine or some other righteous mill. It was worth checking out.

In the meantime he mustered a rationale for keeping the dog.

CHAPTER FIVE
MEET THE LOCALS

DONNIE WAS UP WITH THE SUN CHECKING ON THE DOG, which greeted him with the sound of tennis shoes squeaking on linoleum. Donnie gave it the last of the meatloaf. Good thing Kate always made the portions too big. He didn't have more than five bucks and Kate couldn't spare a dime, what with the move and getting her old Camry fixed.

Dog food wasn't free unless you spent all day driving around looking for roadkill.

The only surefire way Donnie knew was gathering bottles and aluminum along the highway or the creek and trading them in at the recycling plant. Paid a nickel a unit. Well, what else did he have to do?

He got a big garbage bag from under the sink and walked up and down Merriman Road picking up discarded cans and bottles. Within an hour he'd filled half the bag, and he wondered about Gunderson's youth. He'd heard them roaring up and down the road last night, music blaring, laughter, the clink of cans hitting the asphalt. As he dragged his booty into the apartment,

Kate came out of her bedroom wearing jeans and a T-shirt.

"What's that?"

"Cans and bottles. I can sell them at the recycling center for five cents apiece."

"I wasn't aware we even had a recycling center."

"Yeah. It's on Truman Street. Can you drive me?"

"I'm sorry, hon, I'm running late. I have breakfast with Kim. Maybe later."

"No sweat," Donnie said. "I'll take my bike."

"Will you please do the dishes? They're piling up."

Donnie sulked, hating himself. "All right."

"Good boy." She planted a kiss on his cheek and was out the door, feed bag swinging.

Donnie hefted his bag of cans and bottles. It weighed about twenty-five pounds and was the size of a bean bag chair. If he strapped it to his back, he might be able to ride his ten-speed Trek the four miles to the recycling center. He heard insistent yipping through the open window over the sink.

Donnie went into the barn and took the dog out.

"Come on," he said.

It followed him across the yard, entered the apartment building and struggled after him up the stairs, laboriously mounting each one. It couldn't have been more than eight weeks old.

"Just don't piss on anything, okay?" he said, eyeing the dog.

The pup grinned happily, squatted and urinated on the tile floor.

"No!" Donnie yelled, seizing the terrified dog and running downstairs and out the back. He put the pup on the lawn.

"Outside, numbnutz! Jeez, it's a good thing Mom isn't home."

The pup grinned and wagged its tail, hindquarters shaking.

"I should call you Twerk," Donnie said, holding the door for the dog.

They returned to the apartment. Donnie turned on the kitchen radio and searched until he found a Milwaukee station playing The Cry! Twerk got up on its tiny hind legs, paws on Donnie's blue jeans, and whined. Donnie filled a bowl with water and set it on the floor. Twerk lapped it up.

Donnie stared in disgust at the food-encrusted dishes piled five deep in the sink. He was supposed to wash the dishes. He hadn't asked for the job; he'd been volunteered. He looked from the dishes to the dog. He set a dinner plate with dried meatloaf on it on the floor. Twerk went to work. Donnie set all the dishes on the floor in a circle around the pup, who went from dish to dish until they all sparkled in the morning sun.

Donnie put the dishes in the cupboard.

"All right, you have to go back in the barn and I have to get this shit to the recycler."

Donnie returned the pup, made sure it had plenty of water, and then he used duct tape and rope to affix the bulky package to his back. He looked like the Hunchback of Notre Dame. When he tried to swing a leg over his bike, the whole thing shifted with a horrendous clatter to one side. It took him fifteen minutes and an entire roll of duct tape to achieve equilibrium. He set off like a Vietnamese chicken farmer on his way to market.

Donnie went everywhere on his flashy red Trek, because he and Kate had not settled anywhere long enough in his teenage years for him to apply for a driver's license. Kate had been too preoccupied with new jobs and new men to teach him to drive, and none of the men—certainly not the most recent loser—had taken much interest in him. Even worse, Kate was reluctant to risk letting a rookie driver take the wheel of their only car. It wasn't as if she could afford a new one if Donnie got into an accident. Gradually, on his own, Donnie had compiled sufficient hours in driver's ed classes at his previous high schools to qualify to take the driver's test here in Gunderson, if only he and Kate could stick it out long enough.

These thoughts haunted Donnie, now burdened with the huge pack obscuring any vision he might have had to the rear, as he kept his head down and pedaled straight ahead, being careful to stay on the gravel shoulder and off the cracked asphalt highway. A truck passed on the way into town, nearly blowing him into the ditch. The slightest cross-breeze would have blown him off course.

Some goobers in a tricked-out Honda whizzed by on the way out of town, leaving a receding trail of Fatboy Slim.

Donnie had 186 cans and bottles in the bag. At a nickel a pop, that came to $9.30. He should be able to get a bag of dog food. It wasn't a big dog. How much could it eat?

He wasn't aware of the Honda's return until death metal exploded five feet behind him. The goobers had snuck up on him. Startled, Donnie went into a wobble, leaning one way and then the other trying to maintain balance until the whole mess slid to the right, pulling him over like an anchor. He crashed ignominiously into the ditch.

The Honda stopped while the three boys inside laughed hysterically.

"Duuuuude! What are you doin'? Hauling trash?"

"He's a rag picker!"

"YOU'RE A BUM!"

Cheeks burning, Donnie ignored them as he extricated himself from the downed bike. He lay in the shallow ditch, unkempt grass sticking up between his wheel spokes. He'd landed on the same shoulder he'd hurt running from the bull, but he gave no sign of his discomfort as he looked at his sack. Good. It hadn't torn.

"Hey, faggot!" one of them screamed. "What's in the bag? Your panties?"

Donnie looked up from where he was sprawled in the grass. Two faces protruded from the Honda's shotgun seat and rear window, both red with laughter. One was buzz-cut, pudgy with a spray of freckles like a brown Milky Way across his nose and cheeks. The other had a spiky purple Mohawk, sunglasses and a nose ring.

"Very funny," Donnie said.

"Huh? What?" belched Mohawk. "Whadja say, faggot?"

Donnie kept his mouth shut as he pulled his bike upright away from the road and leaned it against a fence post. They'd stopped in front of a farm. A car passed, heading out of town, slowing for a minute before speeding up.

Donnie kept his mouth shut as he checked the bag and ropes, trying to figure how he was going to remount it.

"Enough of this," the driver said, putting the car into gear. As it moved off, Donnie saw the license plate: BDAZZ. Yeah, right.

Mohawk fired his Carpathian shot. "Bye, bottle boy!"

Donnie reflexively flipped him the bird.

The car chirped to a stop.

Shit!

The car backed up so fast, Donnie leaped to avoid being struck. The doors opened and out poured the goobers.

Only they weren't goobers. They were so fucking hip, you could puke. Freckles wore a Headburst T with the sleeves cut off. Mohawk's jeans were sliced like a cheese grater, and he wore Doc Martens. The driver, the tallest of the three, with his hair made to look like an onion, wore a Dethrone wife-beater, pants down around his ass, a silver earring and an Elvis sneer.

Mohawk got in Donnie's face. "Did you just flip us the bird, fuckwad?"

"Well yeahhhhh. You ran me off the road."

Mohawk's hand shoved out so fast, Donnie gasped. The blow to his sternum instantly sucked out all his air as he landed hard on his ass in the ditch.

"Oooh," Freckles said. "Lester shoved the little pussy on his ass!"

"Get up, little pussy!" screeched Mohawk. "Get up and fight like a pussy! Oh, look at him. He's gonna cry."

Mohawk reached in his front pocket and removed a balisong, which he flipped open in a well-practiced move. For an instant Donnie feared for his life. They were going to gut him by the side of the road like fresh-caught trout.

Mohawk stepped across the shallow ditch and slashed the garbage bag holding Donnie's booty diagonally, allowing cans and bottles to spill out.

"Shit!" Freckles said. "Those are your Mountain Dews, Lester!"

Mohawk pointed the blade at Donnie. "I see you again, I'm gonna kick your ass."

Onion Head turned and got back in the car, followed by the other two. The front tires chirped as they roared away, trailing laughter and a booming bass.

CHAPTER SIX
GIRL MEETS PUP

BRUISED AND ACHING, DONNIE LEFT THE CANS WHERE they lay and pedaled home. He rode back into the barn, whose roll-up door was open as the farmer who kept his gear there worked his land. And there he was, Arthur Brown, a wizened nut of a man in coveralls and a straw cowboy hat crouched in the straw playing with Twerk.

"Hi, Mr. Brown," Donnie said as he rode up, doing a gliding dismount. "It's just temporary until we can find him a home."

Brown looked up from where he crouched in the straw. "She's a girl, and you can keep her in here so long as she doesn't start chewing on anything important. She's gonna chew; you know that, son. They all chew. You gotta provide her with quality chewables, or she's gonna chew up your shit."

Brown stood and got a better look. "What happened to you?"

"I crashed my bike. I was carrying a load and I fell over."

"Load of what?"

"Cans and bottles. I was gonna sell 'em to pay for dog food."

Brown looked from the dog to Donnie. "Don't that beat all. They still pay for empties?"

"Nickel a can."

"Huh." Brown returned to the tractor, which had a panel up over the engine.

Donnie walked Twerk around the yard until she did her business, then led the way inside. Twerk managed the stairs better, eagerly scrambling from step to step. Kate usually followed breakfast with Kim with a trip to the Goodwill store, sometimes a hop over to the mall in Wauwatosa, where she'd comb T.J. Maxx for bargains. She wouldn't be home for hours.

One thing for sure. No one was going to mess with his pile of cans and bottles. They'd still be there when he went back. He had to devise a better method of transport or wait for Kate to take him. Pup at his heels, he went down into the basement, which contained four separate storage lockers. None were locked. Donnie opened their storage locker and rooted among the unpacked boxes, end tables and rolled-up rugs, discovering a large back-pack Kate must have used in her student hippie days. That's when she met Donnie's father, a cipher about whom she refused to talk.

Donnie never knew his father. It took years to realize what he was missing. As usual, he had to figure it out for himself. He'd seen good fathers and bad. The good ones set an example and offered guidance. Bad fathers some-times did the same thing, but more often they just weren't there.

He took Twerk back to the barn and set out on foot toward his cache of cans. They were as he had left them with a possible addition or two. He got most of the pile into the backpack and two garbage bags and trudged wearily back toward the apartment complex, pack and bags jingling and clinking with every step. He went straight to the barn, shifted out of the pack and checked on Twerk. The pup had curled up in its nest of rags and was sleeping.

Donnie entered the building by the back door and was surprised to find Kate in the kitchen putting away groceries.

"Nice job on the dishes, kiddo," she said. "What have you been doing?"

"Gathering cans."

She turned and looked at him, her mouth forming a small "O." "What happened to you?"

"Ah, I crashed and fell in the ditch. I couldn't carry all that stuff on the bike. Hey, if I could get my driver's license, I could drop you off at work and drive my cans to the recycling center."

It was a tired argument.

"You don't have enough experience. I don't know what we'd do if anything happened to the car. Wait till we can afford one of your own."

"I'm not gonna crash the car, Ma! Jeez! You think I'm some sort of spastic!"

"No, dear, I just think you're young and inexperienced."

"Well how am I supposed to get experience?"

"Get a job to earn money toward your own car, then we'll talk. Is that dog still here?"

"Yeah."

"Well Monday I'll see if I can break away at lunch and we can take it to the Humane Society."

"Ma, I got no car, I got no friends. Let me keep the dog."

"Don't say that, Donnie. You're one of the most personable young men I know. You're new in town, I understand that. I know it's jarring to jump from place to place. Hopefully, we'll find a home here and you'll make new friends in high school. Just give it a chance."

"You wanna see her?"

Kate's eye roll morphed into resignation. "All right. Let's view this spectacular beast."

Hands on hips, Kate took one look at the butt-wagging black ball and sank to her knees. "Oh, isn't he adorable!"

"It's a she. I call her Twerk."

"Anybody who names a dog Twerk shouldn't have one." She picked Twerk up, and it immediately began licking her face. She set it back in the box. "It looks hungry."

"Yeah, I was gonna buy dog food from the money I made with the cans, but I never got there. What have we got she can eat?"

Kate let out a huge sigh. "All right. We'll go to that 7-Eleven near town and get some dog food."

"Can I drive?"

"You never give up, do you, kiddo?"

CHAPTER SEVEN
DARK ENCOUNTER

WERNER'S MEATS WAS AN IMMENSE REDBRICK CUBE ON the southwest edge of town that reminded Donnie of Scrooge McDuck's money bin. As they got out of the car in the employee parking lot, the stench hit them like a tidal wave. Pens out back held several hundred pigs. Frank Werner had gambled on north winds when he set up the party area, and lost.

A large white party tent stood on the acre lawn behind the plant, sheltering six picnic tables and several dozen employees and their kids. A deejay played Bruno Mars. Children squealed as they rode the slide in the inflatable castle, entertained by a hired clown who performed magic tricks. Frank Werner himself in white toque and apron manned one of the long half-barrel barbecue grills, turning Werner's wieners and corn cobs with a pair of tongs.

Kate wore crisp blue jeans and a man's plaid shirt with the sleeves rolled up. Donnie had showered and was wearing fresh blue jeans and a Jellyfish T-shirt. As they made their way to the grill, Kate introduced Donnie to several of her co-workers. Donnie saw how the men looked at his mother.

Frank greeted them with upraised tongs. "Kate! So glad you could make it. Hello, Donnie." He set the tongs down and stuck out his hand.

Donnie shook firmly the way Kate had told him to. "Hello, sir."

"Well Donnie, some of the kids are playing volleyball over there."

Donnie glanced to where a group of kids ranging in age from twelve to late teens, some of them bare-chested, were batting a white volleyball over a net. He'd never been good at team sports. Just running. He got the message and wandered toward the group, hovering on the fringe, studying the players and eavesdropping. It was five against four. He had no interest in participating until a boy in a dirty Punisher T-shirt with tousled black hair turned to him.

"Hey, kid! Want to play?"

Donnie shrugged and took his position, bringing the team to five members. A lanky kid on the other side yelled, "Serve!" He tossed the ball in the air, leaped up and spiked it straight and hard over the fence right onto Donnie's head.

"Point!" he cried.

The kid in the Punisher T-shirt sneered in disgust. Donnie shrugged and left the field. He wandered back toward the holding pens, where hundreds of pigs milled about, rolling in dust and mud, crowding the water trough and stinking up the place. It wasn't so bad once you got used to it. Pigs grunted and jockeyed for position. They ate things off the ground Donnie didn't want to know. Made him think about what they put in the sausage.

Donnie didn't care. He loved Werner's Smoky Links, of which there was an unlimited supply. If Kate had wanted to serve sausages for the rest of her life, she would have a free source of protein. Werner was very generous with its employees. The pig smell had pretty much killed his appetite, so he followed the fencing toward the back of the property, where a rail spur ran into the slaughterhouse. The corrugated metal gate had retracted into the ceiling, leaving the slaughterhouse open on a warm August day, exhaling the scent of the hecatomb.

Donnie wandered into the huge enclosed space. Two stock-hauling trucks were parked parallel to the far wall. The railroad spur ended at a concrete abutment protected by a necklace of old tires. Dark shapes lurked in the shadows, incomprehensible machines, stacked pallets, fifty-gallon drums. Donnie wandered into the depths of the vast building, noting rows of lockers and numerous doors, squeezing between bulwarks until he came to a dark space nearly filled by a huge hulking shape draped with overlapping tarps.

He felt along the wall until he found a switch plate, and flicked all the switches on. Twenty feet overhead, a series of fluorescent tubes in aluminum shrouds blinked reluctantly to life. Donnie stepped back to look at the covered behemoth. Its top arched downward like a swayback horse, and two enormous wheels extended below the tarps.

The Weenie Wagon!

As Donnie lifted the tarp, mice ran squeaking. He found the door near what he presumed to be the front, slipped in under the tarp and pulled it open with a hair-raising screech. In the faint light of a ceiling bulb, the interior breathed coolly of dust, old vinyl and motor oil.

Donnie used the handrail and boosted himself up into the interior. The tiny light dimly illuminated the driver's and passenger's seats, separated by a gap and a free-standing console. The curving dashboard contained a plethora of gauges. Donnie turned around and looked to the rear. A freezer-type door was set into the bulwark. Donnie grasped the handle and pulled it open. The interior smelled like ham. He shut the door and sat in the driver's seat, gripping the fat-rimmed wheel and making engine noises.

The thing was no dragster. It was no sports car. It was a freak vehicle designed to go slowly while singing the benefits of sausage. He was in love.

Dimly through the walls, he heard Frank Werner over the PA system.

"Okay, folks, gather around! It's time for our first lottery drawing."

Sighing, Donnie realized he'd better get back to the party before Kate freaked. He let himself out of the bizarre vehicle, walked out of the warehouse around the holding pens to the party, where close to a hundred people chowed down on grilled sausage, coleslaw, potato salad and dozens of side dishes, while drawing beer from two barrels.

Donnie looked around. The beer kegs were unattended. Taking a red Solo cup from a nearby table, Donnie drew himself a beer, stood with his back to a pickup and cautiously drank. He wandered back to the volleyball court, now six on a side with a dozen kids cheering. Donnie watched from afar. The same sorry sad sacks with their hats turned backward and sagging pants. They leaped and grunted like monkeys trying to impress the girls. A couple of the girls might have been cute, but Donnie didn't want to get close enough to make sure. They'd only make him nervous.

"Oh, there you are, kiddo!"

Donnie turned to see Kate coming his way, holding a cup of beer and smiling. Donnie quickly put his beer in the back of the truck.

"Having a good time?"

"Sure, Ma."

"There's a volleyball game going on."

"I know."

"You know, kiddo, it wouldn't kill you to make some friends around here."

"I know."

"Listen," she said. "Frank says you can work in the warehouse. He'll pay you seven fifty an hour."

"That's great."

"You can stop in on the way back from school tomorrow and work after school or weekends, as much as you like."

"Great, Ma."

"And we'll drop that pup off at the Humane Society."

Donnie's stomach clenched.

CHAPTER EIGHT
AND SO TO BED

BY THE TIME THEY LEFT, DONNIE WAS BORED BLIND. THEY were halfway home when Kate turned to him and asked, "Do you think Frank's coming on to me?"

"Maaa! How would I know?"

"Of course. You're right."

"'Sides, he starts hitting on you, that's sexual harassment. You could sue him."

"That's how you make it in America, kiddo. You find some deep pockets, carry a banana peel, do a one-and-a-half gainer on it in their foyer and sue them for seven figures. Easy peasy."

When they got home, Donnie went straight to the barn to check on the pup.

"Twerk no more," he said as he pulled her out of the box. "You need a name with more dignity. I'm making up a list. I'm inviting all my Facebook followers to make suggestions. Meanwhile, this is Social Studies 101. Sit."

He worked with the pup for an hour, feeding it sausage from the picnic. By the time he had gone upstairs and showered, it was seven o'clock.

"You'd better get your kit ready for tomorrow, kiddo," Kate said. "No torn jeans or T-shirts."

Donnie pulled out a selection of T-shirts, including one from the NRA. Kate came in to review. She pointed to the NRA shirt.

"Ixnay. You'll get kicked out on your first day."

"Ma, this is rural Wisconsin! Everybody hunts."

"Ixnay. Even that Def Leppard shirt is questionable. Why don't you wear this one from Banner Health?"

"Jeez! I might as well wear a Kick Me sign."

Kate held her chin, brow creasing. "I know. Just a minute."

She went out of the room and returned a minute later with a crisp brown T-shirt bearing the Werner's Meats wiener logo, a surrealistic pig-shaped dirigible flying over San Francisco at night. Donnie picked it up.

"Sure."

"You hungry?"

"No thanks. I ate about eight of those sausages."

Kate smiled, went in her room and went on Facebook. The apartment had a living/dining room, kitchen and two bedrooms. Donnie went into the living room, where the only TV, a flat plasma job, hung from the wall. They carried basic cable, which was about twelve stations. They had no newspaper, no way to know what was coming. Donnie flipped aimlessly from reality show to singing competition to a documentary about a paraplegic lesbian of color who made exquisite dolphin jewelry from fish bones.

Quietly letting himself out of the apartment, Donnie went to the barn and returned with the now nameless pup. They sat on the sofa and he turned the TV back on.

Jackpot. *Hannibal*, a show about a round robin of serial killers stalking one another. He'd never seen it, but at his last school a kid had told him the show featured all sorts of gnarly shit—bodies sewn into vast tapestries, murder victims sliced up like deli ham, people buried alive sprouting fungus. He and the pup had just settled in when Kate came out of her room, eyes flashing from the TV to the sofa.

"Oh no," she said, striding to the sofa and grabbing the remote. "You can't watch this." She turned the television off. "And she has to go back to the barn."

"Oh come on, Ma! That show's on NBC! How bad can it be?"

"No way, José. You want to watch something else, fine."

"Can I use the computer for a minute?"

Kate looked dubiously at the puppy. "What about that?"

"She won't do any damage. She just piddled."

"All right, but you know the rules. Just Facebook! And don't buy anything."

"As if!"

Donnie went into Kate's darkened bedroom and sat at the computer. He went on Facebook, where he was known as Scrawny Donnie and had thirty-five followers, most of whom he had never met. He listed his interests as comic books, movies and skating, although he did not have a board.

Donnie had twelve notifications, mostly kids goofing off. Nine of his followers were girls. A girl named Nina had threatened to kill herself all summer while her friends tried to talk her out of it. Of course there was always some asshole urging her on.

"Does your dad have any guns? Stick the barrel in your mouth."

"Shut the fuck up asshole. I'm reporting you to Facebook."

"What are you a fucking snitch? A fucking internet Facebook troll bitch snitch?"

"Stop it both of you! This is my page. We discuss what I want! And we are discussing whether or not I should kill myself."

"Do it!"

"Fuck you," etc.

Then there was Roberto, a black Milwaukee kid who posted pictures of his bling and his guns. A grinning Roberto with gold grillework that spelled "BERTO." Berto posing with an ivory-handled .45 automatic. Donnie private-messaged him: "Dude! Stop showing that gun before Homeland Security busts down your door!"

Roberto PM'd back: "Word, my brother."

He posted a picture of himself clutching an enormous pair of hedge clippers.

"Time to trim the fat."

Donnie jumped over to CBR.com and the Diamond page to check the action. With comics at four bucks a pop, he was pretty much priced out of the market, but there were always the school libraries. The last school he'd attended, Eugene Clark High in Edgerton, Wisconsin, had an entire section devoted to graphic novels, which was fancy talk for big, expensive comics. He particularly enjoyed the work of Alan Moore and had his own copy of *Watchmen*.

Someone had told him of a porn site, not too gross, but he couldn't take the chance. Not on Kate's computer. He was tempting fate just going to CBR.com. He signed off. It was past ten.

When he went out into the living room, Kate was

zonked out on the couch with the pup curled up in her arms, softly snoring.

CHAPTER NINE
THE LADY IS NO TRAMP

WHEN KATE WOKE, THE DOG WAS BACK IN THE BARN. AS she made breakfast, she made no mention of taking the dog to the Humane Society. It was the first day of school. As Donnie exited the apartment complex, the yellow Gunderson School District bus drove past. Once the weather changed, he'd be on it.

Dressed in fresh blue jeans and his Werner's wiener T, Donnie pedaled to school wearing a small backpack, which contained several notepads and a lunch Kate had made for him. It took fifteen minutes to reach his new school, a blond brick complex plunked at the edge of town, girdled in green, with a football field that doubled for soccer circled by a cinder track.

Donnie shackled his bike to the rack with his Kryptonite bike lock amid a wild selection of bikes, including mountain bikes with suspension at both ends that cost thousands, one-speed Schwinns and Huffys and some homemade jobs that reflected the low-rider culture. He joined the throng of eager pilgrims flowing in a reverse delta through the broad front doors. He reported to the school office, where he filled out forms and cooled his heels until an assistant principal who looked like one of *Dilbert*'s downtrodden office workers came out clutching a clipboard.

"Donnie Waits?"

"Yes, sir."

"You've been assigned to Homeroom 212, Mrs. Brautigan. Go up the stairs and to your right."

The bell sounded as he went up the stairs, late on the first day. He arrived at 212 as Mrs. Brautigan, a gray-haired matron, was closing the door.

"You must be Donnie Waits," she said.

"Yes, ma'am."

"Well take a seat. We're about to get started."

The only empty desk was in the back row next to Mohawk, who elbowed Freckles in the ribs and stage-whispered as Donnie sat, "It's the ragman!" Only Ryan— Onion Head—was absent.

Mrs. Brautigan clicked her fingers in their direction. "No talking unless spoken to. I am Mrs. Brautigan, and this is your homeroom. I also teach American history, so I'll be seeing some of you later in the day. What is the purpose of homeroom? The purpose of homeroom is to allow you to marshal your thoughts, finish up that homework assignment and get to know your fellow students. Those of you who've had me before know that I like to start the school year by having each student stand and introduce yourself. You don't have to make a speech; just tell us who you are and a little about your-selves. Hobbies, interests, that sort of thing. We will go in alphabetical order. As I call your name, please stand and introduce yourselves."

Great, Donnie thought. *Last again.* Fine with him. It would give him time to figure out what he wanted to say.

"April Abramson, you're up," Mrs. Brautigan said.

A thin girl in anachronistic pigtails and glasses stood and said in a mousey voice, "My name is April Abramson..."

"Turn and face the class please," Mrs. Brautigan said.

April turned and fixed her eyes on the back wall, featuring a map of the world and a poster showing a food pyramid. "My name is April Abramson. I have two sisters, Ann and Audrey, and I plan on becoming a vocational nurse."

Mohawk scribbled in his lined pad and showed the result to Freckles, who giggled like a girl. Mrs. Brautigan snapped her fingers.

"What are you doing, Lester?"

Butter wouldn't melt in Mohawk's/Lester's mouth as he said, "Nothing, Mrs. Brautigan."

Mrs. Brautigan headed down the aisle like a dreadnought. Lester ripped the offending page out of his notebook, jammed it in his mouth and began chewing. Mrs. Brautigan stopped by his desk, hands on her hips, and watched. Halfway through, Lester stopped chewing.

"Go on, Lester," Mrs. Brautigan said. "Finish your snack."

The class hooted and guffawed. Sheepishly, Lester removed the sodden mass from his mouth and put it inside his lift-up desk.

"One more stunt like that and you're on detention. Come on, people! Wake up! This is your senior year, not kindergarten. It's time to get serious about who you are and what you want to be. In the Middle Ages, boys your age were considered men and drafted into the king's army, or they already had wives and children to feed. Come on—you won't be seventeen forever."

She returned to the front of the class and consulted a clipboard. "John Brady, you're up."

And so it went, a tentative, stumbling presentation of blood stock, confused ambition and the occasional howler. Donnie's mind drifted until it went to the girl with short black hair and black fingernails sitting diagonally from him two rows up. She turned at one of Lester's snarky comments with a wry smile, and Donnie saw that she was pretty in a dark, Goth kind of way. The backpack at her feet bore numerous patches, including of Neil Gaiman's *Death Girl* as rendered by Michael Zulli, Brian Pulido's Lady Death, the Grateful Dead, Jellyfish and Foo Fighters.

Romantic thoughts jostled with earthy urges.

"Lester Barnes," Mrs. Brautigan said.

Mohawk stood. In Donnie's previous school, Mohawk would have been sent home for a haircut.

"My name is Lester; I'm a party tester. You want to get down, I'm your clown!"

"Lester, just the facts please."

"My brother Travis is training to be an MMA fighter. I like smokin' blunts, hangin' with bootylicious and par-TAY."

"Only booty you hang with…" Freckles said and was drowned out by Mrs. Brautigan.

"Lester, what do you want to be when you grow up?"

"Ahmina be a master deejay and rapper."

Gee, Donnie thought, *I'm not the only one.*

"Thank you. Lester, you may sit."

And so it went until Mrs. Brautigan said, "Keely Van Metre."

The Goth girl rose and flashed a dazzling smile. "I'm Keely Van Metre. Our family has owned Van Metre Stables for over fifty years, and we are ready to serve all your horse needs. I like to read comics, listen to rock and ride horses. I plan to go to college and major in business administration. I may take over the family business. Oh yeah. My dad also builds things."

She smiled again, hesitating for an instant on Donnie before sitting.

Whap between the eyes.

Other players took the field. Donnie envisioned his future together with Lady Death.

The class tittered. Donnie woke up.

"Donnie Waits, hello! It's your turn."

"Huh?" he said, to the class' amusement.

"Come on, Mr. Waits. Stand and tell us about yourself."

Donnie stood, a red tide creeping up his neck. "Donnie Waits. We just moved here from Edgerton. I like comics, drawing and rock too."

He sat.

"Well that was succinct," Mrs. Brautigan said. "Okay, we only have a few minutes. In the future I will call roll, and you will raise your hand and respond 'here' when I say your name. Please consult your schedules for your next class, and I'll see some of you back here at one for American history."

The bell rang.

CHAPTER TEN
SWALLOWING WHOLE

KEELY WAS LONG GONE BY THE TIME DONNIE MADE IT TO the exit. He was about to cruise when Mrs. Brautigan called him back.

"Mr. Waits, I see you've been in three schools in the past three years."

"Yes, ma'am. We move around a lot."

"Why is that?"

Donnie shrugged. "Kate couldn't find a job she liked. Hopefully we're here for a while."

"Kate's your mother?"

"Yes, ma'am."

"If you have any scholastic problems, or even problems having nothing to do with school, I want you to know you can talk to me anytime and I'll give you an honest hearing. I raised three boys, all happily married and gainfully employed, thank the good Lord."

"Thank you, ma'am. I appreciate that."

He ducked out on her warm gaze and looked at his chart. Curses. Gym class. Donnie knew from bitter experience that gym class most often consisted of ritual humiliation of any who deviated from the accepted male norms. He'd often considered going Goth as a means of isolating himself from his peers. He'd even thought about a tattoo, but Kate would shit.

He found the gym and sat in the bleachers with two dozen other seniors. A poster said GUNDERSON GIANTS at one end of the room over a large black scoreboard on which nothing showed. The room smelled of sweat and linseed oil. A thin, wiry guy with a neat Van Dyke wearing gray sweats and carrying a clipboard entered and stood in front of them.

"Greetings, seniors," he said in a reedy voice. "I am Mr. Pagel, the wrestling coach, and this is phys ed for boys. This year we will learn the basics of good cardio, coordination, the importance of teamwork and the will to excel. You will all need to bring gym shorts and plain white T-shirts, jockstraps and tennis shoes that won't mar the floor.

"Here at Gunderson High, we encourage you to try out for sports! Sports will teach you teamwork, make you friends, increase your wind and fill the empty hours until you play sports again."

Titters.

"Good to see some familiar faces. Ryan?"

And wouldn't you know it, fucking Onion Head was sitting at ground zero. Donnie hoped he wouldn't turn his head.

"Okay, everybody," Mr. Pagel said. "Let's count off, beginning with Ryan."

Donnie was last, at twenty-six.

Mr. Pagel gestured to his side. "Everybody remove your shoes. Even numbers here, odd over there."

Soon the two lines confronted each other with Mr. Pagel in the middle. Ryan saw Donnie and did a double take. He whispered something to his companion and they snickered. Mr. Pagel reached behind the bleachers and removed a laundry hamper filled with brightly colored sponge rubber balls, eight inches in diameter. He passed the balls to Ryan's team. There were six balls.

"You know the drill. Neither side can cross over those lines. If you're hit, you sit. If you catch the ball, the thrower sits. The last team standing wins." Mr. Pagel backed off to one side, stuck a whistle on a lanyard in his mouth and gave a sharp tweet.

Ryan immediately rolled back like Russell Wilson and hurled the ball straight, striking Donnie flush in the face.

"SIDDOWN RAGMAN!" Ryan hooted to the delight of his teammates.

A guy on Donnie's side who looked like a crow, with a thick thatch of glossy black hair and a beakish nose, caught the next ball. Then another and another until all of Ryan's side was on their asses. Now it was Donnie's side's turn. Each boy gripped his ball with feverish antic-ipation. At the coach's word, Donnie wound up and hurled the ball diagonally across the gap, striking the end player.

Coach Pagel stood on the sidelines keenly observing, making notes on his clipboard. Time went fast as the balls changed sides again and again until the bell sounded the end of the second period.

On the way out, Ryan stepped from behind the bleachers and elbowed Donnie painfully in the ribs.

"Oops, sorry Ragman! See you around."

Third period was science taught by June Byrd, a tall black woman with broad shoulders and horn-rimmed glasses. Donnie sat at the back of the room, as was his wont. A chubby boy wearing an XXXL Green Bay T-shirt put his hand before his mouth, side-snark style, and whispered, "Gooney bird." Mrs. Byrd handed out text-books: *Asimov's Chronology of the World From the Big Bang to Modern Times.* Donnie couldn't believe it. He'd read Asimov's *Foundation Trilogy* and had never, in his wildest dreams, expected to encounter Asimov in the classroom.

Mrs. Byrd spent the hour describing the scientific process and inquiry. About halfway through, an earnest young man with neatly combed blond hair raised his hand.

"Yes, Adam?"

"Will you also include the theological origins of the universe as stated in the Bible?"

Hoots and whistles.

"No, Adam. This is science, not Bible class."

"But my mom says—"

"Please, Adam. That's enough. Feel free to have your mother contact me outside of class."

Even from the back row, Donnie could read Adam's hunch. Adam wasn't pleased.

At the noon bell, Donnie followed the queue into the cafeteria, making a beeline for the table farthest from the food. He sat by himself and unpacked Kate's lunch, a tuna salad sandwich, a yellow apple, a granola bar and a pint of chocolate milk. The kid in the XXXL Green Bay shirt came toward him like a Macy's parade float, holding a cafeteria tray with two hot dogs and a Coke. He wore Coke-bottle glasses and had big pores and several blackheads.

"Mind if I sit?"

Donnie gestured. The kid sat.

"I'm Malcolm Lipschitz."

Donnie shook his cold, clammy hand.

"Whatcha think of the Pack's chances this season?" Malcolm said.

Donnie shrugged. "I'm not really into football."

"That's all anybody cares about around here. Football, getting high and getting laid. You into shooting?"

"Not really."

"Well maybe we'll go shooting sometime. It's lots of fun. I hunt with my dad. Pheasant mostly, but he's promised to take me deer hunting in the fall. Ever eat deer?"

"I don't think so."

"Well shit, dude. We can fix that. Hey. Watch this." Malcolm put his index fingers to his nose and squeezed, causing tendrils of grease to protrude from the pores. "I'm a mole!"

Donnie kept his head down and ate his lunch, watching Keely Van Metre sit down with a couple of Goth girls.

Suddenly, like a raptor bird, Ryan swooped down on the table, grabbed one of Malcolm's hot dogs, stuffed the whole thing into his mouth like a snake swallowing a mouse and chewed it in Malcolm's face.

"Mm-mm good!" he declared, swallowing with a glottal punctuation. He sashayed away.

"Prick!" Malcolm said, clutching the other hot dog. "Fucking prick!"

"Yeah he's a real prize all right," Donnie said.

Mohawk, aka Lester Barnes, chanted, "Fatty, Fatty two-by-four, couldn't get through the bathroom door. So he did it on the floor, licked it up and did some more!" Creeps laughed. Malcolm turned red with anger and frustration. Donnie put a hand on his shoulder. *"Illegitimi non carborundum."*

"Huh? What's that?"

"It means 'Don't let the bastards grind you down.' It's all the Latin I know."

Between sixth and seventh period, as Donnie walked the crowded halls, a sudden crushing force smacked him in the shoulder, causing him to bang off the lockers. He turned and watched Ryan walk away with his hands behind his back, whistling.

At the final bell, Donnie gathered his books, put on his backpack, got on his bike and pedaled home. He rode straight back to the barn to check on the dog. The cardboard box was on its side, the water bowl spilled.

"Here pup!" he said and whistled, hearing a rhythmic slurping sound from the back of the barn. Following the sound, he found the pup with its head in a can of Crisco.

"Crisco," he said. "That's a good name."

He found a bigger box, refilled the water bowl and put the pup back in.

He carried his backpack upstairs, went into Kate's room and went on Facebook. Keely Van Metre had twelve followers. Donnie sent her a friend request.

"I'm the new kid," he messaged.

CHAPTER ELEVEN
SERIOUS ABOUT LIFE

KEELY ACCEPTED HIS FRIENDSHIP. "YOU WERE THE LAST guy to speak in Mrs. Brautigan's homeroom, weren't you?" she messaged.

"Yes."

"Short and sweet, lol! I like comics too! Which are your favorites?"

"Sandman, Copra, Shutter and Badger because you know Wisconsin..."

"Cool! Do U like the Beatles?"

"Luv the Beatles!"

"Do you ride horses?"

Donnie heard the front door open.

"Gotta run. Talk to you tomorrow!"

He came out of the bedroom as Kate set a bag of groceries on the kitchen counter. "Hi, Ma."

"Hi, hon. How'd it go at the factory?"

A yawning chasm opened beneath Donnie's feet. He'd spaced on the job. "Shit!" he declared. "I spaced on it."

Kate turned toward him in full mom mode with fists on hips. "I thought you wanted a job."

"I do! I'll go tomorrow! I swear! It's not like I'm essential personnel; he's just doing it as a favor to you."

"And to you. You're a senior now, Donnie. You've got to start getting serious about life."

"I know."

Kate field-stripped a frozen lasagna and put it in the microwave. "How'd the first day of school go?"

"Fine."

"Make any friends?"

"Maybe," Donnie said, thinking of Keely and Malcolm. "I met this kid. Says he's Jewish. Malcolm Lipschitz. Does that sound Jewish to you?"

"Yes. What's he like?"

"Not what you'd expect. For one thing, he goes hunting. He has a nose like a mole."

"Excuse me?"

Donnie put his fingers to his nose and squeezed, just like Malcolm had showed him. "Like this. See? See all the little tendrils?"

Kate turned away in disgust. "That's enough. Are you trying out for any extracurricular activities? Debate? Track?"

"How'm I gonna do that and hold a job after school?"

"Hmm. You have a point, kiddo. Why don't you set the table?"

Kate took her briefcase and went into her bedroom while Donnie set the table. At least she hadn't brought up the dog, Crisco. After dinner, Kate sat on the sofa with her glasses on going through files from work.

"Can I bring the dog up?" Donnie said.

Kate looked up, peering over her glasses. She pursed her lips. "All right. But no messes! He's still got to go to the pound."

"She, Mom. It's a her. And her name is Crisco."

"Well that's better than what you had."

As soon as it entered the apartment, the pup went crazy, shooting from place to place like the Road Runner, leaping up on the sofa, licking Kate's face until she pushed it away laughing.

CHAPTER TWELVE
TRUCE

DONNIE RODE HIS BICYCLE TO SCHOOL IN THE MORNING, vowing to stop by the meat-packing plant on the way home. In Mrs. Brautigan's homeroom he sat next to

Keely, who looked more like Lady Death than ever, right down to the black eyeliner. Mrs. Brautigan took roll while Donnie sketched monsters and hot rods in his spiral pad.

Keely took out her pad and started sketching as well. Donnie looked around the room. Mohawk bopped to his iPod. Freckles drew dueling penises in the margin of his history text.

At lunch he looked for Keely, but she wasn't around. Malcolm headed over with his cafeteria tray of spaghetti and meatballs. Setting aside his meal, Malcolm peered deep into his smart phone.

He held the phone up for Donnie. It showed some kind of automatic pistol. "Look at this! Isn't she sweet?"

"Dude, if a teacher sees that, they're sending you home."

"This is still America, isn't it? I can look at a fucking gun on my own phone on my own time, can't I?"

"I'm just sayin'."

Donnie took out his spiral pad and began sketching. At first it was just a goofy figure, but it abruptly morphed into a hulking Ryan with exaggerated muscles and onion ridge looming in front of an aghast Malcolm, stuffing Malcolm's hot dog into his mouth.

Donnie showed it to Malcolm, who took out his earbuds and stared in amazement.

"Hey! That's pretty good!"

Donnie snatched it back. "It's crap." He folded it into a paper airplane and tossed it toward the center of the teeming cafeteria, where it caught an unexpected updraft and sailed farther than he'd intended.

"Hey!" a guttural voice sounded.

Ryan stood rubbing his eye and clutching the paper airplane. He looked around. "Who did this?"

Faces and hands turned in Donnie's direction. Donnie froze as Ryan stalked over and glared.

"I might have known," he said, picking up Malcolm's dish of spaghetti and meatballs and dumping it on Donnie's head.

"You!" A tall teacher wearing glasses, a short-sleeve white shirt and a blue tie headed their way with his hand in front. "You, Cutler. You're going to the principal's office."

Ryan turned aggrieved. "Come on, Mr. Haskins! He sailed a paper airplane into my eye!" Ryan held out the offending missile. Mr. Haskins took it, opened it up, examined the cartoon.

"Both of you. Let's go."

Like two cons heading for solitary, Donnie and Ryan preceded Mr. Haskins out of the room while everyone looked. They passed Keely in the hall, her head swiveling to follow them. Donnie winked at her.

Mr. Haskins marched them into an antechamber with some vinyl furniture and a coffee table holding copies of *Scholastic*, *People*, *Us* and *National Geographic*. The inside door said HOWARD PENNER, ASSISTANT PRINCIPAL.

"You boys have a seat." Mr. Haskins knocked, went into Mr. Penner's office and closed the door.

The two boys sat opposite each other. Donnie picked up a *National Geographic* and looked at photos of volcanoes.

"Yo faggot," Ryan said in a low voice. Donnie ignored him.

"Yo faggot, I'm talkin' to you."

Donnie looked up. "You know what a blivet is? It's ten pounds of shit in a five-pound bag."

"How'd you like me to come over there and punch you in the mouth?"

Donnie set the mag down. "Go ahead."

Mr. Haskins came into the room, sensing the tension. "Both of you, in Mr. Penner's office."

Mr. Haskins held the door while the condemned filed in. Mt. Penner was shaped like a Russian nesting doll with a laurel of gray hair surrounding the back of his head. He wore a bow tie and had some files open on his desk. "Have a seat, gentlemen."

They sat.

"Ryan, give me your version."

"Yeah, Mr. Penner, I was sitting there minding my own business when out of nowhere this drongo sails a paper airplane right in my eye. I could have been blinded."

"And?"

"I was a little peeved, y' know? Maybe I got carried away."

"What did you do?"

"I dumped a plate of spaghetti on him."

Mr. Penner turned to Donnie. "Mr. Waits, I understand you're new this year. I have some sympathy for your predicament. This is your third school in three years, is that right?"

"Yes, sir."

"Well go on."

"I never intended to hit anyone in the eye, sir. It was just a paper airplane."

Mr. Penner held up the offending sketch. "Not a bad likeness, actually. Have you thought about contributing to the school newspaper, the *Gunderson Gavel*?"

"No, sir."

"Well think about it. Gentlemen, the school year is young and we have a long way to go. I'm willing to overlook this one time. Now what say you shake hands and let bygones be bygones."

Ryan swiveled toward Donnie and put out his meat hook. Donnie took it, and Ryan squeezed hard. Donnie let his hand go limp until it would no longer compress, and Ryan let go.

"Good," Mr. Penner said. "You may proceed to your fourth-period assignments."

CHAPTER THIRTEEN
PIERCING REVELATION

DONNIE DIDN'T THINK RYAN WOULD TRY ANYTHING ELSE that day, but he was wrong. Between fifth and sixth period as Donnie headed for history via the hall, Ryan punched him so hard in the shoulder, it went numb. Malcolm saw and cringed on Donnie's behalf.

Donnie shrugged it off and went to class. There was no trouble after class, because Ryan had football practice. Donnie pedaled out to Werner's, backpack heavy with books. Leaving his bike in a rack by the employee parking lot, he followed the receptionist's directions to Human Resources, where a dot-Indian woman named Samantha had him fill out several forms that already contained Kate's signature.

"You know how to find the warehouse?" Samantha said.

"I think so."

"Okay. Ask for Roddy; he'll show you what to do. Don't forget your time card."

Roddy was a pink bald fireplug. "Hey, kid, get a pair of leather gloves. Ya see all those boxes in that truck? Put 'em on those pallets over there. Come see me when you're done."

It was mind-numbing, back-breaking labor. Every time he carried one of the heavy cardboard boxes to the pallets, he looked to his right, where the Weenie Wagon lay under its canvas shroud. It was past six by the time he finished unloading the truck. He reported to Roddy.

"I have to go, Roddy. I have homework."

"Go on, kid. See you tomorrow."

The lights were on in the apartment when he arrived home. Crisco was happy to see him but hungry. Donnie went inside to forage.

Kate was in her room on the phone. A bag of Purina Puppy Chow sat on the counter. Donnie returned to the barn and poured some of it. Kate was making màc and cheese when he returned with the pup under his arm. He set her down on the floor.

"Does this mean she can stay?"

"She's your responsibility. It's up to you to see she's fed and doesn't cause any trouble, understand, buster? She makes a mess, you clean it up."

"Thank you, Ma! Thank you, thank you! I'll take good care of her."

"Frank said you worked hard all afternoon."

"Just a couple of hours. Hey, maybe this weekend you'd let me drive around the parking lot."

Kate held a hand up in warning. "Don't push your luck, kiddo."

The next day Keely joined him and Malcolm in the cafeteria. She wore black eyeliner and a Hellboy T-shirt.

"I got a dog," Donnie said.

"Ooh, can I see?" Keely said.

"I don't have any pictures. I don't even have a phone.

I'll get my mom to snap one, and I'll post it on Facebook tonight."

"What's his name?" Keely said.

"It's a her. Her name is Crisco."

"When can I see her?" Keely said.

"I gotta work Saturday, but what about Sunday? We could meet at that park by the courthouse. The one with the war memorial."

"Sure."

"So are you trying to look like Lady Death?"

Keely made an exaggerated shock face. "No, you fool! I'm Neil Gaiman's Death! Brian Pulido created Lady Death. She's got long blond hair. Death's hair is short and black like mine."

"But, like, they both bring unspeakable horror."

"Exactly."

"What's that tat on your arm?"

Keely proudly lifted her shoulder. "It's an ankh, an ancient Egyptian symbol that means life."

"But you're Death!"

"I wanted to get my tongue pierced, but my dad wouldn't let me."

"People die from piercings."

Keely did an exaggerated double take. "They do not!"

"They most certainly do!" Donnie said. "I read about this one dude who had his ears, nose, tongue, nipples and eyebrows pierced, and each one got infected, and all the infections joined together like that scene in *Les Mis*, and when they found him his body was the consistency of Jell-O."

The bell rang.

Donnie dreaded the break between fifth and sixth period. There was no way to avoid Ryan and his club-like fist. Malcolm sidled up to him after the hit.

"Y'know he's gonna keep doing that until you fight back."

"Yeah, thanks a lot. What am I supposed to do? He could break me in two."

"I'd like to shoot him," Malcolm said through clenched teeth.

"Don't even talk like that," Donnie said.

"I could. I've got my own twelve-gauge. My dad takes me hunting."

"Don't talk about guns, don't look at guns, don't draw pictures of guns," Donnie said.

After school Donnie rode to Werner's, punched in and went to work. Roddy showed him how to operate the forklift, and he unloaded pallets for the rest of the day.

At least I'm driving, he thought. Werner's had a small fleet, including a pair of boxy white vans with the Werner's logo, a flying pig. At quitting time he asked Roddy if he could drive one of the vans around the parking lot.

"You ever drive before?"

"Last place I lived, my friend Steve would sneak his parents' VW out when they were gone, and we'd take turns practicing."

"Hit anything?"

"Just the mailbox, but we fixed it."

"Okay. See me Saturday."

Donnie got home at seven and went straight to the barn. No dog. Frantically he cruised the barn calling, "Crisco! Good doggie! Here, Crisco!"

He went outside circling the barn in a widening gyre. He heard a sliding door open on the second floor and looked up. Kate came out on the little balcony, on which sat a Weber grill and a wicker love seat.

"She's up here!" she called.

Donnie went up. Kate had set out two bowls, food and water. Crisco caromed around her ankles like a Shriner on a mini-bike during a parade. She ran to Donnie and furiously licked his face.

"Come on, kiddo. Dinner's on the table. How was school?"

"School was okay."

"Make any friends?"

"Maybe."

Kate didn't push it. "Take care of the dishes, please. I have a little homework myself." She went into her room and closed the door.

Donnie set the dishes on the floor and watched Crisco do her thing. He put the sparkling-clean dishes back in the cupboard and opened up the utility door in the cabinet. Inside he found a thick cardboard square holding nine green thumbtacks.

He went into his room, Crisco at his heels, and dug out the shaggy Norwegian sweater his grandmother had given him for Christmas three years ago. He'd never worn it.

That was about to change.

CHAPTER FOURTEEN
SHARP SWEATER

DONNIE'S SHOULDER WAS STILL SORE IN THE MORNING. Thursday was cool and overcast, with a snap of fall in the air, as Donnie pedaled to school wearing the off-white Norwegian sweater whose valleys and whorls mirrored the surrounding countryside. The leaves had begun to change.

Only Malcolm showed for lunch. Keely had an activity.

"She's kind of cute for a Goth," Malcolm allowed.

"She's cute, period," Donnie said.

"Is she your girlfriend?"

"Not yet."

Donnie anticipated the late-day class break with a mixture of dread and glee. But first he had to get through Mrs. Brautigan's history class, which involved a long discussion between the teacher and Veronica Seale, a straight-A student and the head cheerleader, insisting that Columbus was a racist usurper and should not be honored.

Donnie busied himself drawing a flip book in the

margin of his history text. The first drawing showed the little black dog sitting. By making the same drawing in the same place on subsequent pages with slight changes Donnie constructed an analog cartoon of Crisco getting up, running, leaping into the air and snagging a bird. Feathers flew.

There were twenty-six drawings. It was better than the animation on Adult Swim. He showed it to the boy at the next desk, a lunk named Leonard, who expertly flipped the pages, running the whole clip several times.

"Excellent," Leonard hissed.

Mrs. Brautigan aimed her gimlet eye. "What's going on back there, boys? Donnie Waits, did you read your homework assignment?"

"Yes, ma'am."

"Can you name the thirteen original colonies?"

"Delaware, Pennsylvania, New Jersey, Georgia, Connecticut, Massachusetts Bay, Maryland, South Carolina, New Hampshire, Virginia, New York, North Carolina, Rhode Island…"

"And?"

"And, and…" Donnie vamped.

"Providence Plantation. Still, that's pretty good."

Veronica Seale raised her hand.

"Yes, Veronica?"

Veronica stood, her long blond hair hanging straight to her ass. "Isn't it true that the Providence and Jamestown colonies handed out smallpox-ridden blankets to the Indians to exterminate them?"

"I hadn't heard that, Veronica. If you would like to make that the subject of your term paper, please make sure you cite all your sources."

Veronica picked up her heavy text and opened it. "It says right here on page 174 of our textbook that British colonists deliberately handed out smallpox-ridden blankets to rid the area of Native Americans."

Donnie noticed Malcolm poking intensely at his smart phone. He raised his hand.

"Malcolm?"

Malcolm stood and read from his phone. "There is only one documented instance in which disease was proposed to be used as a weapon against Native American tribes. During the French and Indian War, Jeffery Amherst, first Baron Amherst, Britain's commander in chief in North America, suggested using the smallpox disease to wipe out their Native American enemy."

"And what is your source, Malcolm?"

"Wikipedia."

Snickers. Malcolm looked around like a Borscht Belt comedian. "What?"

"Siddown, Dipschitz!" Freckles brayed. Half the class laughed.

Mrs. Brautigan brought her yardstick down with a loud report.

"Mr. Conklin, you are out of line."

Freckles looked around, grinning.

"One more outburst like that and you're going to detention."

Big roundelay about what constituted a legitimate source. Donnie retreated to a daydream in which he rescued Keely from a band of Indians astride his mighty stallion. The funny thing was, she was the horse rider. He'd never ridden one and had no intention of doing so. Look at Christopher Reeve.

The clock ticked down. The bell rang. Feeling giddy, Donnie joined the throngs in the halls. Sure enough, here came Ryan grinning in anticipation. They passed in the hall. *Kawango!* Ryan punched Donnie hard in the shoulder.

Donnie looked behind him, Ryan's mouth and eyes open in shock as he stared at his bloody hand, having slammed it into five thumbtacks hidden inside the sweater.

CHAPTER FIFTEEN
LORD VILE

AFTER DINNER DONNIE WORKED WITH CRISCO FOR A HALF hour on basic commands: sit, come, stay. The dog sat like a frog with her hind legs splayed. For the rest of the week he went to school, went to work and went to sleep exhausted around ten, looking forward to the weekend. He managed to avoid Ryan, or perhaps it was just that Ryan had better things to do.

On Friday he reminded Keely about Sunday.

"I'll be there," she said.

Donnie arrived at Werner's at eight Saturday morning and went to work loading and unloading. At ten Roddy told him to take a break.

Donnie got some corn nuts and a soda from the vending machines and joined Roddy and two other workers at a picnic table out back.

"Hey, Roddy, that's the Weenie Wagon in there, isn't it?"

"Yeah, the Weenie Wagon. It was in there when I got here, eight years ago."

"What do you know about it?" Donnie said.

"Why? You want to drive it? It would cost thousands of dollars to get that monstrosity in working condition, and then what are you going to do with it?"

"I heard it had a blown hemi mill," said a Mexican kid named Hernandez.

"Where'd you hear that?" Donnie said.

"My older brother. He's into low riders and hot rods. Said he read about it in an old issue of *Rod & Custom*."

"Think he's still got it?"

"I don't know, man. I could ask."

Donnie worked until four, when Roddy let him drive one of the vans around the parking lot, riding shotgun and offering tips.

"Training for your license, huh? Okay, the important thing to remember is to be smooth. That's what they're looking for. Keep it smooth, no sudden moves. When you signal your turns? Turn your head like this and look over your shoulder. They go crazy for that."

Kate had brought Crisco up when Donnie arrived at five. "Look at this," she said, tossing a peanut to the pup, who snatched it out of the air like Willie Mays snagging a pop fly to center field. She held a peanut three feet off the ground. Crisco leaped straight up and took it out of Kate's hand.

"Where exactly did you find this dog?"

As Donnie told her, she put a hand to her mouth. "I can't believe people can be so cruel. It's a good thing you were there."

"Yeah. I keep listening for that car."

"Well if they show up, don't do anything. Just tell the cops."

Donnie sat on the floor playing with the pup. "As if."

"Wash your hands, kiddo. I'm starving."

Hamburger Helper and steamed broccoli. After

dinner, Kate grabbed her purse. "I'm going to the mall. Want to come?"

"No thanks, Ma. Can I use your computer?"

"Don't buy anything and don't visit any porn sites."

"Ma!"

"And do the dishes."

After she left, Crisco did the dishes. Donnie went into her room and went online. With the addition of Malcolm and Keely, he had fifteen FB followers.

"I named the dog Crisco."

Malcolm posted, "What kind of name is that?"

"She likes Crisco."

"What kind of dog?"

"Some kind of little black dog."

Donnie's notification symbol dinged. He had a friend request from Lord Vile. Clicking on Lord Vile's page, he saw a picture of a comic book monster. There was no information about Lord Vile except ASK. Donnie added Lord Vile to his friends. Instantly he got a message.

"Why don't you kill yourself, you ugly faggot?"

Donnie felt a chill in his chest, and his heart shriveled. He unfriended Lord Vile.

CHAPTER SIXTEEN
THE DISC

DONNIE GOT UP THREE TIMES DURING THE NIGHT TO TAKE Crisco outside to pee. They stood side by side in the moonlight pissing into the bushes. Kate slept in on Sundays, so Donnie made himself a breakfast of Rice Krispies, milk and a banana and parceled out half of Crisco's recommended daily allotment of kibble. At ten thirty he put Crisco in his backpack and pedaled into town. At first she squirmed, throwing off his balance, but shortly she settled in, jaw on Donnie's shoulder, grinning. Keely had agreed to meet him at eleven in Boyd Park, which served as the town square. Boyd Park covered a city block. In the center was a band cupola with crosshatched latticework and a bronze monument to Gunderson's sons who'd served in the world wars.

Donnie wheeled his bike over to a bench that bore a brass plate reading IN LOVING MEMORY OF HERBERT AND NANCY SCHUBERT. Crisco leaped from the backpack before Donnie could take it off and ran around sniffing. Donnie sat on the bench.

"Here, Crisco!" he called. The little dog came running.

At ten fifteen Keely pulled up to the curb in an old hatchback Mazda. Donnie stood grinning.

"Hi!"

"Hi," Keely said, swinging her backpack with Lady Death on the back. She wore cutoffs and a men's button-down tied across her taut belly. Crisco ran up to her, tail wagging, and she knelt to coo.

"Oh! He's beautiful!"

"It's a she."

"She's beautiful! Where did you get her?"

Donnie told her, watching her mouth curl in disgust. "I can't believe people can behave like that."

"I know," Donnie said. "One of these days I'm going to find that creep…"

He left the rest unsaid. In truth he didn't know what he would do. Like all teenage boys, he was fixated on power, violence, fighting and his own shortcomings. He'd been in several fights over the years, wild, hair-grabbing, swinging affairs that all ended without resolution. He was drawn to Gunderson's lone karate shop, John's Martial Arts, but no way could he afford the fees or the time. Someday.

Keely scooped Crisco into her arms and sat Indian-style holding her. "She's so squirmy!" she declared.

"I know. What kind of name is Keely?"

"I'm named after Keely Smith. She was a jazz singer. Do you like jazz?"

"I don't know," Donnie said. "What is it?"

Keely did a slo-mo double take. "Jazz is like, it's swinging improvisational music with a hip beat! My dad says America has created only three legitimate art forms: jazz, movies and comic books."

"Comic books for sure."

"You'd dig jazz. I know you would. My dad has a huge collection all on vinyl. The sound is much better than CDs or what you can download. Have you ever listened to vinyl?"

"What do you mean?" Donnie said.

Keely rolled her eyes and described vinyl records to him.

"Oh sure! I saw some of those at my grandparents' house. They like the big bands—Bennie Goodman, Duke Ellington."

"That's jazz!" Keely said, as Crisco wiggled free of her grip and ran off to sniff the base of a pine tree.

A familiar thumping bass emanated from across the park. Donnie watched with growing apprehension as Ryan's tricked-out Honda pulled to the curb opposite, gangsta rap cut off mid-beat as he shut down the engine. Ryan and Lester got out carrying a six-pack of beer and a plastic flying disc.

"Great," Donnie said.

"Ignore them," Keely said. "They don't even know we're here."

"Maybe we should go somewhere else."

Keely turned on him with anger. "Do not let those pricks run us off! We have every right to be here. They're not going to spoil our weekend."

"Yeah," Donnie said dubiously. "Okay. Do you know who Lord Vile is?"

"No. Who is he?"

Donnie told her. Keely's forehead creased with horror and sympathy.

"It's either Ryan or one of his asshole buddies," Donnie said.

"You should report that."

"I'm not a snitch," Donnie said. "I don't want to be one of those crybabies who goes running to his parents or a teacher. I can handle my own problems."

Karate, baby!

Keely grinned. "I like that! What does your mother do?"

"She's executive secretary to Frank Werner, president of Werner's Meats."

"Oh! I love Werner's wieners!"

Donnie held back about the Weenie Wagon. He didn't want to appear grotesque or bizarre. "What's your dad do?"

"My father is a real estate developer. We also have horses. You should come by sometime. We'll go riding."

"They're big, stupid animals!" Donnie said. "Look what happened to Christopher Reeve."

"Who?" Keely said.

Donnie told her who Christopher Reeve was and his love for the Superman movies. Keely had never seen one.

Ryan and Lester stood about fifty yards away, partially blocked by oak and elm, tossing the plastic disc to each other. Donnie watched as Ryan popped the incoming disc up with his fist, spun around and caught it behind his back. Ryan skimmed it back to Lester, who ran after it with a finger in the air like a French waiter, catching it on the rim, where it twirled around before he gripped it. Donnie had never seen anyone do that with a flying disc.

The little dog sat at Donnie's and Keely's feet watching the flying disc, swiveling her head like a spectator at a tennis match. Without warning, Crisco took off like a cannonball toward the middle of the park.

Donnie felt a sense of dread clutch his gut as he automatically stood and shouted, "Crisco!" He watched in horror as Crisco made a beeline directly toward Ryan, who turned his head at the shout, taking his eye off the flying disc. Crisco ran by him, leaped and caught the disc in her jaws five feet off the ground. She turned and raced straight back to the bench, Ryan in hot pursuit.

CHAPTER SEVENTEEN
A WALK IN THE PARK

DONNIE KNELT AND SCOOPED UP THE DOG AS RYAN arrived, blood in his eye. Crisco turned her head away as Ryan reached for the disc, so Donnie gently pried it loose and handed it over. Ryan stood quivering, a breathless Lester right behind.

"I might have known," Ryan spat, handing the disc to Lester. "A fucking douchebag has a douchebag dog."

"Douchebagggg," Lester said, drawing it out.

Crisco squirmed and Donnie set her on the ground. Ryan handed the disc to Lester.

"I owe you one for that stunt you pulled last week," Ryan said.

"You mean that stunt where you punched me in the arm for no reason?" Donnie said, oddly oblivious to the sense of physical danger.

"Kick his ass!" Lester said.

Ryan puffed up. Donnie could feel an ass kicking coming on.

"Hey!" Keely said. They all looked at her. She stood

ten feet away with her smart phone to her eye trained on them. "Go ahead! I'm recording."

Ryan sneered at her. "You dumb bitch! I could run you down, take that out of your hands and make you eat it."

Lester waved the red plastic disc. "Do it!"

Donnie looked at him. "What are you, his cheerleader? Is he taking you to the prom?"

Lester made a fist and took a step. Crisco leaped up, tore the plastic disc from his hand and ran toward the cupola in the center of the park. Lester ran after her, but it wasn't much of a race.

"Okay," Ryan said, "this time I'm going to drop-kick your fucking dog like a field goal," and took off running.

Donnie and Keely ran after him.

"I'm still filming!" Keely cried with the phone to her face.

Crisco circled the cupola with the disc firmly clamped in her jaws, like a quadruped Ubangi. Ryan took off after her. Lester arrived red-faced and panting and circled the cupola in the opposite direction to catch the dog between them. As Lester and Ryan converged, Crisco juked like Jim Brown running for daylight straight back to Donnie, where she leaped into his arms. Donnie caught her, staggering backward, laughing as the little dog triumphantly waved the flying disc.

Ryan ran toward them, followed by a plodding, gasping Lester. Keely scooted and scoped like Lucien Ballard. This was going to be the greatest viral YouTube sensation ever!

Donnie pried the disc loose from Crisco's jaws and sailed it at Ryan, who fumbled the catch. With a grimace he stepped forward and shoved Donnie hard on the shoulder, knocking him down and spilling Crisco, who growled at Ryan and showed her teeth.

A black-and-white Dodge with a light bar pulled up to the curb thirty feet away. GUNDERSON POLICE was emblazoned on the door. A tall man in a Smokey hat got out. Ryan backed off and waited.

Chief Robertson had an avuncular face and wore wire-rimmed glasses. "Is there a problem, Ryan?" he said.

"No sir, Chief Robertson, sir," Ryan replied.

The chief nodded at Lester. "Lester." He turned toward Donnie and stuck out his hand. "Chief Robertson."

Donnie took it. "Donnie Waits. We just moved to town. My mom works for Frank Werner."

"How do you like Gunderson?"

"It's okay, I guess."

Robertson noticed Keely. "Miss Van Metre. Are you filming this?"

Keely came forward smiling. "You bet. I'll send you a copy if you like."

Robertson took four cards from his shirt pocket and handed them out. "You kids have any trouble, please don't hesitate to call. Ryan, I'd appreciate if you'd keep that bass down in town."

"Yes sir, Chief Robertson, sir."

Robertson stared at him a beat, turned and walked away. Seconds later he drove off.

"Come on," Ryan said. "I'll figure out what to do with this douchebag later."

"Douchebag!" Lester said, stumbling to catch up.

Keely and Donnie looked at each other and burst out laughing. Minutes later Ryan and Lester drove away, bass booming. Keely keyed up her video and showed it to Donnie. She'd caught Crisco snatching the disc from Lester, the Keystone Kops chase with Lester and Ryan, and Crisco's triumphant return. She'd filmed right up to Chief Robertson's turning toward her.

"Now I'm going to upload it to Facebook and YouTube," she said, grinning.

Donnie put a hand on her wrist. "Seriously? Don't you need people's permission to film them?"

"Let 'em bitch," she said. "What are they doing to do? Sue me? It will only make them look ridiculous."

Donnie watched as Keely made good on her pledge. They walked around the park, the little dog buzzing around their feet, talking about movies, comic books and music. Keely launched into a lurid exegesis of Ed Gein and Jeffrey Dahmer.

"So proud of Wisconsin!" she said.

Donnie didn't believe her. She vowed to show him the books and magazine articles. When Donnie looked at his watch, it was three o'clock.

"I'd better get back," he said.

"Come on. I'll give you a ride."

"I rode my bike."

"Not a problem," Keely said. "I'll lift the hatch and we can store it in the back." It fit nicely with the front wheel removed. It took ten minutes to reach Donnie's place.

"I always wondered who lived out here," Keely said, turning onto the driveway.

Donnie removed his bike and reattached the front wheel. Crisco went straight to the front door. "Want to stay for dinner? Let me check with Kate."

"Can't," Keely said. "Sunday dinner's a big deal at my place. See you tomorrow."

Donnie couldn't stop grinning. "Okay."

Keely was about to close the door when she stopped and looked at him. "You know, disc dogs are a big sport these days."

"What disc dogs?" Donnie said.

Keely pointed at Crisco. "That one."

CHAPTER EIGHTEEN
HOT STUFF

AFTER DINNER, DONNIE PUT CRISCO IN HIS BACKPACK AND pedaled to Nate's, crossing the Arliss Street Bridge. Nate's old pickup was in the yard, and Nate was in the kitchen banging pots and howling to The Spinners' "Rubberband Man." Donnie held the screen door for the dog and followed her into the kitchen, which smelled like grease, cumin and bourbon. Donnie noticed the open bottle of Jack Daniel's and the tumbler at Nate's elbow.

Suddenly Nate caught sight of the dog and jumped back with a shout. Then he saw Donnie.

"What are you laughing at? Come in a man's house uninvited with some misbegotten mutt..."

Donnie leaned over and turned down the music.

"Whatsa matter? Don'tcha like The Spinners?" Nate said.

"Never heard of them."

Nate stared at him like he was a rat. "Son, your cultural patrimony is sorely lacking. Listen to this." He jumped to "Games People Play" and turned up the volume.

Donnie forced himself to listen, but after the first couple of bars, it wasn't a problem. They listened to "One of a Kind," "Then Came You" and "Working My Way Back to You" before Nate reached over and turned it back down.

"Okay," Donnie said. "I gotta have that."

Nate removed the CD from the boom box, put it in its case and handed it to Donnie.

"Wow! Thanks, man!"

"Is you hip to the blues?"

Donnie looked confused.

"I think so."

Nate reeled back like Richard Pryor. "Son, if you don't dig the blues, you got a hole in your soul! If you must choose, let it be the blues!" He reached over, plucked a disc and slid it in. "Son Seals. Learn it, love it, live it."

Crisco stood on her hind legs, paws against Nate's knee.

"What the hell is this?"

"This is Crisco."

Crisco leaped into Nate's lap. "She's a cute pup, that's for sure. I'm makin' chili. Want to try some?"

"I just ate dinner."

"You can at least try it."

Donnie sat. Crisco jumped from Nate's lap to his. Nate spooned out a bowl.

"I can't have that dog sittin' there when we're eating."

Donnie dumped Crisco to the floor as Nate set a bowl in front of him. "Where you been?"

"Started school last week," Donnie said, eyeing the chili for insects.

"How'd that go?"

"Everywhere I go there's always some asshole giving me shit."

Nate scooped out his own bowl. "Ain't that the truth. Same in the Army. Got outta high school, tried a year of college; it wasn't for me. My old man was in the plumber's union. Wanted me to join. That wasn't for me. I wanted to see the world. So I signed up. Next thing I know I'm humpin' sixty pounds through a rice paddy. Lucky I didn't get my balls blowed off."

He sat at the table and looked down at Crisco, who looked up with bug eyes. She had a chesty little Jimmy Cagney body, and her forehead met her snout at a right angle.

"Sits like a frog, don't she? Look at them legs."

"Yeah, she's kind of boneless. Were you ever married?"

"Three times, last time for five years to a ball-breaking bitch named Brenda. Met her in a bar in San Diego. Two days later I wake up in a cheap motel in Las Vegas with her next to me wearin' a ring. To this day I don't recall proposin.' Took me six years to get rid of her. Son, take my advice. Get to know her sober. You gonna eat that chili?"

Donnie dipped his spoon in the chili, blew on it and slipped it into his mouth. In a nanosecond his eyes bulged, sweat popped on his forehead and scalp, and a furnace ignited in his mouth and belly. He got up breathing hard, went to the kitchen sink, turned it on and stuck his mouth directly under the faucet.

Nate regarded him placidly as he chewed and swallowed. "Too hot?"

"Holy shit, Nate! What did you put in it?"

"Friend of mine grows chili peppers. He warned me

these were a little hot. Maybe I shoulda tested them before adding."

"You could melt glass with this shit!"

Nate's face went red, and he'd begun to sweat as he tried to maintain his cool. Nate lasted one more spoonful before sliding the bowl away and pouring himself a big glass of water, which he emptied. "Damn! I *knew* I should have tested those chili peppers! Well sheeit. It's too goddamn hot to give a dog!"

"This is what happens when you cook drunk," Donnie said.

Nate shuddered and put a lid on the gently boiling pot. He turned the stove off. "I wasn't that hungry anyway." He picked up a small paper bag. "These ain't fit for man nor beast."

He opened the cupboard beneath the sink and tossed the paper bag in the trash.

"Can I have 'em?" Donnie said.

Nate looked at him quizzically. "What for?"

"I can use 'em in science class. We gotta do a project. Ahmina do mine on the world's hottest foods."

Nate reached beneath the sink and handed the paper bag to Donnie. "They're all yours."

Donnie zipped them up in an outside pocket of his backpack. "Thanks, Nate. I'd better get back. School tomorrow."

"See you around, youngblood."

CHAPTER NINETEEN
WHAT TO DO

IN THE CAFETERIA ON MONDAY, DONNIE OBSERVED TWO things: one, he had a raging boner for Keely, sitting opposite, happily oblivious to the effect she was having; and two, Ryan Cutler swooping down on another hapless nerd, stuffing the nerd's hot dog into his maw like a breechloader, chewing and swallowing a foot from Nerdface. The poor shmuck could only stare in fear, trying not to cry while Ryan's butt-boy Lester hooted.

Mr. Haskins was nowhere to be seen. Millie Childs was on cafeteria duty, and she was about as effective as a pet rock. She looked like a feed sack and had an itsy-bitsy voice that inspired derision. She buried her face in a book by Anaïs Nin. It was a miracle the cafeteria hadn't broken out in riots.

Keely's foot brushed Donnie's. They got in a footsie battle, which did nothing for Donnie's hard-on. He thought about sex most of the time. Was it like this for everybody? How did anybody get any work done? He looked at Miss Childs, wondering if anyone had ever desired her. Had to be freaks who went for that sort of thing.

It was a relief when the bell rang and Donnie went to English. Elizabeth Dowling, a tall middle-aged woman with cat eye glasses and a curly bun, taught English. As she shut the door, Donnie looked around him. In a class of two dozen, at least half had their noses buried in their smart phones. Mrs. Dowling whacked her desk with a yardstick, drawing their attention. Donnie figured they issued yardsticks to all the teachers.

"Listen up, class! Put those phones away now. Do not put them in your backpacks or pockets; lift up the desk tops and put them inside the desk. Now, Elisha and Ron."

Sheepishly the class complied.

"You're seniors now. Next year you will all hopefully graduate. Some of you will go on to college, some of you will go to work right away, so it's time for you to plan your future. You will each write a two-thousand-word essay on what you plan to do when you graduate from school."

Groans and shuffling. *Wham!* went the yardstick against the desk.

"You are not here to gossip or play games. The purpose of school is to prepare you for adult life. You will learn to write an essay if it kills you. An essay is a point of view, an argument, but it need not be argumentative. You can think of it as an expression of purpose. It will have a beginning, a middle and an end and will come to a conclusion.

"Start small and grow it from there. State your goal in a single sentence. 'I want to be a race car driver.' 'I want to be a news anchor.' Then tell us why and how you plan to achieve your goal."

Mrs. Dowling snapped her fingers at two girls

giggling in the last row. "Pay attention, girls, unless you want to end up on *Judge Judy*. You may start now. I will be happy to help, but for starters, take out your notepads and write down what you want to be."

A skinny boy in glasses raised his hand.

"Yes, Brett?"

"What if we don't know what we want to be?"

"Well figure it out. Write down two or three possibilities and narrow it down. Come on, people. You won't be schoolkids forever. The purpose of school is to prepare you for adult life, and by God I intend to do just that."

"You said 'God,'" said one of the giggling girls.

"Thank you for pointing that out, Brenda. Are you going to report me to the school board?"

Giggles.

"Get to work, people!"

Donnie stared at his blank page. Famous skateboarder, like Tony Hawk? Successful rapper, like Eminem? He knew at some level that these were unrealistic goals, but he couldn't imagine himself wearing a suit and tie and going to an office job every day. He wasn't blind to reality. Most of his friends had come from broken families, many of them on welfare. The kids who had two parents seemed better adjusted.

Nobody grew up hoping to become an insurance salesman. It just happened because people had to make a living. Even celebrities made a living. They had to produce the songs or movies or create some internet company before they became famous, so wanting to become famous by itself was not an option.

Except for people like Paris Hilton and the cast of *Jersey Shore*.

Well what?

Donnie made a list. Policeman. Fireman. Join the

Army. He stared at it in loathing, ripped it out, crumpled it up and tossed it in his desk. Mrs. Dowling was on him like a hawk on a June bug.

"Having trouble, Donnie?"

He looked up at her friendly gray eyes. "Mrs. Dowling, I have no idea what I want to be when I grow up."

"Well what do you enjoy doing? Start by making a list of that."

He would have written "fucking," but he'd never done it.

He wrote "veterinarian." Then he crossed it out and wrote "race car driver."

CHAPTER TWENTY
FUN COOKING

By the time he got to work, he'd changed his mind a dozen times. He'd dismissed juggler, guitar god and comic book artist as too ridiculous and now favored jet fighter pilot and/or race car driver. His forklift became a Brabham Formula One car, the wide row between the aisles of shelving became the back straight at Mulsanne.

"Here came the steely-eyed, cool-as-a-Popsicle, impossibly young and handsome Donnie Waits threatening to take the lead from the current leader, Giuseppe Monte Carlo! That Brabham pentacle engine generates a thousand horsepower, folks, but so far no one has been man enough to wrestle it around the circuit without exploding!"

"Look out!" a spectator cried from the stands as Donnie drove the forklift into a towering pile of discarded boxes.

Donnie snapped out of it, turning red and throwing the ugly metal cube into reverse as boxes plummeted. He looked over to see who'd busted him. Thank God! Just a grunt named Paco. Paco, who was in his early twenties, with jet black hair and mustache, stared at him for a minute.

"Didn't choo see that?"

"No, sorry, man."

Donnie put it in his rearview, finishing his assignment with the utmost care. As he was putting the forklift away, he saw Roddy.

"Hey, Roddy! Who do I talk to about getting that Weenie Wagon running?"

Roddy stared at him in consternation. "Nobody. You don't talk to nobody!"

Donnie got down and walked over to the time clock. "Why not?"

Roddy looked around to see if anyone was within earshot and lowered his voice. "This fuckin' meat plant is hanging on by a thread. If Werner's doesn't turn it around in the next year, we'll all be out of jobs."

Donnie experienced a sucking void in his gut at the thought of Kate's losing her job and their having to move again. "Seriously?"

"Listen, you know how to do a Google search, don't you? Look it up. Look at the share prices over the past five years. You didn't hear it from me." Roddy pointed a finger at him.

Donnie shook his head. "Gotcha."

It was dark by the time he entered his apartment. Kate was online and Crisco was on her bed.

"She was barking, so I let her in. How was school?"

"Great. I saw Ryan Cutler jam this kid's hot dog in his mouth and swallow it all in one motion."

Kate's eyes remained glued to the monitor. "How was work?"

"Great. They say the company's going broke and we'll all be out of work."

Kate looked at him. "Who said that?"

Donnie waved. "I'm just joking. Just a test to see if you were listening."

Kate made a face and held out her arms. "Gimme a hug. You hungry?"

"No, I had some sausage at work. I brought some home for you guys if you're interested."

"I'm not but she might be. You know, I think we ought to call her Cisco. That way people won't be confused."

"They're not confused now, Ma! Cisco?!"

"You know!" Kate said. "It's friendlier. "The Cisco Kid was a friend of mine. He drink whiskey, Poncho drink the wine."

Donnie squinted at her.

"Never mind. Do you mind? She won't know the difference, and I'd feel so much better."

"Ma, I know you hate to cook."

"I'm serious."

"You're gonna give her a complex."

Kate swiveled to the bed. "Here, Cisco!"

The pup bounced up, butt wagging, and went to Kate.

"Whatever!" Donnie said, heading for the kitchen. Cisco, as she was now known, followed at his heels. He took a smoky link out of the plastic bag they'd given him and held it five feet above the ground. "Sit!" he commanded.

Cisco leaped straight up and snagged the sausage like Charles Barkley going for a rebound. Donnie sat on the sofa and turned on the television. *The Voice* was on. On the coffee table was a little pamphlet, "Werner's Meats Cookout Fun." The washed-out colors screamed early '60s.

"Hey, Ma, what's this?"

"What's what?" she shouted back.

"This wiener pamphlet?"

Kate appeared in the doorway to her bedroom. "Frank wants me to redesign it. He hired a PR group out of Milwaukee to chart a new direction for the company."

"Roddy says the business is in trouble and may shut down."

A pained look crossed Kate's face. "Is that who told you?"

Donnie shrugged.

"There are all sorts of factors at work, but it's true the company has experienced a downturn. That's what the redesign is all about. That's why Frank hired me."

"I thought it was the vegans," Donnie said.

"Very funny, kiddo. Take a look at that pamphlet. See if you can think of anything."

With the dog in his lap, Donnie opened the pamphlet.

"Fun cooking never stops when you have Werner's Meats. Even during the unfriendliest weather, you and the family can share many happy times having a cook-in! Simply build the fire in your fireplace and grill these flavorful meats to your heart's content. You can buy a flip grill, or a grill that fits over the fire basket. Or a few bricks with a metal grid laid on will serve just as nicely.

"Liver Sausage Pickle Dip: 1 package Werner's Wiener Liver Sausage, 2/3 cup minced garlic dill pickles, 1/3 cup minced celery, 2 Tbsp. minced onion, 1 Tbsp. pickle juice, 1 tsp. lemon juice, 1/4 tsp. garlic powder, 1/4 tsp. Tabasco sauce. Cream liver sausage. Add ingredients in order listed. Blend well. Chill."

"MA! I don't think this pamphlet can be saved."

CHAPTER TWENTY-ONE
WALK/RUN

KATE STAYED UP SO LATE THAT DONNIE DIDN'T GET A chance to check his FB page. He met Keely in the cafeteria at noon. She pulled a plastic disc from her backpack and handed it to him. On the back it said SELECT SIRES with the address and contact information for a breeding company.

"That's for Crisco."

"She's Cisco now," Donnie said.

"Since when?"

"Since last night. Kate wanted it. I don't care. Crisco, Cisco, she's still the same dog."

Kate leaned in conspiratorially. "You know that video I took of Cisco snatching those jerks' Frisbee? It's got over a thousand hits."

"Wow," Donnie said. "Maybe we should make one on purpose. I wonder how high she can jump."

"Look up 'disc dog championship' when you get home," Keely said.

A cry of outrage split the lunch room. Keely and Donnie turned to see Ryan, back arced in an ecstasy of gluttony, facing the ceiling and tamping in the vestiges of Malcolm's hot dog that Ryan had swiped on the fly. Donnie looked around and saw Miss Childs with her face buried in a book about doll collecting.

"I warned him not to eat the hot dogs," Donnie said.

"Who? Malcolm or Ryan?"

Phys ed was next. Mr. Pagel addressed the assembled in the locker room. He wore cotton shorts and a cotton knit shirt with a collar, carried a clipboard and had a whistle around his neck on a lanyard.

"Today is the six-hundred-yard walk/run we conduct twice a year, in the fall and in the spring, to ascertain your level of fitness. You're all young men. I assume we don't have anyone with a heart condition or some other excuse to avoid this common high school test. Change into your shorts and running shoes and meet me outside by the track."

"Bataan Death March," Malcolm whispered to Donnie in the locker room.

Twenty-two kids lined up at the track behind Mr. Pagel, who had exchanged the clipboard for a stopwatch. "We'll run six at a time. Ames, Butler, Cutler, Carruthers, Davidson and Erving, to your marks."

Coach blew his whistle and the six took off, Cutler effortlessly taking the lead. The remaining boys stood around shifting their feet, punching one another on the shoulder and gossiping. Malcolm said, "I hate this crap. I hate it! Last year I almost seized a piston. I came in dead last."

"It's called walk/run for a reason, dude," Donnie said. "Just walk. What do you care if you post a good time?"

"If I don't cooperate, they call my old man in for a consultation. They'll tell him he has to get on my ass at home. Eat less! Exercise more! I call bullshit."

"I feel your pain. Saw you skipped lunch today."

"That motherfucker!" Malcolm wailed. "Would I love to fix him."

"Your day is coming, my friend," Donnie said.

"Whaddaya mean?"

"Can't talk about it. Trust me. He will be hoist with his own petard."

The first group rounded the final corner and stretched for home, Cutler several lengths in the lead. Coach crouched with his stopwatch at the finish line, pressing down with brio and pumping a fist in the air as Cutler flew by. He barely noticed the other boys.

"Excellent, men. Excellent. Except for Harris. Here he comes now."

The hapless Harris dragged his sorry ass across the finish line a half minute behind the others.

"Cutler," Coach said. "You just tied the school record. Three minutes and twelve seconds!"

Cutler tucked his thumbs into his armpits and did the chicken strut. He wasn't even breathing hard. Mr. Pagel called six more and blew the whistle. Donnie and Malcolm hung back.

"You see that latest *Ghost Rider*?" Malcolm said.

"Nahh. I don't even know where to buy comics around here."

"I get 'em at Capital City in Madison. Anyhow, now he's Latino and drives a hot rod."

"What?!" Donnie exclaimed.

"Yeah. I wrote 'em a letter. I ain't that crazy about the new Batman either."

Donnie put his head in his hands and moaned. "What have we come to?"

"That's not all. Marvel's turning Thor into a woman."

"No!" Donnie gasped.

"Waits!" Coach snarled. "Wake up! You and Lipschitz to the line!"

"Move it, Jewboy," Freckles urged.

"Don't hang with me," Malcolm muttered. "I seen you run. Go ahead and run."

Mr. Pagel made plain through his cavalier attitude that he did not expect much from this last group, which coincidentally was made up of stoners, losers and fat boys. When he blew the whistle, Donnie took off like a particle beam, channeling all his frustration and pent-up adolescent anger into his legs. At the first turn he couldn't even hear the others, they were so far behind. He was vaguely aware of some kids pointing and Mr. Pagel scratching his head. By the time Donnie rounded the final turn, Mr. Pagel was crouched and ready like a hungry tiger. As Donnie blazed by, he heard the coach say, "Wow!"

Donnie slowed to a walk, chest a little heated, breathing hard.

"Waits!" Mr. Pagel boomed. "You just posted a new school record!"

Ryan glared at Donnie in rage.

CHAPTER TWENTY-TWO
STAR TURN

"Waits," Mr. Pagel said on the way into the locker room, "I want you to try out for the track team. Can you come by after school?"

"I'm sorry, Coach, but I've got a job."

They entered the humid locker room to the sound of banging doors and jabber. "Oh? Where you working?"

"Werner's Meats every day after school."

"Hmmm," Mr. Pagel said, following Donnie toward the shower. "Is this a matter of economic necessity?"

"Well, yeah, if I want money."

"Suppose I could get you a job working for the athletic department. What do they pay?"

"Seven fifty an hour."

"Hmmm," Mr. Pagel said. "Let me look into that."

Donnie had no interest in joining the track team. He didn't seek glory and had participated in track at the previous school only because he had a crush on a girl and tried to impress her. It had come to nothing. He was relieved when Mr. Pagel left him to his shower.

Several people congratulated him on his run between fifth and sixth period, and Ryan passed without a punch, eyes straight ahead. After school, Donnie rode his bike to Werner's and punched in, wondering if he would still have a job in the coming months and if so, how he would get to work when the weather changed.

His plan was to save enough money to buy a cheap used car. He would pass the driver's test come hell or high water. If Kate wouldn't take him to Motor Vehicles, he'd ask Nate, but he couldn't imagine Kate turning him down. He'd mustered his arguments. With a license and his own car, he could run errands. She wouldn't have to worry about him getting around during the winter. He could take Cisco to the vet.

The vet!

The dog needed vaccinations before she was bitten by a rabid bat and killed them all! Donnie worked like a madman unloading crates off a truck and stacking them in the warehouse. It was close to six, quitting time during the week, when he saw Frank Werner talking to Roddy.

Donnie parked the forklift and waited until Frank noticed him.

"Donnie?"

"Sir, have you thought of restoring the Weenie Wagon? I think it could convey a powerful message about sausage to today's youth."

Frank grinned. "What's the message?"

"Eat more wieners," Donnie said earnestly.

"It's kind of low on our priorities right now," Frank said, "but I'll give it some thought."

"I have some ad ideas," Donnie said.

"Let's hear 'em."

"Want a leaner, meaner body? Eat a leaner, meaner wiener."

"O-kay."

"Also, you could give away free condoms with the Werner's logo."

Frank clapped Donnie on the back. "I like the way you think. Keep it up."

Donnie couldn't wait to get home. Kate was meeting her friend Kim for drinks and had left him instructions to heat a frozen meal in the microwave. Donnie brought Cisco up and went online. Keely was online too.

"Need a vet for Cisco. Know any?"

"We use Morton's Veterinary. They're good with horses and dogs. Hey! Is it true you set a new school record?"

"I guess. Pagel wants me to join the track team."

"Will you?"

"Don't think so. I need my job."

Donnie watched the Cisco video—two and a half minutes of pure joy, including the sound of Ryan and Lester cursing. He reposted it on his own page, and as he watched it garnered three likes. "Cisco eats only Werner's wieners," he wrote. And beneath that, "Werner's—a meaner, leaner wiener!"

It was still light out when Donnie took Cisco out behind the building to the patchy lawn. He hadn't thrown a flying disc for years, but the technique had never left him. It was all in the wrist and spin. Maximum spin, minimal wrist. If you held the disc too long, it would invariably rotate to a vertical position and ignominiously fall to earth.

Cisco tried to wrench the disc from Donnie's hand. He skimmed it lightly over the crabgrass and Cisco took off, leaped and snagged it out of the air. She returned, sat at his feet with the disc in her mouth, butt wagging.

"Well all right," Donnie said.

He threw the disc until it got dark. The little dog was twenty for twenty. Upstairs he went back online and looked up "disc dogs," and that's where he learned about Ashley Whippet and the World Disc Dog Championship.

CHAPTER TWENTY-THREE
KEELY'S INSPECTION

DONNIE TOOK OFF WORK AFTER SCHOOL ON THURSDAY SO Keely could drive him and Cisco to the veterinarian. Louise Morton, young and beautiful with long honey-colored hair, examined Cisco minutely with her hands on a stainless-steel table as Donnie pinched himself under the arm to take his mind off his boner. He dreamed of a world where Dr. Morton begged him not to stop, a world in which he was suave and charming. He was pretty certain he'd know what to do. He'd been practicing for years.

"Very healthy pup," Dr. Morton said.

"Do you know what kind of dog she is?"

"She's a Heinz 57 Variety dog, but I would guess Boston terrier and pug, although where that tail came from I don't know. I'm going to give her shots for rabies and distemper, which will be good for three years. You need to have her spayed in the next couple of months."

Keely sat in a corner hunched over her phone.

The bill came to sixty-five dollars, which Donnie paid from his first paycheck. On the way home, Cisco perched proudly on his lap, displaying her new bright red nylon collar with accompanying honors and awards.

"I think we're going to train for the World Disc Dog Championship."

"The WDDC?!" Keely said in awe.

"Yeah."

"Never heard of it," she sneered.

"You are so sarcastic!"

Keely grinned. "It's my default mode. So what do you do, exactly, in the World Disc Dog Championship?"

"There are several competitions, including freestyle and long distance. Freestyle, you do a routine to music—catching, dance, doggie acrobatics, jumps and catches, me catching the dog in mid-air."

"You could train with a medicine ball," Keely said.

"Doc says there's no telling how big she'll get."

"What if she tops out at two hundred pounds?"

"Dubious."

Keely turned onto the gravel drive at the edge of town.

"Want to see her catch?" Donnie said.

"Yeah. But you've got to stop calling her Cisco. Her name should be Disco."

Donnie squinted in consternation. "Not you too!"

"I'm serious. She won't notice the difference, and it fits."

Donnie opened the door; Disco leaped out and he followed. "This is the fourth name she'll have! And God knows how many names she had before this. We'll give her a complex!"

Keely knelt in the grass. "Here, Disco! Good girl!"

The dog ran to her, butt wagging, got up on its hind legs and licked her face. "See?"

Donnie waved a plastic disc over his head. "Whatever!"

In the fading afternoon light, he tossed the disc, starting short and increasing the distance with each throw. Disco didn't miss a beat. Keely and Donnie turned at the sound of a second-story window's cranking open.

"Donnie, dinner! Ask your friend if she wants to eat, too."

"Okay, Ma!" Donnie turned to Keely, who already had her phone out. She spoke briefly.

"I can stay," she said.

"Great!"

Upstairs, Donnie introduced Keely to his mother.

"May I set the table, Mrs. Waits?" Keely said.

"Call me Kate, Keely," Kate said. "Donnie will set the table."

Donnie rolled his eyes and went to the silverware drawer. He picked up a fork and held it up, pinkie extended. "Shall we use the Queen Anne or the gold plate!"

There were at most three matching pieces; odds and ends from over the years, picked up in thrift shops, comprised the rest. Kate had made some kind of dish with Italian sausage, mushrooms, onions, tomatoes, garlic and pasta.

Kate was a quizzer. She would wait until your mouth was full before asking a question. "What do your parents do, Keely?"

Keely chewed and swallowed. "My father is a developer, and my mother is a Realtor. We also have stables."

"Do you have any brothers or sisters?"

"My older brother's in Afghanistan with the Air

Force. Did Donnie tell you he set a school record for the six-hundred-yard run?"

Kate put her fork down. "Why, no! Donnie, why didn't you tell me?"

Donnie shrugged. "No biggie. Probably just a fluke."

"I swear, this kid never talks to me! How was Cisco?"

"She's Disco now, Ma."

Kate raised her eyebrows. "Since when?"

"Since I decided to train her as a disc dog."

After dinner, Kate excused herself. "I'm going to the mall. I should be back in an hour. Donnie, will you take care of the dishes?"

"You bet, Ma. Have a good time."

As soon as she was out the door, Donnie set the dishes on the floor and Keely watched with delight as Disco slobbered them clean. When Donnie returned them to the cupboards unrinsed, she got up.

"Gross. See you tomorrow."

CHAPTER TWENTY-FOUR
THE EXPERTS

THE CONFERENCE ROOM ON THE TOP FLOOR OF WERNER'S had an expansive glass wall that looked out on rolling farmland and the holding pens. Eight people sat around the immense mahogany table, including Frank Werner, Kate, Sales Vice President Herbert Woytciwicz, Marketing Vice President John Howard and four representatives from Kramer Advertising, including CEO Alan Kramer, the young and beauteous Bethany Schultz and two young yes-men in glasses and ties.

They all had laptops set up in front of them. A sideboard held coffee, tea and a selection of doughnuts. A large flat-screen TV was mounted on the inside wall and depicted a graph of Werner's sales over the past ten years. The line slanted downhill.

Kramer did not come cheap. Frank had had to extend his personal credit to bring them in. If he could not turn around sales in the next twelve months, that would be it, an ignominious end to the company his grandfather had started in 1949.

Frank straightened his shoulders, and the conversation ceased. "I'd like to introduce Alan Kramer of Kramer Advertising and his assistants, Bethany Schultz, Jessie Klingensmith and Jim Brooks. We've known for some time that our current message isn't reaching the customer base we need, so I've asked Alan to take a look at our situation and postulate a few solutions, because these guys are the experts. Alan?"

Kramer was a big, buff guy in a dark blue suit with long, wavy silver hair combed back in a pompadour, hair that belonged on a TV lawyer. "Thank you, Frank. Our team has gone over your advertising for the past ten years as well as researched the successful techniques not only of meat packers but of other major food providers, including General Mills, Newman's Own and Whole Foods.

"Werner's faces a number of challenges in this century, including changing public tastes and perceptions and changing health habits. You've all heard the slogan Meat Is Murder. You all dismissed it as utopian hyperbole. Unfortunately, this kind of thinking permeates our culture to the point where vegetarians now comprise 30 percent of the general population.

"You will never get the vegetarians. The goal is to raise awareness of not only the taste of meat but its nutritional value. Meat is good food! Sausages and other prepared meats have gotten a bum rap over the years due to nitrates, carcinogens, etc., etc. We have a few scenarios. Bethany?"

Bethany had long, lustrous black hair and wore a simple sleeveless shift with a moderate neckline at which John Howard stared. "Is it possible to make sausage without nitrates?"

Frank's jaw tensed. "Not really. Not only do they give

the meat its characteristic flavor, they also provide the color."

Bethany dismissed it with a flip of her locks. "Not a problem. Meat is good food." She paused and looked around.

"Go on," Frank said.

"Meat Is Good Food could be the centerpiece of your new advertising campaign."

"Meat Is Good Food," Frank said with exaggerated diction. "What else you got?"

Jessie tentatively raised his hand. He was soft, with a receding hairline and plump lips. "Man is the top of the food chain. Man was meant to eat meat. Meat is natural."

"Can't say 'man,'" John said. "We mean, people are the top of the food chain. People were meant to eat meat."

A crease of irritation appeared on Bethany's forehead. "We've prepared some visuals. How do I..."

Kate rose and came around the table, pointing to an input port at the base of the wall-mounted screen. "Plug in here."

Bethany plugged her laptop in and fiddled with the keyboard. A series of images appeared briefly: HuffPost, TMZ, a picture of Bethany naked on a bed belly down, smiling at the camera. Bethany colored and hurriedly changed the picture until she came to a page labeled "Werner's" showing a series of folders. She clicked on one, and the screen filled with the bright black-and-white image of an elegant couple in *The Thin Man* mode, he in a tux, she in a cocktail dress, in a hoity-toity restaurant straight out of a Fred Astaire movie. The waitress wore a white apron, her hair piled high, with bee-stung lips.

"Your choice of wine?"

"We'll have the '38 Chateau de Rothschild Merlot."

"May I tell you about our specials?"

"Never mind the specials," the woman said in a tough newsgal voice. "We'll have the Werner's Polish sausage and kraut!"

ELEGANCE IS BACK IN STYLE appeared at the bottom in blood-red script.

Bethany froze the image while Kramer and the two yes-men applauded. John Howard joined in.

Bethany brought another image up, a sales chart related to celebrity endorsements. American Express, pre- and post-Samuel L. Jackson. Reverse mortgages with Fred Thompson, Breck with Beyoncé. "Studies show that celebrity endorsements can be highly effective with a targeted audience," Bethany said. "We have very good relations with a number of Hollywood agencies, and the following celebrities are open to pitches: Val Kilmer, Lindsay Lohan, Christian Slater, Sean Young, Danny Bonaduce and Heather Graham, just for starters."

Kate jumped into the hole. "Maybe Werner's needs a spokes–cartoon character, like the GEICO gecko or the Michelin Man."

"We have some thoughts on that," Kramer said. "Bethany?"

A cartoon flying pig appeared on the screen. "Porkton Van Ham," Bethany said.

"GEICO already has a flying pig," Frank said.

"But it's an anthropomorphic pig," Bethany said. "Ours is a real flying mammal."

"You mean a real flying cartoon pig," Frank said. "Been there, done that."

"No one will mistake Porkton Van Ham for the GEICO pig," Bethany said tendentiously. A picture of green sausage with red lettering on a green plate appeared onscreen. The lettering said ORGANICALLY GROWN.

"Green sausage," Bethany said. "This could open up entire new markets for you, boutique food emporiums like Whole Foods, Sprouts and Organic Joe's."

"Green eggs and ham," Kate muttered.

"Expanding on that idea," Kramer said, "have you thought of reconfiguring your sausage so that it is made of free-range chicken, wild turkey or feral hogs? I understand there's a huge feral hog problem down South."

Only Kate noticed the signs of deep chagrin on Frank's face. He did his best to maintain a poker face throughout the rest of the hour-long meeting, at the end of which Kate caught his eye and said, "Remember your three o'clock."

"Oh my gosh, you're right! Well I hate to cut this short..."

CHAPTER TWENTY-FIVE
WHOLE NEW IMAGE

SEPTEMBER STRETCHED INTO OCTOBER WITH UNUSUALLY pleasant weather. Donnie went to his job every day after school and then raced home to work with Disco for an hour before eating dinner and hitting the homework. On September 22 he couldn't find his time card, so he sought out Roddy.

Roddy had a pained expression. "Sorry, kid. I just got word we got to cut expenses across the board. You've been pink-slipped."

Donnie was not exactly devastated. It was just a job. He'd known all along it was a make-work favor for Kate, and now he worried about Kate's job. She couldn't lose her job, not again. Donnie didn't think he could take another frantic search for employment followed by uprooting and traveling to another city.

He rode to Nate's and leaned his bike against the front porch. Nate sat in a lawn chair at the end of his pier with a line in the water, a pint bottle of Jack at his side, a black cheroot in his mouth. Lightnin' Hopkins played through an open window.

"How's it goin', youngblood?" he said.

"I just lost my job."

"What job?"

Donnie told him.

"Hell, I'd hire ya but I'm barely making ends meet as it is."

"Hey, Nate, can I drive your pickup? Just down the road. I'm gonna be sixteen in six weeks, and I need to practice for my test."

Nate fished in his pocket and tossed Donnie a set of keys attached to a plastic float. "Knock yourself out. Don't hit nothin'."

Donnie practically leaped behind the wheel. The Ford pickup was at least twenty years old and had a floor-mounted stick shift. He started the engine, put it in first and with the utmost care let the clutch out. The truck lunged and died. It took him four more tries to get it moving forward in first. His upshift was greeted with grinding gears. He eventually got into fourth, by which time he'd traveled a half mile and had to turn around in a field entrance. Parking the truck in front of the shop, Donnie walked around to the pier and found Nate bent over his knees coughing spasmodically into a hand-kerchief.

Spots of red appeared on the soiled cloth.

"You okay?" Donnie said.

"Fine. I got an appointment with the VA next month."

"I thought you said it was this month."

"They pushed me back. Don't worry. I'll get in there. It's that fuckin' Agent Orange."

"Hey, Nate, if Kate can't make it, can you take me to my driver's test?"

"Gonna be sixteen, huh? Yeah, no prob. Hey, you know where I can get any reefer?"

Donnie hadn't smoked pot since the first week of school. He'd seen kids dealing in the parking lot. They were sketchy, not serious about life, and he stayed away from them. "I got a couple doobies I can lay on you."

"That'd be great but I'm lookin' to cop like a couple ounces. Come on. You must know somebody at school." He reached into his cargo pants pocket, withdrew a frayed fabric wallet and handed Donnie two C-notes. "Here. See how much you can get for that. And you know how to check if it's good pot, right? I don't want any ditch weed."

"Come on," Donnie said, pocketing the bills. "If there's one thing I know, it's pot."

The light was fading by the time Donnie pulled up at the apartment building. Kate was still at the office. Donnie could hear Disco's hysterical ululation as soon as he entered the building. Somehow the dog knew. Disco was there to greet him at the door leaping, lapping and licking. He went down on his knees to squeeze her, then tossed his things on the dining room table and shut the door.

Out on the balcony Disco had neatly deposited her poop and piss on the spread newspapers. Donnie held a plastic disc and Disco went crazy, running in circles and yapping. They worked the disc in the fading light in the field next to the apartment building, Donnie perfecting his release, Disco going for longer and longer flights.

They were still out there at twilight as Kate pulled around to the back and parked in the gravel lot. Donnie and Disco met her at the door.

"Hi, Ma! Uh-oh."

She had that face—mouth turned down, creases in her forehead.

"What's wrong, Ma?" A bolus of dread formed in his gut.

Kate forced a smile and hugged him. "Nothing, kiddo. Hard day at work. The big-bucks ad agency Frank hired was as useful as a Ouija board. You could do better."

"Yeah, they eliminated my position."

"I heard about that, kid. So sorry. I hope you know it had nothing to do with your performance."

They went upstairs into the apartment.

"I know, Ma. I'm worried about your job."

"Well don't be. We've been in this situation before."

Yeah, Donnie thought. *That's why I'm worried.*

"So what do you need? Like an advertising slogan or something?"

Kate tossed her briefcase on the sofa and went into the kitchen, pulling things from the refrigerator. "They need a whole new image. They need to sell sausage. Something to convince people that Werner's sausage is hip, with it, a fun food."

"I got some ideas!"

"They couldn't be any worse than what we heard today."

"I think they should refurbish the Weenie Wagon and show up at sporting events handing out free wieners."

"Free doesn't make money," Kate said, stirring things in a pan.

"Get 'em hooked," Donnie said. "Then they have to pay for the next one."

CHAPTER TWENTY-SIX
JIHAD

IN TOWN, FAKE TOMBSTONES, WHITE SHEETS AND BLACK bats appeared on lawns, porches and in windows. It was Halloween week. Zombies, werewolves and vampires lurched, slunk and flitted through the halls. In home-room Keely texted Donnie: "Party at my house on the 31st! Can you come?"

"Donnie Waits, I see you staring at your phone. Put it away before I take it away," Mrs. Brautigan said.

Sheepishly, Donnie put it away. As Mrs. Brautigan turned to the blackboard, he caught Keely's eye and gave her the thumbs-up. Halloween fell on a Friday that year, and it would be business as usual at Gunderson High.

In phys ed the coach divided his class in two, and they played soccer on the field inside the track. Ryan played forward on the opposing team and wanged the ball at Donnie's head every chance he could. Donnie caught most of them on his forehead, but one struck him in the side when he wasn't looking. There wasn't any pain, but it caught him by surprise. He stumbled and went down to howls of delight from the other team, including the odious Lester, who brayed like a jackal.

On the way into the locker room, Ryan "accidentally" shouldered Donnie into the lockers with a resounding bang. Donnie and Malcolm hung back until the jocks were through even though it made them late for the next period. Donnie noticed red marks on Malcolm's unfortunate chest. Man boobs. No getting around it.

"What are those?" he said.

Malcolm made a pained expression. "Ryan's been giving me titty twisters. Thinks it's funny."

A dark cloud descended on Donnie. Malcolm was somebody with whom he could identify. Malcolm was about the only school friend he had, not counting Keely, whom he had begun to think of as his girlfriend. This would not stand.

It was time for the nuclear option.

After school, Donnie went from business to business on the small Main Street until he came to a Help Wanted sign in the window of the Piggly Wiggly. He applied as a bagger to work twenty hours a week. Just as he was returning home, the phone rang. He had the job, and they wanted him to start Wednesday afternoon. Kate phoned to tell him she was working late and he was on his own for dinner. Donnie zapped a personal-size pizza and gave half to Disco. He went online and watched disc dog competitions for an hour and read the rules.

On his FB page, the Disco video had eighty-four likes and had been shared twelve times. Donnie visited each page and wrote, "Powered by Werner's—a meaner, leaner wiener." He ended up with twelve friend requests.

Having made up his mind to avenge Malcolm, Donnie slept well.

The next morning at school, kids pushed the envelope leading up to Halloween by wearing all sorts of risqué and outlandish costumes. The principal sent two girls home for inappropriate dress. Malcolm showed up in a wizard's cape he'd ordered from a catalog, along with a five-foot oak walking stick.

"Dude," Donnie told him during the break, "I'd leave that in your locker or sure as shit somebody's going to take it away from you."

They stood outside Malcolm's locker in the crowded hall. "You're right," Malcolm said, putting the staff in the locker and removing a stuffed parrot that he affixed to his shoulder with Velcro. Donnie cringed.

"Dude, you wear that and sure as shit somebody's going to swoop up on your ass from behind, rip it off and start tossing it around."

Malcolm's face fell. "Well shit. I can't do anything."

"The robe's bad enough, but don't worry. You shall be avenged."

"What do you mean?"

"Just make sure you're in the cafeteria at noon."

The morning stretched to infinity. Algebra was particularly grueling. If Donnie couldn't do it on his calculator, it wasn't important. He laid low, along with two-thirds of the students, hoping Mr. Heuer wouldn't call on them.

In social studies, Ms. Ott was on a tear. After assigning *I Know Why the Caged Bird Sings*, she said, "You are the future. It's up to you to reverse the tide of racism that has scourged this country since its inception. I am calling on each and every one of you to monitor your parents for racial attitudes and insensitivity."

Incorrigible wiseass Greg raised his hand.

Ms. Ott wore Coke-bottle glasses and had a mass of hair that almost obscured her face, causing students to refer to her behind her back as Cousin It. "What is it, Greg?"

Slumped in his chair like a hipster, Greg said, "So, like, if they only serve me white chicken meat, does that count?"

Ms. Ott considered the question. Fortunately the bell rang.

This was it. Showtime. Donnie headed for the cafeteria. The careful student would have observed it was the first time he had not brought his own lunch. He stood in line. He purchased a hot dog. He took that hot dog to the farthest corner of the cafeteria and performed minor surgery. He waited until he saw Ryan sitting with his sycophants Lester and Dylan, picked up his tray and headed their way, seemingly oblivious. As he approached their table, he saw Keely coming toward him.

Perfect.

Donnie innocently held his tray next to Ryan's head while looking the other way. The predator snapped up the dog, tamped it into his mouth like a python swallowing a goat, chewed and swallowed.

"Mmmm, good!" Ryan exclaimed.

Donnie turned to him placidly and watched. Ryan stared back with a "fuck you" smile that suddenly began to quaver. A look of alarm crept over his face just before it turned red, and sweat appeared on his forehead like battleship rivets. Ryan lurched back from the table, knocking over his chair, and ran for the water fountain.

Mr. Haskins saw the whole thing.

CHAPTER TWENTY-SEVEN
BACK ROOM DEAL

MR. PENNER WAITED PLACIDLY BEHIND HIS DESK LIKE A Buddha, hands neatly folded on what Donnie could only assume was his permanent record. "This is a very serious matter, Mr. Waits. Very serious indeed."

Donnie sat before him in a straight-backed wooden chair left over from some previous school. "What? I like my meat tangy. Did I ask him to steal my food? Did you talk to any witnesses?"

"You knew Cutler couldn't resist you waving your hot dog in his face. What did you put in it?"

"I did not wave my hot dog in his face, sir. I was holding my tray while talking to a friend, and Ryan just grabbed it and stuffed it in his mouth."

"What did you put in it?"

"Chili peppers. The kind people eat."

"Well it must have been a hell of a strong pepper, because that boy is now at the hospital having his stomach pumped."

Donnie felt a cringe of guilt, but then he remembered how he'd first met Ryan.

"Sir, this high school is supposed to be a bully-free zone, isn't it?"

Mr. Penner looked uncomfortable. "It is."

"Are you aware of the extent to which Ryan Cutler has been bullying kids throughout his entire school career? I'm not talking about myself. I'm new this year. I'm talking about kids who dread school like the slaughterhouse because they know Ryan and his gang are going to make them feel awful. Every day."

Mr. Penner reached for a mug of coffee at his elbow and sipped. "There is some question whether Ryan will be able to take the field next week for our kickoff game."

"I've been interviewing his victims. I'm going to post my notes on Facebook."

Donnie saw fear in Mr. Penner's eyes. There was only one thing authorities ever feared: bad publicity. School administrators didn't fear discipline. The unions had their backs. Students didn't fear their teachers. All they had to do was cry "discrimination" or claim they had some sort of psychological problem. They certainly didn't fear their parents.

"Don't do that. I'm sure we can reach an amicable solution. I would like you to take five detentions."

Donnie tried not to gloat. He had this weasel on the run. "May I have one of your cards, sir?"

"Why?"

"So my mother will know to whom I'm speaking."

Mr. Penner swallowed. "What do you suggest?"

"I'll apologize and we'll forget this ever happened."

Mr. Penner stared above Donnie's head. Perhaps he saw his retirement. "Very well. Will you write a letter of apology?"

"No, sir. That is the coward's way out. I will apologize to Ryan in person right here."

Mr. Penner cleared his throat. "Very well. I'll let you know the next time Ryan is back in school."

"Thank you, sir!" Donnie said sincerely.

"You are a very impressive young man."

"Thank you, sir!"

"Do you have any career plans?"

Ach! Again.

"I'm thinking of being a writer," Donnie vamped.

"What kind of writer?"

"An investigative writer, someone who makes a difference, like those guys in *All the President's Men*."

Mr. Penner's egg-like skull split into a smile. "Well now, that's an admirable goal, Donnie. I wanted to be a reporter myself one day. I actually worked for a suburban weekly in Milwaukee for several years."

"That's great, sir! Maybe you can give me some pointers. Did you cover any important stories?"

"I sold ads. All right. Will you give me your word you won't pull anything like this for the rest of the school year?"

"What do you mean, Mr. Penner?"

"Look, Donnie. You're a smart kid. This is my last year. I just want to retire quietly. You scratch my back, I scratch yours. I got enough trouble with kids smoking and selling dope in the parking lot. Don't add to my work."

Donnie stood and extended his hand. "Deal, Mr. Penner."

They shook. Donnie exited the assistant principal's office with head held high and proceeded to the library. He didn't want to make a scene barging into Mrs. Dowling's English class halfway through.

In the library Donnie sat at the computer and watched disc dog competitions. The current Sky Dogz

World Freestyle Champion was an Aussie shepherd named Cactus Jack handled by Lily Carruthers. Cactus Jack looked like some kind of greyhound/monkey mix, while Lily resembled a young Sigourney Weaver. They performed their routine to the tone poem *Thus Sprach Zarathustra*, and Donnie had to admit it was dynamic: Cactus Jack leaping off Lily's back, grabbing discs ten feet in the air; Cactus Jack doing a propeller off Lily's back and catching the disc in the air; Cactus Jack doing a backward somersault and catching the disc in the air.

Donnie smelled Britney Spears perfume and knew the librarian, a pale young woman named Deb Romero, stood behind him. It was Deb's job to see that no one accessed the Kanye/Kim sex tape or *Soldier of Fortune*.

"What's that you're watching, Donnie?" she mewed in a voice that belonged to a timid ten-year-old.

"Disc dog competition, Miss Romero. I'm thinking of competing with my dog."

"What kind of dog do you have?" she minced.

"Some kind of Boston terrier/pug mash-up."

"I wish I could have a dog," Deb said. "My landlord won't let me."

"I'll bring you a picture. There's the bell. See you later, Miss Romero."

At the edge of the parking lot, he purchased an ounce of dope from Greg.

CHAPTER TWENTY-EIGHT
SEALED WITH A HANDSHAKE

THE NEXT DAY, RYAN WAS OUT OF THE HOSPITAL AND good to go. Donnie suspected histrionics and emotional problems from the way Ryan had flopped around like a carpet worm. The apology was set for three o'clock. Donnie worked on it in English class. Mrs. Dowling cruised his desk.

"What's that you're writing?" she said.

"I have to apologize to Ryan Cutler for him swiping my hot dog."

"Yes, I heard about that. I don't know what to say. On the one hand that was very irresponsible of you. What if he'd been allergic? On the other, I am not unaware that Ryan has certain bullying proclivities."

"It was my hot dog, Mrs. Dowling. On my plate. No one asked him to take it."

Mrs. Dowling smiled. "You have elevated passive aggression to an art form."

In phys ed they had moved on to swimming, in which Donnie excelled, scoring the fastest times in the Australian crawl, backstroke and sidestroke in the

Olympic-size swimming pool. Ryan and his cabal stayed away. After showering and dressing, Donnie went to Mr. Penner's office, where Ryan already sat reading an issue of *Sports Illustrated*.

"Ready for your apology?" Donnie said.

Ryan looked up with a funny expression. "I guess. But first I would like to apologize to you for being such a jerk, and in particular for running you off the road last summer."

Donnie was dubious. "Seriously?"

Ryan stood and stuck out his hand. "Seriously."

They shook.

"Well fuck! This apology is no fun," Donnie said, aware that he was watching a transformation.

Mr. Penner opened his door. "Come on in, boys."

They entered. Mr. Penner sat behind his desk.

"Ryan, I apologize for baiting you with a chili-laden hot dog."

"Donnie, I apologize for stealing your hot dog."

"Boys," Mr. Penner said. "Well done. Please proceed to your final-period assignments."

In the hall, Ryan said, "You ought to try out for track, dude. Seriously."

"I have no time for track. I'm training my dog to compete in the World Disc Dog Championship."

"Yeah, I can see that. Hey, a bunch of us are gathering at June Skerritt's house Friday night for a Halloween party. Tell 'em I sent ya."

"Thanks, man, but I got another party to attend."

"Yeah? Whozat?"

"Keely Van Metre."

"Man would I like to fuck her. She's hot, for a Goth."

Donnie just smiled.

Buoyed by the encounter, Donnie floated through

final period and rode his bike to the Piggly Wiggly, where they gave him a white apron and the fundamentals on bag packing and put him to work. It was nine and dark by the time he got home. Disco spotted him from the balcony and emitted a high-pitched squeal, black Goth fingernails on a blackboard scraping inexorably toward Armageddon.

She leaped at him the moment he entered the door. Kate, wearing her reading glasses, sat at the dining room table with her laptop open, amid stacks of papers and brochures.

"How'd it go, kiddo?"

"Well it's easier than unloading pallets, that's for sure. It's a good place to meet people. Whatcha doin'?"

"Frank fired the Kramer Group and said I could do better. So I'm trying to come up with an ad campaign."

"You?"

"Don't act so surprised. I majored in communications."

"Get in shape with Werner's meaner, leaner wiener."

Kate wrote that down.

"The more you scarf, the more you barf."

"That's not helpful."

"You never saw such a sausage."

"Say, about Friday night, do you think you can get yourself to that party? Frank asked me out."

Alarm bells went off in the back of Donnie's brain. Kate's romantic involvements invariably ended in disaster. "That's great, Ma."

"I see that look on your face. I know, I know, I shouldn't date co-workers. But he's not really a co-worker, he's my boss. And he's a good man. He treats people with respect and knows what it is to be a gentleman. He holds the door for women. I trust you're doing the same thing?"

"Every chance I get, Ma."

"This girl you're dating. She's quite the sex kitten."

Donnie flushed.

"I know we've had this talk before, and I'm sorry your sorry-ass father isn't around to give it to you. I could tell you to do as I say and not as I do, and you don't have to tell me. But if you're going to have sex, use some protection."

"MA!"

"All right, I've said my piece. Do you need condoms?"

Donnie clapped his hands over his ears and bent over. "La la la—I can't hear you!" Virgin though he was, he did want condoms but was too embarrassed to ask his mother. He'd ask Nate. Which reminded him—his birthday was in two weeks, and he needed to put in his request, but Kate beat him to it.

"Oh, I almost forgot." Kate stood and hugged him. "Happy birthday, baby! I have something for you."

"Condoms?"

She laughed. "No. Sorry I haven't had time to wrap it." She went into her bedroom and returned with an Ace skateboard with a hand-painted samurai wielding two swords.

It was heavy. "Ma! This is awesome! Thank you!"

"Don't break your neck. What are you going as on Friday?"

"The Badger and Bat Dog."

"You mean Bucky Badger?"

"No, Ma! The *Badger*! Wisconsin's very own superhero!"

"I want you back home by eleven."

"Maaaaaaa!"

CHAPTER TWENTY-NINE
FIRST KISS

DONNIE'S COSTUME WAS A RED MUSCLE SHIRT WITH THE Badger claw stenciled in black, baggy black kung fu trousers, kung fu slippers and black marker on his face. The Badger mask was actually makeup—two black stripes extending upward from the eyes, and two black stripes on either side of the face from under the chin.

Donnie had found a Bat Dog outfit in a thrift store that fit Disco perfectly. He'd traded gigs at the Piggly Wiggly with a boy named Jim who normally worked on Sundays. Keely picked him up at five o'clock on a mild evening dressed as Buffy with a bandolier of wooden stakes over her shoulder.

"Oh!" she said. "You're bringing Disco. Shouldn't you have a leash?"

"Don't need one. She follows me everywhere."

Donnie sat and Disco leaped into his lap. Keely lived on a ranch five miles outside of town. They entered between two brick gateposts supporting a wrought iron trestle. The sign read RANCH DE BLANCHE.

"Blanche is my mother," Keely said, pulling up in

front of a rambling house with curved gables and a shingle roof. There were a half dozen cars parked out front, including a new BMW and a Porsche Boxster. Behind the house was a red barn that opened onto a white-picket-enclosed pasture in which two horses grazed. Donnie was no expert, but the horses were beautiful—white and brown and sleek as seals. The entryway was hung with orange plastic pumpkins lit from within, and the front-facing windows were adorned with spiderwebs and spiders. The Byrds' "Chestnut Mare" spilled through open windows.

Costumed revelers spilled out the open front door onto the flagstone porch, clutching drinks. Donnie saw two vampires, three zombies and a man wearing a Nixon mask. Taking his hand, Keely led him inside, Disco at their heels. People nudged one another and pointed at the dog, who immediately sought out the Van Metres' German shepherd and stuck her nose in his rump.

"That's Chuck," Keely said, leading Donnie to a cluster of four and introducing him to a tall man dressed as Zorro with black domino mask, black *vaquero* hat and a saber at the belt of his pantaloons. "Daddy, this is the boy I've been telling you about, Donnie Waits."

Donnie stuck out his hand. "Pleased to meet you, sir."

"Call me Van. Keely's told us all about you. This is my wife, Blanche, and this is Bob and Sally Prendergast." Blanche was dressed as Snow White, which Donnie thought was pushing it a little, and the Prendergasts as Fred and Wilma Flintstone. Bob had Fred's build.

"Who are you supposed to be?" Bob said.

"The Badger!" Donnie said, as if it were self-evident.

"Well I'm a UW alumnus, and you don't look like Bucky," Bob said.

"Not Bucky, the *Badger*! Wisconsin's own superhero!"

He explained about the comic book. Bat Dog ran up and sat at Donnie's feet, tail wagging.

"I know who she is!" Van Metre declared. "Bat Hound!"

Mrs. Prendergast stooped to pet. "Oh, she's adorable!"

Keely grabbed Donnie's hand. "Come on. I want to show you the barn."

The barn was nicer than some people's houses. They entered through a glass door into a vast, well-lit space with a series of stalls against one wall and a wood floor that included a ground-level pool with a concrete ramp. A wiry man the color of burnished mahogany, with white hair in a crew cut, stood at the side of the pool holding a pole attached to a bridle on a sorrel treading water. He looked up and smiled when he saw Keely.

"There's my sheila! This looks like a rum bunch!"

"Cully, this is Donnie. Cully is our horse trainer. He's from Australia."

Cully stooped to pet Disco. "Why ain't you dressed as Batman?"

"You can't swing a dead cat up here without hitting four Batmen and a Wolverine. I'm the Badger."

"Who's the Badger?"

"Wisconsin's own superhero. He fights crime and talks to animals. Actually, he's a multiple personality, only one of which is a costumed crime fighter."

"Sounds like me!" Cully said. "I talk to animals."

"What's wrong with Jolyanne?" Keely said.

"Bit of a limp. I think she's soaked long enough." Cully picked up the staff and led the horse slowly up the ramp. "I got to rub her down now. You go back to the party. I'll be along directly."

"What do you do with those horses?" Donnie said on the way back.

"I compete in dressage. It's horsy stuff. Want to see my trophies?"

"Sure."

She led him around the back of the house, where footlights illuminated a flagstone patio with a built-in barbecue grill. Disco capered along. Chinese lanterns were hung from the trees, and about a dozen people in costume were talking and drinking. She slid open a sliding glass door and pulled him into a darkened room. The dog followed. She shut all the blinds before turning on the lights, revealing a pine-paneled wall covered with gold, red and blue ribbons, and pictures of Keely in jodh-purs and jockey regalia standing proudly next to her horse, jumping a hurdle, strutting in front of a bleacher filled with people. A wall-mounted shelf contained a dozen trophies.

"Holy shit!" Donnie said. "I had no idea."

"I like to keep a low profile."

Donnie was acutely aware of her proximity, her scent and her short-skirted, tight-sweatered vampire-slayer outfit. Keely used a rheostat to turn the lights down, turned and faced him with a hopeful upturned face. Even Donnie could read this one.

He pulled her close and kissed her.

The dog watched, tail wagging.

CHAPTER THIRTY
OLIVE LOAF

"WIENER'S—A LEANER, MEANER WIENER," KATE SAID TO Frank Werner at the Metropol Cafe on the Milwaukee waterfront.

"Hmm," Frank said, studying the wine list. "What else you got?"

Kate consulted a legal pad.

"Nitrates, shmitrates."

"Go on."

"Werner's, more than just sausage."

The waiter, an olive-complexioned young man with a light beard, hovered. "We'll take a bottle of the Coppola Merlot."

"Excellent," the waiter said, and faded away.

"How bad is it, Frank?" Kate said.

Frank leaned forward and regarded her with his brown eyes. "I sold my condo in Cabo to pay third-quarter taxes and salaries. I'll sell my father's Ferraris if I have to. I'm not going to be the first Werner to run this business into the ground."

"Tell me there's some good news."

"The good news is that I love you and want you to marry me. I have enough set aside that neither one of us will ever have to work."

Kate gave a pained smile. "I need more time, Frank. I like you. I might even love you, but we've only known each other five months. I'm not going anywhere. It would be awkward for you to announce our engagement and then have to give up the company."

Frank smiled. "I understand. Not another word until we resolve the situation. I can't believe how inane their ideas were."

"You know, GEICO runs a whole raftload of campaigns. They've got the lizard, the flying pig, the banjo pickers. Maybe you should spread it out a little more."

"I've only got so much for advertising," Frank said. "I have to tread carefully. If I go with something too abstruse or geeky, I'll lose traditional customers."

"If there were only some way," Kate said, "to make Werner's the food of choice among young people. Hip, young people who ride skateboards and bikes and ski and run and raft."

The waiter returned with a wine bucket, their wine and two goblets. He expertly uncorked the wine and decanted a half inch into Frank's glass. Frank didn't bother to sniff. "It's fine." The waiter poured.

"Let me tell you about our specials," the waiter said.

"We'll have the chateaubriand for two. Mixed lettuce salads with the pesto dressing on the side." He looked at Kate. "That all right with you?"

"Fine."

"Perfect," the waiter said. "I'll get those started."

"What about bringing back olive loaf?" Kate said after

the waiter left. "I don't understand why you stopped making it."

"People don't like olive loaf."

"What about pickle loaf, or radish loaf? I know! Arugula loaf! Infused. Infused with arugula! Whole Foods could go for that."

"Hmmm," Frank said.

"Portobello loaf infused with chai! Winter sausage."

After dinner, they got in Frank's Cadillac. "My place?"

Kate's mouth turned into a slit. "I hate this sneaking around. I told Donnie to be home at eleven."

"Donnie strikes me as an exceptional young man. Surely he can be at home by himself."

Kate sighed, but it was a sigh of pleasure. "All right. But I have to be home by midnight or I turn into a pumpkin."

CHAPTER THIRTY-ONE
NINJA ATTACK

DONNIE AND KEELY SPRAWLED ON THE BIG LEATHER SOFA in the trophy room. Donnie had his hand on Keely's breast but didn't know how to proceed. The problem was solved when Cully unexpectedly opened the patio door and turned on the lights.

"Whoops!" he said. "Fuck me, I was just leavin'."

He exited, turning off the lights. Donnie and Keely burst out laughing. He wanted to ask her if she was still a virgin but didn't have the nerve.

Keely got up, straightening her white blouse and reattaching her stake bandolier. "Come on!" she said, pulling Donnie up. "Let's get some food." Disco leaped off the end of the sofa and grinned, tongue lolling.

The Van Metres had a groaning board laden with grilled hamburgers, hot dogs, fruit and potato salad. Donnie loaded two dogs with ketchup and relish, gave one to Disco.

"I wonder if Gunderson High serves Werner's hot dogs."

"I doubt it," Keely said. "I think they get all their food

from a government warehouse in Kenosha. I think these hot dogs are left over from the Vietnam War. Hey, are you working tomorrow?"

"Yeah. Why?"

"I've got to do some shopping. I'll come by and say hello."

"Great," Donnie said without enthusiasm.

"What?"

Donnie set the hot dog down. "I'm worried that Werner's is going to go under and Mom's going to lose her job. Then we'll have to move."

"I don't even know what that's like," Keely said. "I've lived in this house my whole life."

"Must be nice. Someday I'm going to own my own home, and I'm never going to move again."

Cully sat down next to Keely, plate laden with cheeseburgers and salad. "'Ow you two lovebirds getting along?"

Donnie turned crimson; Keely laughed. "Daddy has nothing to worry about, if that's what you're asking, Cully."

"Not me. Live and let live, that's my motto."

"Donnie's training Disco to compete in the World Disc Dog Championship."

Cully raised his eyebrows like a humping caterpillar. "Wot, this dog?"

Sensing she was being discussed, Disco sat at attention, tail wagging.

"Yeah," Donnie said. "She can leap tall buildings in a single bound."

"I used to date a sheila did that. Now she's world champion."

"Lily Carruthers?" Donnie said.

"That's the one! How do you know about Lily?"

"I've been researching the sport."

"She's a right terror, that one. Raises Aussie shepherds for a living. Since she won the world championship, she's got clients from all over the world. Arab princes, Russian billionaires, they all want an Aussie shep from Lily's kennel."

"How long's the barn?" Donnie said.

"'Bout two hundred feet. Why?"

"I was just thinking, when the weather gets cold, could we train in there?"

"Aw sure, mate. We got three dogs of our own. They're in kennels right now, or they'd be all over that buffet table like journalists at an open bar."

"The Monster Mash" emanated from the house.

"Come on!" Keely said, getting up. "It's time to do the Transylvania Stomp!"

Inside, a dozen people had formed a conga line in which they lurched or slunk according to their costumes. The Universal Monsters danced spasmodically: Frankenstein's monster, Dracula, the Wolfman and the Mummy all in a row. Donnie and Keely joined in as the music morphed into Greg Pope's "The Yeti."

By ten thirty Donnie was all spazzed out. "I told Ma I'd be home by eleven."

"Come on, Badge," Keely said. "I'll drop you."

They spent ten minutes kissing and groping in the back parking lot before Donnie reluctantly disengaged himself. "See you tomorrow, I hope, I hope."

"You will!"

Donnie watched her taillights round the building and disappear.

"Let's go, Disco." He walked toward the rear door, oblivious to two shadows that detached themselves from the bushes. Disco whirled, growling. Something violently yanked Donnie back and slammed him to the ground, knocking the wind out of him.

He barely saw the boot that waffle-stomped his face.

"Faggot!" a voice hissed.

Donnie looked up and glimpsed two figures dressed in black, like ninja, with black masks covering all but their eyes.

A sickening jolt in Donnie's ribs nearly lifted him off the ground. "This is for Ryan." A different voice, a different hiss.

"EEEYAH!" the first assailant screamed, kicking out madly with his left leg. Disco circled, snarling, darted in and sank her teeth into his calf again, ricocheting back and crouching, fangs bared.

"I don't fuckin' believe it! It's that fuckin' dog!"

Donnie's hand grasped a rock the size of a billiard ball and slammed it into the ninja's knee.

"Let's go," he grunted in pain. They took off running. Donnie remained curled.

Seconds later he heard the deep burble of glasspacks as an engine roared to life and peeled out, spraying gravel all over the yard.

CHAPTER THIRTY-TWO
MISSED STEPS?

BLEEDING PROFUSELY FROM HIS NOSE, RIBS BROADCASTING lightning bolts, Donnie endured Disco's non-stop licking for a minute, then slowly uncurled, pulled himself up by the doorknob and somehow dragged himself inside. Disco whined with worry.

Mrs. McGillicuddy opened her door to the limit of her chain and stared. "Go back to bed, Mrs. McGillicuddy," Donnie croaked.

Great, he thought. *First the screaming boyfriend and now this.* Donnie couldn't live with himself if he got them kicked out of the apartment.

One step at a time, Donnie pulled himself up the stairs, pausing to sit several times while Disco licked. "Good girl," he said hoarsely, wincing as he petted her. "Hadn't been for you, they might have killed me."

He didn't believe Ryan was in on the attack. Ryan's apology had been heartfelt. Whoever had done it was the same evil bastard who'd tried to drown Disco. That left Ryan's fawning sycophants, Mohawk and Freckles, aka Lester Barnes and Billy Clanagan. Donnie had never seen their cars and never heard that distinctive exhaust note anywhere around Gunderson High.

The thought that it was a third, unknown party was chilling. No. It had to be Billy and/or Lester with unknown confederates. Whoever it was had made a deliberate effort to disguise their voices, as if Donnie couldn't figure it out.

He knew he should call the cops, but that would just earn him a snitch jacket, and never mind that crap about going to a responsible adult. Being a man meant handling your own difficulties. Donnie wasn't a man yet, but he was determined to be one. He would find out who attacked him and serve them a cold dish.

Slowly, painfully he hunched into the bathroom and took a shower sitting on the shower stool. After he dried himself, he used a whole spool of adhesive tape on his ribs, round and round. Now he could be the Mummy. He looked in the mirror. He was going to have a serious mouse in the morning. There was no use exciting Kate. Then he'd have to tell her the story, and she'd get hysterical and insist they call the police. He downed four ibuprofen pills and went to bed knowing he would be unable to sleep.

Kate came home at one thirty, quietly opened his door to find him and the dog feigning sleep, and went to her room. In the morning, Donnie did his best to keep his face averted, but there was no way to disguise the difficulty he had moving.

"Why are you limping?" Kate said at the stove, frying bacon.

"I fell down a flight of stairs. I'll be all right."

Kate saw the bruise on his face. "My God! You did that falling down stairs?"

"They were big stairs. Don't worry. I'll be all right."

"All right? You can hardly move! Do you need to go the hospital?"

"Ma! I'm fine, okay! I'm just a klutz."

"This happened at the Van Metres'? How did it happen?"

"I was goofing around, playing spook in the darkness, you know? I didn't see the stairs."

Kate put her hands on her hips and gave him a hard look. The look softened. "You know if you're in trouble you can always come to me; you know that, don't you?"

"Sure, Ma."

"I'm so sorry your father wasn't man enough to stay and raise you. That's on me."

"Don't worry about it. Can you give me a ride to the Piggly Wiggly?"

"You're not going to work in that condition, are you?"

"I need this job."

Armed with tape and painkillers, Donnie was at the grocery store by nine. His co-workers noticed his stiff movements and marks, which he explained as falling down stairs. Rather than hoist bags, he used a grocery cart to deliver them to Buicks driven by little old ladies. He hoped Keely wouldn't see him like this, but there was nothing he could do about it, and when he saw her walk in the store at two looking for him, he raised his hand.

Keely's eyes and mouth went round. "What happened?"

He couldn't very well tell her he'd fallen down her stairs, so he told her the truth.

"You have to go to the police!" she said.

"No way. That will only bring me more grief. I've seen it. Don't worry. They'll be sorry they did this."

"Do you know who did it?" Keely said.

"I have my suspicions."

Keely returned at five and drove Donnie home. She helped him up the stairs, where Disco greeted them effusively.

There was a note from Kate: "Donnie dear, I'm at work, home around eight. Dinner in fridge. Love you!"

"What can I do?" Keely said.

"You mind cleaning up Disco's guano on the balcony?"

Keely took care of business without complaint, washed her hands and opened the refrigerator. It was filled with Werner's meats. She made macaroni and cheese with Werner's honey-cured ham. Afterward she did the dishes.

"You don't have to do that. Disco can do that."

"No she can't! Her mouth's full of bacteria. It's a miracle you haven't contracted diphtheria or the bubonic plague." She pulled all the dishes out of the cupboard and washed them all. There weren't that many.

"I gotta get back," she said. "Stacy and I are going to see that new vampire movie."

"What new vampire movie?"

"The one with all those young actors."

She kissed him on the lips and was gone.

CHAPTER THIRTY-THREE
LIKE A GENTLEMAN

DONNIE RETURNED TO THE PIGGLY WIGGLY ON SUNDAY at nine to spell Jim, who'd agreed to work for Donnie on the previous Friday. Kate gave him a ride. She'd come in after he'd gone to bed. She wasn't fooling him. She was seeing Frank Werner, and it wasn't all business. What kind of business meeting lasts until one in the morning?

Maybe she liked him. Kate didn't have a great track record with men, but Frank was different. Not only did he have a real job, but he was the boss. Sure, the company was sliding into the river, but that wasn't necessarily Frank's fault. Donnie wasn't stupid. He understood how the zeitgeist had moved away from processed meats in recent years. Now there were greenies in your face everyplace you turned, trying to tell you how to live. Gunderson High had recently announced that they were instituting a new lunch program in compliance with the First Lady's guidelines. Henceforth, there would be no hot dogs, hamburgers, chili or pizza. Henceforth, there would be spaghetti squash, stewed beets, seaweed and gluten-free croissants.

There would be no more peanut butter. Any student who brought peanut butter to school, even in their own sandwich, was treated as if they'd brought a loaded .44 magnum.

Donnie thought about how to save Werner's almost as much as he thought about winning the World Disc Dog Championship, which he thought about almost as much as having sex with Keely. Scratch that. Gentlemen didn't have sex. They made love. He was trying to think like a gentleman.

Mrs. Murphy, a gray-haired widow, came through the checkout lane with a full cart, including twenty pounds of cat food, twelve canned soups and a gallon of milk. Donnie winced loading her bags, and she said, "Let me help you with that, dear."

He body-blocked her. He wasn't going to have an octogenarian do his job. "It's nothing, Mrs. Murphy. Really." He sucked it up, followed Mrs. Murphy to her Buick and loaded the groceries. She fumbled in her purse.

"I appreciate it, Mrs. Murphy, but this is what I'm paid to do. There's no need to tip me."

Louise Morton the vet came through the checkout lane with a thirty-five-pound bag of dog food. Donnie positioned the cart at the edge of the counter and dragged the bag into it, wincing.

"What happened?" Dr. Morton said.

"I fell down a flight of stairs."

"When are you bringing your dog in to get fixed?"

"What's that cost?"

"For you, a hundred twenty dollars."

Donnie did a quick mental calculation. "I should have the money in a couple weeks."

"Well don't delay. You don't want her going into heat around other dogs."

"Right, right."

As Donnie struggled to lift the dog food into the back of Dr. Morton's Mazda, she came around and helped. "What happened to you? Really. You didn't get that from falling down stairs."

"I got jumped last night."

Dr. Morton looked grim. "Did you tell the police?"

"No. Don't worry about it. It's my problem."

A distinctive burble insinuated itself. Donnie watched with apprehension as an old Camaro with mag wheels, gangsta rap blasting, pulled into the A&W across the street. He stood partially behind the Mazda's raised tailgate, although he needn't have bothered. The two who exited the car never looked his way.

One of them was Lester. The other was Lester-sized, had a shaved head and neck tats and was cut from the same cloth. Dr. Morton followed his gaze.

"Those are the guys, aren't they?"

Donnie shook his head. "Don't say anything."

"It's your call," Dr. Morton said, getting into her car.

CHAPTER THIRTY-FOUR
AN UNLIKELY ALLIANCE

BY THE END OF THE DAY, DONNIE HURT TOO MUCH TO toss the Frisbee. A co-worker gave him a ride home. On Monday, he looked in vain for Lester. Usually the adenoidal freak followed Ryan like a gull after a fishing trawler, but that day was conspicuous by his absence.

On Tuesday, Donnie sat next to Ryan in the bleachers while Coach Pagel ran one-on-one basketball drills.

"Are you thinking of playing pro football?" Donnie said.

Ryan kept his eyes fixed on the kids shooting from the free-throw line. "It crossed my mind, but my dad says two hundred thousand other high school grads have the same idea. I'm going to keep it up through college and see what happens, but I'm majoring in business. I want my own car dealership. You?"

"I'm going to be a writer."

"What, comic books?"

Donnie burned.

Ryan smacked Donnie lightly on the back of the head. "Just joshin', hoss."

"I like comics. Don't you read comics?"

"Nah. My brother had a big collection, all this weird Vertigo shit. And *Sin City*. He loved *Sin City*. The movie's cool. He left it to me when he joined the Marines, but I just haven't gotten into it. Maybe you want it."

"What? Are you serious?"

"I don't know. Why don't you come take a look one of these days? I don't know when, because I'm so busy between school, football and Marlene. You haven't met Marlene. She goes to Rosa Parks in Waukesha."

"How come you're being so nice to me?"

Ryan looked at him. "That was stupid of me to run you off the road like that. It was Lester's idea."

"Where is Lester?"

"Fuck if I know."

"Cutler! Waits! Get down here," Coach Pagel bellowed.

They lined up behind two other kids. When Ryan reached the line, Coach tossed him the ball. He bounced it once, leaped up on the balls of his feet and tossed a perfect swoosher through the hoop.

"Waits! Let's go!"

The coach did a double take. "What happened to you?"

"I fell down some stairs."

"His mother crossed her legs," some wag said.

Coach Pagel snapped his fingers. "Shut your mouth, Harris. Waits, let's go!"

"Waits is right," some wag said.

Coach Pagel snapped his fingers and tossed Donnie the ball. Donnie winced as he caught it and fought down a spasm of pain. He'd be damned if he'd look like a pussy in gym. This was what being a man was all about—sucking it up and getting the job done. Ignoring crimson lightning streaking through his body, he took aim and sailed. The ball bounced off the tip of the backboard into the stands. Hoots and laughter. Donnie went to the back of the queue.

"Does Lester have an older brother?" he asked Ryan.

"Yeah. Travis. They call him Bane. He tried out for the Marines same as my brother, but he didn't cut the mustard. 'Not Marine material,' they said. Something psychological."

The very fact that Donnie and Ryan were now on speaking terms had raised his stock. Classmates who previously wouldn't acknowledge him now accepted him as one of them, including him in conversations and jokes. People stopped shouldering him aside and trying to trip him in the halls.

Kate gave him rides to school, after which he would walk to the Piggly Wiggly, where a co-worker—usually Brad, who owned a souped-up Mustang—would give him a ride home. By Saturday he felt well enough to throw the disc, so he and Disco resumed training.

It was all in the wrist. You had to impart maximum spin while releasing the disc quickly with an abbreviated snap. A correct throw had an elegant beauty. The disc skimming parallel to the earth, hovering at the end as if reluctant to touch down. Sometimes its altitude fluctuated—up, down, up, like a playful hummingbird.

Disco chased the plate until it hovered, and leaped to snatch it out of the sky. Donnie had seen videos of dogs performing backward-leaping somersaults. If Disco could do that while snatching a Frisbee, it would make for a dynamic presentation.

On Sunday he phoned Keely and asked if he could use their horse barn to train. He wanted to try skipping the disc off a hard, flat surface.

"Come on over," she said.

CHAPTER THIRTY-FIVE
SPIN!

KATE GAVE DONNIE AND DISCO A RIDE. "CALL ME WHEN you're done. I'm meeting with Frank today to discuss marketing strategy."

Sure you are.

"Okay, Ma. Thanks."

Kate used the turnaround in front of the house to drop them off. "This is quite a place," she said.

"Yeah, they're rich."

Disco followed Donnie into the big barn, doors open at both sides. Keely was inside helping Cully check a horse. Donnie set his backpack down on a table while Disco ran to Keely, tail wagging.

"That's a fair dinkum dog," Cully said.

"She's a purebred wisenheimer," Donnie said. He explained the trick he wanted Disco to learn.

"Here's what you do, then," Cully said. "You start by holding a treat over her head so that she jumps for it. You catch her at apogee, spin her around like a propeller and drop her on her hind legs. Once she gets the hang of it, you start with the disc. It's not a new trick. Cactus Jack does it."

Undeterred, Donnie went to work while Keely held the treat, shouting "spin!" each time. The little dog took to it like a kid to cotton candy, and within ten training jumps performed the backward aerial somersault on her own, snatching the treat from Keely's hand. Donnie started throwing the disc from ten feet away. At first Disco simply leaped and snagged, but then Keely stepped in, caught her at apogee after she grabbed the disc and turned her over. Soon she was performing backward aerial somersaults while catching the disc.

Gradually Donnie increased the distance until Disco was performing at about fifty feet. Spying a round Formica tabletop leaning against the wall, he set it on the wood floor and skipped the disc off it. Disco snatched the spinning plate on the rebound like Cal Ripkin. By now the dog had mastered "catch," "jump" and "spin."

"She's smart, that one," Cully observed.

"So you used to date Lily?" Donnie said.

Cully got a faraway look in his eyes. "Used to be my sheila. But we let time and distance get between us. It was a long time ago."

"What brought you to America?"

"Met Van Metre at Eagle Farm in New South Wales, and we hit it off. I was trainer for the Boorman Stables, and he hired me away."

"You race horses?" Donnie asked, incredulous.

"Not me, mate. I'm just the trainer. Sam Sala's the jockey, although this filly here," he said, indicating Keely, "sits a pretty horse."

"We race at Fairmount Park," Keely said. "Dad's just getting started. We're not making any money at it. Yet."

Cully grinned. "Horse racing is no way to get rich. It's how the rich waste their money."

They broke at noon and went to the main house for lunch. Chuck, the Van Metres' German shepherd, who'd been sleeping in the sun, followed them in. Disco stuck her butt in the air in the classic dog signal for play, and soon they were barking and chasing each other around the yard. Keely let them in. Disco leaped up, snagged Chuck by the collar and dragged him toward the house. For the first time, Donnie noticed the oval track surrounded by a white picket fence. They went into the big kitchen.

"Where do you live, Cully?"

"Old farmhouse other side of those trees. Place used to be a horse farm before Van bought it."

Donnie had never seen such wealth. The Van Metres' rambling home had to be close to ten thousand square feet. He felt privileged to be there. Keely removed a large, lidded plastic bowl from the refrigerator and poured from it into a saucepan on the gas stove.

"She makes the best chili," Cory said.

"Not too hot, I hope," Donnie said.

Disco did her starving-waif act until Keely got up, took out two hot dogs and held them up. "Sit!" she commanded. Both dogs sat, tails wagging, their eyes on the prize. "Spin!" Keely said, tossing a hot dog to Disco, who performed a flying reverse somersault. By the time she landed, the hot dog was gone.

Keely turned to the other dog, holding the treat five feet up. "Up, Chuck!" she said, and the big dog effort- lessly rose like a sounding porpoise to delicately take the treat from her grasp. Donnie flashed on the cafeteria.

"Are those Werner's wieners?"

"Nope. Get 'em at Walmart, eight for a buck."

"Would you like me to get you some Werner's wieners?"

"I don't think the dogs really care what kind of wiener they get."

After lunch, Keely drove Donnie and Disco home. Donnie was excited and frightened by the prospect of him and Keely alone in the apartment until Keely told him she had to get back to work on homework.

"See you tomorrow!" she said.

Donnie let himself into the apartment and went online. He went to FB and entered "Lester Barnes" in the finder. There were dozens, if not hundreds, but his Lester popped like a 3D effect. He went to Lester's page.

"I like smokin' blunts and smokin' hot bitches!" Lester declared in the "About Me" section. There was a photo of Lester forcing vodka down a puppy's throat. The pup was undoubtedly one of Disco's siblings. Donnie wondered what had become of the rest. He wanted to repost that pic on his own page, asking for people to identify Barnes and turn him in, but it was really up to him, wasn't it? What kind of subhuman drowned and tortured puppies? He had to do something.

Bullies had often made Donnie's life unbearable. He was sure it was worse for Malcolm. Donnie didn't wonder why so many kids went on shooting sprees, but even at his darkest, he had never considered killing others. Sure, there were times he wished death on others, but he'd never considered doing it himself. He had too great a sense of personal responsibility and future success. There were times he'd had access to guns, like when Kate had dated a trucker named Schultz, who never shut up about his guns. Schultz had tried to get Kate to take shooting lessons, even tried to give her a gun, but she wasn't having it.

It wasn't that Kate was some great anti-gun activist. She simply did not see herself as a shooter and didn't believe she'd ever need a gun.

"That's what everyone says until they do," Schultz said a couple of days before Kate gave him the heave-ho.

On his own page, 193 people had liked the video of Disco leading the boys on a merry chase in the park. Donnie went to YouTube. The video had over ten thousand hits.

CHAPTER THIRTY-SIX
TEST PREP

THE DAY MOVED AS SLOWLY AS A GARBAGE TRUCK. ALL Donnie could think about was his impending driver's test, for which he'd made an appointment last week. He would be taking it in Nate's Ford. Only Keely and Malcolm knew about the driver's test. Now that Donnie's social status had been elevated, he found it awkward to be seen with Malcolm in the halls. When his new friends bad-mouthed Malcolm, Donnie would politely point out that they wouldn't like it if people said the same about them.

Lester returned to school but remained aloof, exiled from Ryan's inner circle. Every now and then Donnie caught Lester glaring at him with malice. Donnie worried that Lester might strike at Disco. Disturbing reports emanated from Milwaukee of people finding meatballs in parks spiked with rat poison and nails. Disco was safe on the balcony for the time being.

It was a crisp fall day, temperature in the mid-fifties as Donnie joined the swarm flowing from Gunderson High. He paused on the steps, looking up and down the street, until he spotted Nate halfway down the block. Despite lingering pain, Donnie couldn't help breaking into a lope, backpack bobbing. Kate had already signed the papers. Donnie tossed his bag in the back and climbed in, grinning.

"And away we go!"

Nate smelled like bourbon.

"You haven't been drinking, have you?"

Nate pulled out into traffic, eliciting a honk of protest from a suburban hausfrau in a Mercedes SUV. "Of course not! That's left over from last night."

Donnie examined him. Nate was freshly shaven and wore a clean blue work shirt. It was five minutes to the county courthouse on Boyd Park. Behind the courthouse was a large municipal parking lot and the entrance to the Department of Motor Vehicles. Nate parked several rows back, and they entered through the glass doors. Inside was a big tiled room with several rows of folding chairs, six of which were occupied, mostly by young people filling out forms on clipboards.

Donnie waited for his turn at the window and explained that he was there for his test. The clerk handed him a clipboard and instructed him to fill out the questionnaire. Donnie took a seat.

"I'll be out back havin' a smoke," Nate said. "You know where."

Donnie breezed through the written questionnaire like he ran track.

"Unless otherwise posted, what is the speed on residential streets? When you come to a four-way intersection, who has the right of way? What is the fastest posted speed limit in Wisconsin?"

He was done in ten minutes and turned in his answers. The clerk checked them off and handed back the clipboard. "You scored a 90. Take this to Miss Grange at the last window and have a seat. She'll call you when they're ready."

Donnie sat swinging his leg over his knee and looking around, antsy as a colony. There were four other supplicants now, three young people and an older woman with a pageboy cut wearing a Sturgis T-shirt. Tats descended from the bottoms of her sleeves. Of the remaining three, two were Hispanic, both young men with wispy mustaches, and one was a kid Donnie recognized from school. Jessie something.

The walls were decorated with bucolic scenes of dairy operations, forests and streams, as well as posters exhorting citizens to report any suspicious activity. He thought about the Barnes boys. He was temporarily out of tricks. He didn't know them well enough to devise some brilliant passive-aggressive punishment. But he would. Travis Barnes probably had a criminal record. Donnie was getting pretty computer-wise in the library, and Malcolm had boasted that he could tap into school records.

Donnie would get the Barneses' address and put them under surveillance. What business did they have with dogs? Did Lester even have parents, or did he live with his thuggish brother? Donnie wasn't the only one from a broken home. He'd seen some setups that made his own circumstances look like a sitcom. He could always report Lester for throwing around the "fag" insult like confetti.

But Donnie was no snitch.

"Donald Waits," a man said, reading from a clipboard.

Donnie looked up. The man wore a worn gray suit with a blue shirt open at the collar, was bald and had horn-rimmed glasses. He looked like someone had been pushing down on him for twenty years.

Donnie hopped up. "That's me, sir!"

The man looked at him curiously. "I'm Mr. Anderson. I'll be your test supervisor. Where's your mother?"

"She couldn't make it, sir. She works at Werner's Meats, but my friend Nathan Compass, who's a veteran, brought me."

"Let's go," Anderson said, holding the door to the back parking lot. They went outside, where Anderson plucked a triangular sign that said STUDENT DRIVER off the sidewalk. "Will you be using your own vehicle?"

"I'll be using Nate's truck. There it is." Donnie waved. Nate blipped the horn, started the engine and pulled around to where they stood.

Anderson looked at the vehicle. "You'll have to wait here, Mr. Compass. I am required to accompany Donnie during the test."

Nate killed the engine, got out and pulled a folding lawn chair and a paperback book from the bed. "No problem."

"Where'd you serve?" Anderson said.

"Vietnam. 1972 to '75. Army. You?"

"I was in Operation Desert Storm. Okay, Donnie, get behind the wheel." Anderson mounted the Student Driver sign on top of the cab, where it stuck fast with magnets.

Donnie climbed into the seat, heart thudding. He fastened his seatbelt and willed himself to relax, breathing out slowly to bring down his pulse. He took Nate's wraparounds from the rearview and put them on, along with a Packers hat.

"This test will consist of basic traffic maneuvers and parking, and takes place here in the lot and a little bit down Blount Street. Traffic should be light, but that's part of the test."

Anderson got in and fastened his seatbelt. "Start the engine."

Making sure the shift was in neutral, Donnie turned the key and the old Ford came instantly to life.

"Put it in gear, drive straight to the end of the parking lot and turn left."

"Should I put my signals on?"

"That's up to you."

Donnie eased the stick into first, revved the engine and slowly let out the clutch. Practice had paid off. The truck moved ahead with a minute lurch. Donnie got it into second before signaling and turning ninety degrees to the left.

"Pull out onto Mason and take a left on Blount."

Donnie pulled up to the stop sign at the exit onto Mason and then heard a familiar burble. The orange, rusted rat Camaro pulled up to the intersection of Blount and Mason.

CHAPTER THIRTY-SEVEN
CAR CHASE

"Go on," Anderson said. "The street's clear." He noticed Donnie staring at the Camaro as it turned left and disappeared down Mason, trailing thudding bass.

"Doesn't Gunderson have a noise ordinance?" Donnie said.

"Theoretically, although I've never heard of it being enforced. I don't much like it either. Let's go."

Donnie used his turn signal, looked both ways and pulled out onto Mason. He used the signal again to turn onto Blount Street.

"Turn right on Ridge Boulevard and merge with traffic."

Ridge Boulevard was the biggest street in Gunderson, a four-laner that cut through the heart of town, trailing off into car dealerships and fast-food franchises at either end.

"You're doing good. Go two blocks and take a right turn onto Monroe."

There was a slight crunch as Donnie shifted from third into fourth, and then he was cruising down Ridge at thirty-five miles per hour, the posted speed limit. A kid darted between two cars on his board right into their path. Donnie stood on the brakes, and only seatbelts prevented him and Anderson from smacking into the windshield. Anderson made a note on his clipboard.

"Go on," he said.

Donnie put on his left turn signal, looked over his shoulder and pulled into the left lane. Anderson wrote something. Donnie stopped at the intersection with Monroe to let traffic pass. When it was clear, he turned left onto Monroe and worked up through the gears until they were doing forty-five, the posted limit. Anderson scribbled.

"Now I want you to parallel park in front of the hardware store."

Donnie felt a trill of panic. He'd never parallel parked, although he'd read some advice about it on the internet. "Pull parallel to the vehicle in front so that your rear bumper is no farther back than the vehicle. Put in reverse and turn the wheel sharply to the right as you back slowly into the place. Look over your shoulder and align your vehicle with the vehicle behind you."

Easier said than done. Donnie sawed back and forth three times before he got it right. He was sweating when he finally eased the pickup into the spot.

"Don't worry about it," Anderson said. "Most people have trouble with this part. Now I want you to pull out and proceed down Monroe."

Getting out was easier, and soon they were cruising down Monroe headed toward the intersection with Adams Street.

"Pull into the left lane and turn left on Adams."

The light changed as they approached, and Donnie stopped. He glanced in the rearview. The Camaro was coming up on the right, bass booming. Donnie glanced over to see Travis wearing wraparounds, a ball cap with the brim backward and a toothy grin. Lester sat next to him.

Anderson frowned at them, and Travis turned up the bass. The light changed, and Donnie turned left perhaps a tad fast. The Camaro screeched a wide looping left to go around them and veered into their lane, and Travis stood on the brakes. Donnie didn't think they recognized him, that they were focused on STUDENT DRIVER.

"What do I do, Mr. Anderson?"

Anderson took out his cell phone. "I'm calling the cops. This jerk shouldn't be on the road."

The Camaro hunkered down and burned rubber, fishtailing down the road away from them.

"Damn!" Anderson said. "Did you see their license plate?"

"No sir, but I know who they are. That's Travis and Lester Barnes. Lester's in my class at high school."

Anderson wrote it down. "All right, you're doing fine. Now proceed to Washington Street, turn left and circle back toward the County Building."

They returned to the parking lot, where Donnie pulled up in front of the Motor Vehicles door and killed the engine. Anderson remained where he was, making notations. Donnie looked at him nervously.

"Did I pass?"

"Indeed, you did. There were a couple of shaky moments, but all in all you did better than most. If you'll come in with me, we'll issue you a temporary license until your regular license arrives in the mail."

They went inside, followed by Nate, his finger in the middle of *A Rage in Harlem* by Chester Himes. Donnie could not stop grinning as they took his picture.

CHAPTER THIRTY-EIGHT
MALCOLM PLAYS HOOKY

IT TOOK A WEEK TO CONVINCE KATE TO LET DONNIE drive her car, with her quivering in the passenger seat, gripping the grab handle with both hands and trying not to cry out. He drove himself to the Piggly Wiggly, and a co-worker let him drive his old car back home. Donnie was obsessed with obtaining his own wheels, but the money he made at his job barely covered Disco's expenses.

On November 20, Kate let him use the car to take Disco to the veterinarian to be spayed. Not even Louise Morton's proximity could ease his anxiety.

"Go home! She'll be fine," she assured Donnie. "I've done this hundreds of times."

He drove home sick with worry that something would go wrong. He barely slept and couldn't wait for Dr. Morton to open her shop at nine the following day. Of course, he was stuck in math at the time and had no way to make a phone call. It wasn't until noon that Keely lent him her cell phone.

"Disco's fine, Donnie," Dr. Morton told him. "You can pick her up after school."

Donnie thanked her and returned Keely's phone. "I have to work after school. Will you pick Disco up and take her home?"

"No prob. Where's Malcolm? He hasn't been here all week."

Donnie looked around. He'd been so preoccupied, he hadn't noticed. He borrowed Keely's phone again. Malcolm lived with his mother, father and older sister in a rented farmhouse. Irv Lipschitz was a roofer. His wife, Maureen, was a clerk at the Ace Hardware. Their struggle was evident in Malcolm's threadbare clothes and chronic financial difficulties, but Malcolm had his own phone and drove an ancient Neon.

Malcolm's phone rang several times before going to voicemail.

"Dude! Where are ya?" Donnie said.

He quit work at seven and rode his bike in the opposite direction of his house, out lonely County BB to the Lipschitz place, a falling-down farmhouse with a sagging front porch. The ancient Neon sat in the dirt drive, and the blinds were drawn. Donnie brought his bike up on the porch and knocked. He was about to give up when he heard a sound from inside, and seconds later the front door opened to reveal Malcolm with puffed lips and a black eye.

He turned and went into the dark interior. "Come on in," he said. A game console sat on the coffee table in front of an old TV running an early version of Grand Theft Auto. The house smelled like dirty laundry. A gun rack held two shotguns and a rifle. Just sitting there in the living room.

"Dude! What happened?" Donnie said.

"Fucking Lester and his gorilla brother! They got me at the Dairy Queen last week. Beat the shit out of me! My old man told me it was my own fault for being such a pussy."

Malcolm threw himself down on the worn cloth sofa and picked up the game console. Donnie was afraid he was going to break a finger the way he squeezed it, eyes onscreen, shooting at imaginary enemies.

"So what are you doing? You got to go to school, dude. Come on back. Lester hasn't been around much anyway."

"I hate him!"

"Yeah I know. Ryan hasn't been bothering you, has he?"

"No. He stopped. Thank God for small blessings. But that fucker Lester has always been riding my ass! Ever since eighth grade. I'd like to kill him!"

"Perfectly natural. But you gotta come back to school, man. Someday you'll look back on this and laugh. You'll be a successful game designer, and Lester will be working for minimum wage at Walmart if he's not dead or in prison."

Malcolm worked his yoke and stared at the screen, where the sound had been muted so that the explosions and gunfire seemed to be coming from a long way off.

"Seriously. You got to go to school or they'll send the police after you."

"I don't care."

"Yes you do! Come on, man. I'll speak to your teachers and say you were sick. What do you tell your old man?"

"He's so plastered he doesn't give a shit."

"Are you really Jewish?"

"He called me a dirty little kike, too."

"Come on, man! You can't let him do this to you. I'll tell you what. You return to school and I've got your back."

Malcolm looked up. "Donnie, you're a good friend, but you can't be with me everywhere. You don't know what it's like. It's like his whole purpose in life is to make me suffer. You should see what he posts on my Facebook page."

"That's like a cyber crime or something. You need to tell the school."

Malcolm looked up with angry, despairing eyes. "Yeah, right! Like that's gonna do any good!"

Donnie knew Malcolm was right. School administrators were too busy covering their asses to take meaningful action. Then they'd rope Lester's brother and father into it, and who knew what that would bring. If Lester even had a father.

"Can I borrow your phone?" Donnie said. "I need to check on Disco."

Wordlessly, Malcolm forked it over. Donnie phoned Keely.

"Where are you?" she said. "Disco and I are at your place. Your mother let us in. Disco's fine. The operation was super smooth. We're trying not to get her too excited so she won't open the incision. It's turquoise. You should see it."

"I'll be there in twenty," Donnie promised. He hung up and handed the phone back to Malcolm. "You coming tomorrow?"

"I don't know."

"Come on, Malcolm. I've got your back. I know what to do."

"Oh yeah? What?"

"We'll film that fucker and put it on the web."

"Oh great. That'll make him stop."

As Donnie let himself out, Malcolm turned the volume way up so that the gunfire was deafening.

CHAPTER THIRTY-NINE
MOVIE DIRECTOR

Donnie thought about it all the way home. One thing Nate had told him that he knew to be absolutely true was that the one thing everybody feared was bad publicity. Even a lowlife thug like Lester wouldn't want people laughing at him online. Problem: Donnie had no vid cam. He didn't even have a phone. Was it fair to drag Keely into this mess? He thought not. He needed a phone, and he needed it more than a car.

This could change everything. A phone was within his means. He had probably banked enough to get one right away. It would be cheaper if he went in on Kate's plan. He rode up to his apartment building after seven. It was already dark, and the night air chilled him to the bone. Leaning his bike against the back wall, he took the steps two at a time, hearing laughter and Disco's hysterical squeal through the door.

As soon as he entered, Disco was jumping all over him. He sat on the floor and held her in his lap. "Ho shit! Why didn't you stop her jumping around?"

"No prob," Keely said. "The doctor used some kind of cement to heal her up. Says give her a week to recover."

"Where were you?" Kate said.

"I went to check on a friend. Hasn't been to school in a while."

"Malcolm?" Keely said.

Donnie nodded.

"How is he?"

Donnie shook his head. Kate had her back turned, taking something out of the oven.

"I made a mac and cheese casserole, buster. Eat. What about you, Keely? Are you hungry?"

"I could eat something."

Kate put two plates on the dining room table and went into her room to work on the new Werner's campaign.

"What's going on with him?" Keely said.

Donnie told her.

"That's terrible. We've got to do something!"

"I'm gonna get a smart phone and film that fucker acting like a jerk. Then I'm going to put it up on YouTube and link it to the Gunderson High website."

"Seriously?"

"I'm not kidding. I can pay for my own phone now."

Keely pushed her chair away from the table, and Disco popped into her lap.

"Get down!" Donnie snapped. The dog looked at him and wagged her tail. Keely laughed.

"Her table manners need improvement."

"Well I guess we'll resume training next weekend. See you on Sunday?"

"You bet. Gotta go." She got up, kissed him lightly on the lips and danced out the door. Disco leaped into his lap. Donnie eased her back to the floor and started his homework assignment. Algebra. A half hour later, he closed his notepad and knocked on Kate's door.

"Come in."

Donnie found Kate pecking away at her computer. "Ma, I want to get a smart phone."

Kate made a few pecks and turned to him. "Kiddo, I agree with you. I'll put it on my plan."

"Really?"

"Really. I'm so pleased to find you making friends out here."

"I can pay for it!"

"That won't be necessary. Take a look at this."

Donnie looked over Kate's shoulder at a black-and-white picture of Steve McQueen straddling a dirt bike, chomping on a hot dog.

"What do you think?"

"Who's that?"

Kate shook her head. "Steve McQueen! Haven't you ever seen *The Great Escape*, *Bullitt* or *The Magnificent Seven*?"

"No."

"Well I've failed as a mother. Let me see if I can get those for you. Now I need you out of here. I have to have this presentation ready for tomorrow."

Leaving the patio door open for Disco, Donnie went to bed. Just before he fell asleep, he added a new entry to his future resume: movie director.

WHEN MALCOLM FAILED TO APPEAR FOR THE REST OF THE week, Donnie approached Mrs. Brautigan. It was Friday.

"Yes, I'm aware that Malcolm has not been in class, nor have his parents returned any of my phone calls. I'm going to have to inform the administration, and they'll probably report him as truant to the police."

"Are they going to arrest him?"

"No, but they will probably stop over and see if everything's all right. I'm sorry his parents aren't more involved."

"You ever meet them?" Donnie said.

"No. Have you?"

"I met his mother once, right after we moved here. Their house smelled funny, like old laundry. She seemed overwhelmed, y'know. Malcolm says his old man is a roofer and likes to hunt." Instantly he regretted it.

"You say there are guns in the house?" Mrs. Brautigan said.

"So what? This is Wisconsin. Everybody has guns in the house."

"No they don't. Do you have any guns in your house?"

"No."

"Neither do I."

"How is that relevant to Malcolm not coming to school?" Donnie said. "Here's a kid with no violent tendencies who's been mercilessly bullied."

"I admire your debating skills, Donnie. Have you thought about trying out for the debate squad?"

Donnie thought about that group of future politicians. "I have too much to do, Mrs. Brautigan. I have a job and I'm trying to train my dog."

"Yes, at the Piggly Wiggly. I saw you there last week. What's this about a dog? How much training does a dog require?"

"A lot if we want to win the World Disc Dog Championship."

Between fourth and fifth period, Donnie spotted a familiar coxcomb of purple hair bobbing above the heads in the hall. Lester Barnes had returned. He walked alone with a permanent sneer affixed to his face. Donnie tried to catch his eye, but Lester wasn't having any of it. Donnie hoped Mr. Anderson had reported the Barnes brothers to the police.

When school let out, Lester's brother picked him up in the booming Camaro, trailing Tupac and peeling out in violation of several school rules.

Donnie rode his bike to the Piggly Wiggly. The temperature was in the forties, not too bad in his jacket and Hurley knit cap. As Donnie bagged groceries, Kate entered and made a beeline toward him. She waited until Donnie had finished bagging and handed him an oblong rectangular box.

"It's a Razor or something. They tell me it does every-thing you want. Read the instructions please."

Donnie took the box. He would have hugged her, but he didn't want to appear foolish. "Thanks, Ma! I'll be home around seven."

"I won't be there. Can you make yourself dinner?"

"Sure." The affair was heating up.

When he got home, it was dark. Donnie stuck a Salis-bury steak in the microwave, went into Kate's room and went on Facebook. He now had 214 friends, and the video of Disco evading the boys had over 397 likes. He went over to Malcolm's page and began reading. The bottom fell out of his stomach.

"Hitler was right. Too bad he didn't kill your parents."

"Whatsa matter faggot Jewboy? Why don't you kill yourself."

The messages were signed "Lord Vile" with a picture of Humungus from *The Road Warrior*. Donnie went to Humungus' homepage.

"I like smokin' blunts and smokin' hot bitches!"

It was Lester all right. Donnie had a sick feeling in the pit of his gut. Disco sensed it and sat at his feet whining. He didn't know what to do. This was sick shit and ought to be reported, but it really wasn't his call. Didn't Malcolm know he should report this to Facebook, and maybe to the police?

Is that what a man would do? A man didn't go whining to the authorities every time he got butt-hurt. A man took care of his own business. Donnie wanted to help his friend, but he didn't know what to do. He had to reach out. He called Malcolm on his new phone, and it went straight to voicemail.

"Dude, listen. I got to talk to you. It's important. I got a new phone. Call me at this number."

He looked up Irving Lipschitz in the phone directory and called. He hung up after seven rings. He called Keely and told her what he'd seen.

"Maybe we should go out there," she said. "I'd come but we have a mare foaling and I have to help Cully. What about tomorrow?"

"I work until five. I can go then."

"I'll pick you up."

"Okay."

Donnie didn't sleep well. In the morning, Kate had still not come home, and there was a message on his own phone to fix himself breakfast and she'd see him later.

That's how it always started.

CHAPTER FORTY-ONE
IRV LIPSCHITZ

DONNIE HAD BEEN BAGGING FOR THREE HOURS WHEN THE store manager, Luther Burke, came by. "Donnie, you're doing a great job. Keep it up. I like your attitude. Let me know if you want more hours or want to move up to cashier. It pays a little better."

"Thanks, Mr. Burke, but between school and my training, I've barely got time for this job. Don't get me wrong. I'm grateful for the work and I have no intention of quitting."

Burke was the spitting image of J. Jonah Jameson, except he wore glasses. "What training?"

"I'm training my dog to participate in disc dog competitions."

"You mean like Frisbee dogs?"

"That's right, Mr. Burke. The name comes from the Frisbie Pie Company in Bridgeport, Connecticut. Wham-O purchased the rights in 1955 and changed the name to Frisbee."

"I did not know that. Please keep me apprised of your progress."

Donnie told him about the YouTube video.

"Send me a link and I'll put it up on our website," Burke said.

At five, Donnie hung up his apron and stood outside waiting for Keely, who pulled up blasting The Blasters. They loaded Donnie's bike into the back and took off under overcast skies and a chill wind. Donnie directed Keely off the highway onto County BB.

"There it is on the right," he said as they approached the old farmhouse.

"You're kidding," Keely said. "Wow. This is like something out of *The Grapes of Wrath*. I had no idea. I thought he was Jewish."

"He is Jewish."

They wallowed up the rutted dirt road to the sagging house, in front of which sat a beat-up old Lincoln Town Car. No Neon. From outside they could hear a college football game blasting on the TV. Donnie knocked, and when there was no answer he knocked louder. The TV sound receded, and seconds later the door opened. Irv Lipschitz was a big slob with a beer gut, a filthy Packers T-shirt, jowls, a drinker's red nose and short curly hair.

"Mr. Lipschitz?" Donnie said.

"What do you want?"

"Is Malcolm here?"

"Nope." He started to shut the door, but Donnie put out a hand.

"Sir, could we speak to you for a minute?"

"What's this about?"

"We're worried about Malcolm."

With a sigh Mr. Lipschitz dropped his hand and stepped back. "Come on in."

The interior stank of cigarettes, beer and body odor.

Lipschitz slumped in an overstuffed chair like a beaten man.

Donnie and Keely sat on the sofa. Lipschitz straightened up when he got a good look at her.

"Sir, did you know Malcolm is being bullied at school?"

"So fuckin' what? Everybody gets bullied. I got bullied. Weren't you ever bullied?"

"Yes, sir, but this is pretty vicious."

"It's really vicious," Keely said.

"I told him what to do. They push you, you push back. If it were so bad, he woulda said something to me."

Donnie doubted it. "Sir, Malcolm's a great kid. Funny and smart. But these people who are bullying him are nasty. They're giving him a real hard time."

"Then he should go tell someone at school."

"He told me you told him not to be a crybaby."

Lipschitz picked up a can of Miller—*Miller*!—took a slug and belched loudly for effect. "That's right. No kid of mine is gonna go whining to the authorities."

"Sir, we're concerned he might harm himself or others."

"What do you mean?"

"We're worried he's thinking of killing himself," Keely said.

Lipschitz gave them a funny look. "You gotta be shitting me."

"I knew a kid killed himself at the last school I was at," Donnie said. "He was being bullied, too. Never said boo about it. One day he just jumped off a bridge. He left a message on his Facebook page saying he couldn't stand it anymore."

"Do you ever go to his Facebook page?" Keely said.

"I don't even know what that is. He got that fuckin'

computer himself, pays all the bills from money he makes selling shit on eBay. Kid's a self-starter. I don't see him killing himself."

"Why don't you try calling him? Maybe he'll answer you."

Lipschitz stared, sighed, heaved himself up out of the chair and went to the phone on the wall in the kitchen. He dialed, waited, said, "It's your old man. Call me. Couple of your friends over here are worried about you." He put his hand over the mouthpiece.

"What are your names?"

"Donnie and Keely," Donnie said.

"Donnie and Keely," Lipschitz said into the phone, and hung up. He opened the refrigerator, peeled off a Miller, returned to his chair, sat, popped the tab and chugged half the can. "Happy?"

"Has the school called?" Keely said.

"How would I know? I'm not home. Ask his mother."

"Where is she?" Donnie said.

"Workin.' Ace Hardware in town."

Donnie and Keely exchanged a glance. They got up and headed for the door. "Thanks," Donnie said.

Lipschitz turned the volume up on the football game. "I told that kid, someone hits you, you hit 'em back twice as hard. They bring a knife, you bring a gun."

Donnie stopped. "Sir, are any of your guns missing?"

Lipschitz stared at the gun rack. "Oh shit."

CHAPTER FORTY-TWO
THE SEARCHERS

Donnie and Keely drove into town.

"We should tell the cops," Keely said.

"No! What if they shoot him?"

"Come on! We'll tell Chief Robertson. He'll understand."

"No, Keely. We can't. The chief may be a good guy, but he'll tell others and all of a sudden you've got a couple dozen cops all revved up about some kid out there with a gun. Hardly a week goes by you don't read about cops shooting the wrong guy, some poor doofus holding a cell phone, the wrong house. You know Malcolm. What's he gonna do when the cops tell him to drop the gun and get down on the ground? I know Malcolm! He's just as likely to kill himself as someone else. He may throw down on them just to get it over!"

"Well what are we gonna do?" Keely wailed.

"We have to find him first."

"How?" Keely said as they drove by Discount Tires, the outermost outpost of Gunderson. They passed the

A&W, KFC, McDonald's and Burger King and came to the first stoplight at Main and Monroe.

Donnie took out his phone. "I have an idea. I'll tell him I've got that asshole Lester under surveillance."

The light changed. Keely drove until she came to the Piggly Wiggly and pulled into the parking lot. "Try it."

The call went straight to voicemail. "Dude. We've got Barnes under surveillance. Call me."

They sat in tense silence in the parking lot for five minutes, sick with worry. Finally Donnie said, "You may as well take me home."

Keely went with Donnie into the apartment, where Disco greeted them with a crescendo of ululation, running maniacally around the room, leaping on the sofa, leaping on them before settling down belly up in Keely's lap.

There was a note on the fridge. "Working late, kiddo. Make your own dinner. Love, Mom."

"I'll do it," Keely said, going through the refrigerator. She made mac and cheese with Werner's Polish sausage. After dinner they sat on the sofa and watched *The Voice*, but soon they forgot all about *The Voice* and found themselves horizontal, groins thrust together.

"I have a birthday present for you," Keely said breathlessly.

"What?"

"Me."

They went into Donnie's bedroom and shut Disco out. She sat outside the door whining. Keely unselfconsciously took off her shirt, her training bra, and her pants, removing a condom from its pocket.

"Let me put this on you."

Donnie came before he could insert. He fell back,

red-faced and humiliated. Keely took his face in her hands.

"Never mind. It's not important. We'll have lots of opportunities to get it right. I love you no matter what."

Fortunately, Keely had another condom.

KATE WAS BUBBLY AS CHAMPAGNE WHEN SHE CAME HOME at eight. "How'd it go, kiddo? You eat dinner?"

"Yeah, Ma. Keely made mac and cheese with Polish sausage. How's the image overhaul?"

"I don't know what we're going to do. Frank's thinking of selling his dad's Ferrari so we can hire another ad agency."

"Those ad agencies are full of shit, Ma."

"Can we watch our language?"

"Sorry, but you know what I mean. Half the ads I see make me hate the product's guts. Like that GEICO lizard. I'm so sick of that lizard, I would never buy GEICO no matter what! I don't much care for Progressive's Flo either."

"So you're out of ideas."

"I didn't say that. I'm working on it."

"Well let me know soonest, kiddo. I don't know how much longer Werner's is going to be around."

"Frank's your boyfriend, isn't he?"

Kate gave a wry smile. "Is it that obvious?"

Donnie laughed. "We've been down this road before!"

"Frank's a good man and he likes you."

Donnie hugged his mother. "It's okay, Ma. He's a thousand times better than any of your previous boyfriends."

"I'm glad you feel that way. What are your plans for tomorrow?"

"Training Disco at the Van Metres'."

"And all this training is for what?"

"I told you, Ma. I'm entering Disco in the state Flying Dogz Championship in the spring. First we're going to do a few local events to get her used to the crowds."

"Have you given any thought on what you plan to do for a living?"

"Don't rush me, Ma. I just got my driver's license."

"And how would you feel if Frank and I got married?"

"Fine."

She kissed him on the forehead. "I'm going to bed. I'll take you over in the morning."

Keely's scent kept him up for hours. In the morning, Kate made scrambled eggs and fried Werner's maple-cured bacon before driving Donnie and Disco to the Van Metre house. It was difficult for Donnie to take his eyes off Keely's ass. He shifted his pants to hide his boner and, when no one was looking, slapped himself in the nuts.

Keely brought a boom box into the barn, Chuck at her side. "We might as well start working with music so Disco gets used to it. I've put together a little playlist."

Disco capered and leaped as Keely pressed a button. Earth, Wind and Fire's "Sing a Song" played as they went through their routine. Donnie had a stack of five discs, a buck apiece at Petco in Wauwatosa, and flipped them at Disco as fast as she could do a backward aerial somersault. An hour later, Disco was just getting warmed up, sitting at Donnie's feet grinning, tongue lolling. Chuck lay down and watched with a sly doggie smile.

Keely took out her phone. "Do that thing with the backward flip. See how fast she can handle the five discs. I'm going to film it."

As soon as Donnie gripped the disc, Disco let out a series of ear-piercing squeals that sounded like the highest register of an amplified violin. Donnie and Keely looked at each other and grinned. Disco's squeal was unique. It was appealing. Anything that had that much enthusiasm for anything sounded like a winner. Donnie and Disco went to work to a disco beat while Chuck walked up and down the sidelines like an anxious coach, barking. Keely filmed twenty minutes before she stood laughing. "Okay! I think I've got enough!"

"Wait!" Donnie said. "One more thing. Can you get one of those hot dogs from the kitchen?"

Keely returned shortly with two hot dogs, one of which she flipped to Chuck. "What now?"

Donnie took the remaining one. "Okay. Get ready to film."

Donnie faced the camera, hot dog in hand, Disco capering at his feet. "Hi! I'm Donnie Waits and this is Disco! Disco eats Werner's franks! Flip, Disco!" Donnie tossed the hot dog as Disco performed a perfect backward aerial somersault. The hot dog was gone by the time she hit the ground. Donnie faced the camera.

"I wonder if she even tastes it. But don't take Disco's word for it. Werner's franks taste great!"

Keely chopped the air. "Cut! That's a wrap. Okay, I'll edit this with a little music and then we'll post it."

"Can you put together a two-minute clip featuring her doing the stunts first, and then the plug?"

"No prob!"

Cully came by in time for the endorsement. "What's this film for? You trying to raise money?"

"Sort of," Donnie said. "I'm trying to save my mother's job."

"Oi yeah," Cully said. "They was talking about Werner's at the pub last night. Lotta people might lose their jobs."

"Werner's is in trouble?" Keely said. "Now I'm sorry I bought those hot dogs at Walmart."

"I don't think your business would have made a difference," Donnie said. "But if they don't find a way to turn things around fast, there goes the sausage."

On the way home, Keely said, "Check your phone. Maybe Malcolm called."

"He hasn't called. I don't know what I'm going to do."

"Maybe it's time to tell the police."

"If I don't hear from him by tomorrow, I will. When can I see you again? We need to practice."

"Disc training?"

Donnie smiled. "You know what I mean."

"This weekend for sure."

They took so long kissing, Disco whined to be let out.

CHAPTER FORTY-FOUR
FULL-DRESS CAMO

DONNIE TOSSED AND TURNED SO MUCH, DISCO GROWLED at him. His mind was taffy torn in three directions: Keely, Malcolm and Disco, alternating from arousal to dread to hope. When he finally fell asleep, he had a phantasmagoric dream in which he and Keely were at a party looking for an empty room, pursued by Malcolm with a gun while Disco snatched Frisbees out of a Frisbee-launching machine. All to a disco beat.

Kate woke him at seven. "Can you get yourself to school, sweetie? I have an early-morning meeting."

"Sure, no prob," he said, rolling over.

Kate snatched the covers off. "Come on, get up. You'll be late. I made some bacon."

The smell of bacon and coffee overcame his drowsiness. It was a clear, cool morning in late November, temperature in the forties. He wore a jacket and a knit cap as he rode his bike to school, glancing at his cheap Timex watch. Yeah, he was gonna be late. Good thing Mrs. Brautigan liked him.

As the bell commencing the first period rang faintly

through the crisp morning air, Donnie was just pulling up to the entrance to the student parking lot. A familiar rumble caused the hairs on the back of his neck to stand as he turned into the lot. He stared straight at one of the crowded bike racks, and it wasn't until he inserted his front wheel in the slot that he looked to see Lester Barnes exiting his brother's Camaro, whooping and heading for the door.

Donnie didn't even want to be in the same building as Lester. Adjusting his backpack, he headed for the back entrance. He was reaching for the door when movement off to his left caught his attention. Malcolm. Dressed head to toe in camo hunt wear, he had been invisible standing in the trees at the edge of the lot. Hood up, he marched toward the rear entrance clutching a shotgun at port arms. Donnie veered to intercept, catching up with his friend fifty feet from the rear entrance.

"Stop! Stop right there! What the fuck do you think you're doing, Malcolm?"

"I don't care," Malcolm said. "They've made my life a living hell. Now I'm going to show them a little hell before I go."

"Didn't you get my message? I've been calling you for days."

Malcolm tried to get around Donnie, who moved to intercept. "Get out of my way, Donnie. I don't want to hurt you."

"What are you gonna do? Shoot me? They'll put the school on lockdown and pump you full of lead. Listen. I got the goods on Lester. He's going down for all sorts of shit; he won't be around much longer."

"It's not just Lester! It's everybody! That fucker Conklin and Shawn Gunther, and all those cliquish bitches that make fun of me when we pass in the hall-way, and that prick Pagel!"

"What are you going to do? Kill them all? You got enough ammo? Come on, dude! Don't throw your life away! This is all just temporary, trust me!"

Malcolm dug in his heels, leaned forward and pushed Donnie steadily backward. Donnie hunkered down and tried to push back, but since Malcolm weighed over two hundred and Donnie weighed only 135, it wasn't much of a contest. The only sound was their respective grunt-ing. It went on forever but gradually, inch by inch, Malcolm simply slid Donnie backward toward the stairs.

The rear doors banged open and Mr. Haskins appeared. "Malcolm! Malcolm, what are you doing?"

Donnie turned to look and Malcolm shoved him to the ground, heading toward the rear door with the shotgun across his chest. Mr. Haskins put out his hands in a placating manner.

"Son, think what you're doing. Put the gun down now and there will be no charges, I promise. We'll get you the help you need."

Malcolm stopped at the base of the stairs as faces appeared at every window facing the rear parking lot, two stories' worth. Several second-floor windows screeched open so kids could hear.

"I'm sick of being bullied, Mr. Haskins!"

Mr. Haskins took a step down. Malcolm swung the shotgun to his shoulder and ratcheted a shell into the chamber with the sound of a nuclear explosion. "Get out of the way."

"What are you going to do? Shoot me? What have I ever done to you? I'm not going to let you in the school, Malcolm. The police are already on their way."

The sound of a siren insinuated the crisp fall air and grew louder.

"Put it down, Malcolm," Donnie said quietly. "We'll get him. I swear it. I'll get him for you. Look what I did to Ryan."

Malcolm turned toward Donnie, tears streaming down his face. His mouth quivered. "Nothing works for me! Nobody likes me! My own family thinks I'm shit! I can't do anything right!"

He turned and leveled the shotgun at Mr. Haskins as a half dozen uniformed cops appeared, two of them in tan county, three around each side of the building, all of them holding automatic weapons.

Chief Robertson was in front. "PUT THE GUN DOWN, SON! PUT IT DOWN NOW!"

Malcolm swung the shotgun at Chief Robertson and the air erupted, so close Donnie could hear the bullets sizzle. He thought they were awfully quick to fire, and a couple of inches either way, they would have struck him.

Malcolm jerked spasmodically as if dancing, and then he collapsed.

CHAPTER FORTY-FIVE
FREE TO GO

THEY PUT THE SCHOOL ON LOCKDOWN, WHICH MADE NO sense. Malcolm had been the only threat and he was dead. "We have to make sure there are no other shooters," they said.

Kate came as soon as she heard, pulling up at the same time as Van Van Metre in his SUV. They joined several other milling parents at the curb, held there by a line of police officers, including county. A half dozen squad cars crowded the street with lights flashing. A news van from Milwaukee was first on the scene, setting up shop in the parking lot of the retirement village across the street.

All students returned to homeroom, where Principal Molly Price addressed them through the PA system.

"This is such a tragedy, I don't know what to say. We are dismissing all classes, and you will be permitted to leave just as soon as the police give the go-ahead. We will all pray for Malcolm's family, and please remember, we're all in this together. If you are being bullied or know of someone being bullied, please tell us!

"There will be no school tomorrow. We don't know about the rest of the week, so please be patient. You'll hear about it on the news."

Chief Robertson sat with Donnie in the cafeteria, which had become command center for the investigation. Cops helped themselves to coffee in the kitchen.

"Tell me what happened, Donnie."

Donnie told him about the bullying. "It was mostly Lester Barnes."

Robertson waved a deputy over and told him to find Barnes.

"We didn't know what to do. I should have called you Saturday."

"You should have. But we don't know what would have happened. What do you know about this Barnes?"

Donnie told him about the bike incident and Disco. "I think Lester and his brother threw Disco off the bridge. If I hadn't been there, she would have drowned. His Facebook page shows him forcing vodka down a dog's throat."

Robertson pointed at Donnie's backpack. "Can you show me?"

Donnie took out his new phone, went online and went to Facebook. A crease appeared between his eyes. "Lord Vile is gone."

"Excuse me?"

"He was calling himself Lord Vile, and now he's gone."

"Nothing's ever gone on the internet. We'll get a warrant for his electronics. I would say after today, you're a reliable witness. That was a brave thing you did, son. Understand, I don't condone keeping this to yourself for two days, but what you did took a lot of courage."

"Thank you, sir."

"Any idea what you plan to be when you grow up?"

"No sir, right now I'm focused on school and training my dog."

"Oh yeah? What are you training him for?"

"I'm training her to be World Disc Dog Champion."

"That's an admirable goal, son. Ever think of going into law enforcement?"

Robertson's deputy, a prematurely balding, athletic black man in a blue suit, came up. "Lester Barnes never checked in, Chief. There are two outstanding warrants out for his brother Travis: assault and DUI."

"See if you can find 'em. Hang on a minute." Robertson turned back to Donnie. "These people have any guns, weapons, anything like that?"

"Not that I know of. Travis drives an old orange Camaro with fat rear wheels and glasspacks, but you usually hear his bass before you hear the engine."

"Travis is well known to me," the chief said. "I would have picked him up on those warrants if I hadn't been short-handed these past few months." He turned to the deputy. "Go get 'em, Paul."

The deputy nodded and headed toward the door, speaking into his shoulder mic. As he left the cafeteria, the other half of the door swung inward and Kate streamed in like a tugboat, looked around, saw Donnie and headed over. As Donnie rose to meet her, she embraced him.

"Oh thank God! Thank God! Are you all right?"

"Maaa! Of course I'm all right!"

She let him go. "They said you were involved. I was so worried. I came right down but they wouldn't let me in until now."

Chief Robertson stood and offered his hand. "Mrs. Waits? Chief Robertson. Donnie took a great personal risk in trying to prevent the shooter from entering the building. He's a very brave young man."

"Chief, Malcolm didn't shoot anyone," Donnie said. "He's not a shooter."

"I'll leave you two alone for now, but we'll want to talk to you later."

Arm around Donnie, Kate turned to the cop. "We're free to go?"

"Yup."

CHAPTER FORTY-SIX
GIMME SHELTER

Chaos reigned in front of the high school as frantic parents pulled their kids while students with cars formed an impenetrable block trying to get out of the parking lot. Kate had parked down Main in front of the funeral home, but even there, traffic was backed up. As they waited to pull out, a cop went onto the street with sunglasses, gloves and a whistle and began to direct traffic. Kate remained grim-lipped until they were well clear of traffic.

"Tell me what happened."

Donnie told her.

"That's terrible! My God! You saw this?"

"I was so close, I heard the bullets zip past my ear."

"Oh, you poor baby! This is terrible. Just terrible." She began to cry.

"Don't cry, Ma."

"I can't help it. That poor boy!"

Donnie wondered if anyone had notified Malcolm's parents and how they'd react. More police vehicles entered town as Donnie and Kate drove out, as if by their numbers they could somehow turn back the clock. As they pulled into the apartment parking lot, a van with a dish on top that said WMLK on the side with the channel number followed them.

"Shit!" Kate exclaimed, stepping on the gas, deliberately inducing a spinout on the gravel and making a 180-degree turn. She roared past the puzzled news crew and turned right back into town, grimly gripping the steering wheel with both hands. They hit ninety.

"Ma! Where we going?"

"The plant. Dig out my phone and call Frank. Then give it to me."

Donnie did as he was told, using the electronic directory. Frank answered on the first ring.

"Are you all right?"

"It's Donnie, Frank. I'm giving you to Ma." He handed it over.

"Frank? There's a news van on our tail. I'm about five minutes out. Can you close the gates behind us so they can't get in?"

"I'm on it," Donnie heard Frank say.

Great, he thought. *A three-ring circus.* It was exciting! He mentally began to rehearse his interview. His phone rang. It was Keely.

"Are you all right?" she said.

"That's the existential question that's on everybody's tongues," Donnie said. "Am I all right physically, psychically, spiritually or morally?"

"God, you are such a nerd! Are you all right?"

"I'm fine. Malcolm's dead."

"I saw," she said in a subdued voice. "I wish I could be with you now."

"Me too."

The factory loomed on their right, surrounded by

hurricane fencing topped with concertina wire. Four or five men milled near the entrance, prepared to block the van's entry with their bodies. Kate accelerated and turned sharply into the gate. As soon as she was over the rail, the electric gate began to slide shut. The news van stopped in the short driveway. Its doors opened, disgorging a driver, a babe with blow-dried hair—mic already clipped to her collar—and a cameraman with a shoulder unit weighted in back with iron dumbbells.

Frank was just inside the gate. Kate stopped the car, got out and threw herself into his arms. Some of the guys at the gate looked mildly surprised. A flush crept up Donnie's neck. Frank disentangled Kate with as much dignity as he could muster.

"Okay, please no talking to the media. You can admit any legitimate visitors who are here on business."

He headed back to the main building while Kate returned to the car and drove around to the employee parking lot.

"Ma, what about Disco?" Donnie said.

"She'll be fine. She can pee on the balcony, and she has water, doesn't she?"

"Well how long are we going to be here?"

"I don't know, but I don't want a bunch of idiots thrusting microphones in our faces, understand? This is a tragedy. Let's not turn it into a circus."

"It's already a circus," Donnie mumbled. Kate chose to ignore him. She parked the car and then went in through the employee entrance, followed by the stench of hogs. Donnie's phone chirped Bryan Scary's "Flight of the Knife." He didn't recognize the number.

"Hello?" he said.

"Hello, is this Donnie Waits?" said a breathless female voice.

"This is Donnie."

"Donnie, this is Vicki Dukemajian with WMLK in Milwaukee. I'd like to ask you a few questions about your heroic act in preventing the shooter from entering Gunderson High this morning, if you don't mind."

"I'm sorry, Miss Dukemajian, I have nothing to say." He called Keely and asked her to check on Disco. "The key is under the doormat."

After that he shut off the phone and wandered into the vast warehouse past the crates and forklifts to where the Weenie Wagon lurked like a giant shrouded Cheeto. Donnie grabbed a headband flashlight off a shelf, slipped it over his head, turned it on and ducked under the tarp. He made his way toward the rear and found a panel with four ring bolts, like those found on the hoods of drag racers, holding it shut. He undid the ring bolts, popped it off and set it on the ground.

The flashlight revealed a hulking engine connected to a supercharger with a ribbed valve cover that said 426 HEMI.

CHAPTER FORTY-SEVEN
SPONSOR

AN HOUR LATER, DONNIE FOUND KATE IN THE boardroom working on her presentation.

"Where've you been, kiddo? I tried phoning you."

"I turned my phone off because these news people started phoning."

"Smart," she said. "I just tell them, 'No comment.'"

She used the remote to turn on the flat-screen, tuned to a local station. An ambulance chaser shouted at them and then the news came on, somber footage of a devastated Irv Lipschitz in front of their sad-sack house.

"No comment," he said, going inside and shutting the door.

The pert newscaster—was it Dukemajian?—turned toward the camera. "Prosecutors are as yet undecided whether to charge the Lipschitzes with negligence for failing to secure their guns, and may be considering more serious charges."

The scene flipped to a live shot of the packing plant besieged by news vans and official vehicles. "No word as yet from young hero Donnie Waits, whom authorities are crediting with stopping the gunman before he could enter the building. Waits and his mother, Kate, executive assistant to local meat magnate Frank Werner, have taken refuge at the Werner's packing plant. We will continue to pursue a statement, but for now the community breaths a huge sigh of relief even as it deals with its grief.

"This is Vicki Dukemajian for WMLK News in Milwaukee."

Frank strode in looking sharp in a pale gray suit, white shirt and red tie. "I've asked Lon Hargreaves to advise you on media matters. He's our top counsel."

"Why do we need a lawyer?" Donnie said. "We haven't done anything wrong."

"Don't worry about it, Donnie," Frank said. "These media sharks will eat you alive if you're not careful. We've received two dozen requests for interviews. Imagine trying to handle those on your own."

"We'll just say no."

Frank grinned like a shark. "That's not how it works, my friend. The media's like a hungry tiger. They'll just keep coming and coming until you give them some meat."

"What do you mean, meat?"

"Frank means that you're a hot story right now, and they won't give up until we give them something. If we don't give them something, they'll make stuff up."

"They're digging into your past right now," Frank said. "They're turning up Kate's old boyfriends and searching for your father."

Donnie barked derisively. "That's not right! We didn't do anything wrong."

"That's the way it is," Frank said. He looked at Kate.

"He knows," she said. "I told him."

"Your mother and I love each other very much," Frank said.

Donnie raised his hands in benediction. "No prob!"

The console phone on the board table rang. Frank picked it up. "Let her in," he said, turning to Donnie. "A friend of yours is here with your dog."

Donnie clapped his hands. "I'll be right back."

He found Keely in the lobby with Disco on a leash, Disco on her hind legs straining to greet every passerby. People lined up to pet the dog.

"I saw your video," said a young man in a one-piece jumpsuit. "Really cool, man."

"Thanks," Donnie said, leading Kate and Disco to the elevator.

As soon as the doors shut, Keely fell into his arms and gave him a smooch. "My hero!"

"It's no big deal," Donnie insisted.

"That video turned out great. I'm going to put it up tonight."

When Donnie, Keely and Disco entered the boardroom, Frank and Kate were huddled around her laptop. Kate got up and gave Keely a hug; Frank got down and petted Disco, who pawed and leaped at him, grinning. Kate took off her *Lady Death* backpack and set it on the table.

"She loves Werner's wieners," Donnie said.

"I'll bet. Your mother and I have prepared a statement for the press. How does this sound to you?"

Kate read from the laptop. "Donnie Waits was merely trying to stop a friend from hurting himself or others and does not consider his actions particularly heroic. The Waits family requests your respect and understanding during these troubled times, and asks the same for the Lipschitz family."

Kate and Frank looked at him expectantly.

"It's okay but there's nothing about why Malcolm did it. There's nothing about the bullying."

"Let this serve as a reminder," Frank said, "that bullying remains a major concern for young people everywhere. If you are aware of bullying, don't be afraid to tell school authorities—or something like that."

Kate pecked. "I'm on it."

Keely unpacked her laptop and set it up as Donnie looked over her shoulder. She keyed up her video. "This is a little rough but you get the idea."

As "Sing a Song" played in the background, Disco leaped and spun like a yo-yo, the camera steadily circling 360 degrees like in a Martin Scorsese film. It ended with Donnie's endorsement. The whole thing was two and a half minutes.

Frank stood beside Donnie. "Can I see that?"

Keely played it again. Frank turned to Kate.

"Have you seen this?"

Kate watched it.

"What did you say you're training for?" Frank asked Donnie.

"The World Disc Dog Championship. It takes place on the Fourth of July on the mall in Washington, D.C."

"Do you need a sponsor?"

CHAPTER FORTY-EIGHT
"FLIP DISCO"

FRANK AND KATE LEFT THE PLANT AT FOUR VIA A BACK entrance in Frank's SUV, followed by Keely, Donnie and Disco in Keely's Mazda. They followed Frank to his estate in Shady Grove, a gated community outside Hartland.

"Holy shit," Donnie said as they followed Frank through an art nouveau wrought iron gate up the circular brick drive to the hooded front door of Frank's Prairie-style mansion, which resembled a vast brooding prairie hen, wings extending to either side topped with redwood shingles. Vines crawled the brick walls, and hooded gables looked out on the restored prairie. Frank led them through the round foyer, through the living room, down three steps to the rec area with a walk-out to the patio and an oval swimming pool covered by a heavy canvas. The rec area faced a walk-in fireplace and had a pool table.

"I might be living here," Donnie whispered to Keely.

Frank pointed at Disco. "Is she house-trained?"

"She's house-trained," Donnie said.

"Well if you're not worried she'll run away, you can let her off the leash."

As soon as Keely freed her, Disco took off like Speedy Gonzalez, ricocheting from sofa to floor to chair to stair, then collapsed on her back in front of Donnie with her paws in the air, grinning. He crouched and rubbed her belly.

"You folks are free to choose any of the bedrooms in the guest wing." He pointed. "Kate and I will be in my office."

Donnie snapped his fingers twice. "Keep it clean, you two."

"Come on," Keely said, setting her backpack on the oak dining room table. "Let's prep this vid!"

As Donnie watched, Keely used an editing program to fine-tune the vid, zooming in here, zooming out there, bringing up a funky beat beneath Donnie's endorsement at the end.

"What's that song?" Donnie said.

"'Atomic Dog.' George Clinton. What do we call this?"

"Flip Disco."

Keely wrote it in. "Okay, ready? And here we go!" She touched a key and the video uploaded to YouTube. She posted it on her and Donnie's Facebook pages. It was like watching a pari-mutuel board. First one person liked it, then another. Then the numbers spun like a pinball machine. They watched in silence for fifteen minutes while their "likes" climbed into the hundreds. Keely went to post it on Twitter, but it had already been posted.

On FB, comments piled up.

"Rad!"

"Love that dog!"

"Werner's, breakfast of champions!"

Keely found "Atomic Dog" on YouTube and turned it

up, and she and Donnie and Disco danced around, Disco on hind legs, her pink tongue jutting like a pennant. Donnie calculated his chances of getting into Keely's pants under Frank's roof. Not good. It was okay for the grown-ups to sneak off and play house, but not the kids. Fair enough. The grown-ups had jobs and paid for the house.

But a kid had needs, too, and she was so close!

Fuggedaboudit.

"Isn't that airplane awfully close?" Keely said.

The roar made the whole house buzz. They walked through the sliding glass door onto the patio and looked up. A helicopter was circling the house. Seconds later Frank stormed out, looked up and was about to flip it the bird when Kate latched on to his arm.

"Don't do it! I just phoned the police. They're ordering those people to back off."

They could just make out the call letters of MLRA, a Milwaukee-based TV station, on the side.

"Come back in," Kate said. "The police are holding a news conference and they're discussing the rest of the week."

Everyone went inside and faced the wall-mounted big-screen in the rec area. The ubiquitous Vicki Duke-majian appeared before a hastily erected podium in front of the County Building where Donnie had taken his test.

"Gunderson police chief Harold Robertson is about to speak," she said in a hushed tone.

Looking uncomfortable, Robertson gripped the podium. "At approximately eight fifteen this morning, a youth with a loaded shotgun attempted to enter Gunderson High. He was prevented from entering by a fellow student, who held him there long enough for the Gunderson police and members of the Washington

County Sheriff's Department to arrive. Unfortunately, when advised to drop the weapon, the youth turned it on officers, who responded with deadly force.

"Malcolm Lipschitz was described by his classmates as a troubled boy who was obsessed with violent video games and guns."

"THAT'S A LIE!" Donnie shouted. Keely put her hand on his shoulder.

"Donnie Waits, who prevented him from entering, is being hailed today as a hero. The Gunderson School District will remain closed for the rest of the week while counselors are brought in."

Vicki Dukemajian elbowed her way to the front of the howling mob and thrust a mic in Robertson's face. "Chief Robertson! Is there any truth to the rumors that Malcolm was the victim of bullying, and that his repeated complaints to administrators were met with indifference?"

"We are taking those allegations very seriously," Robertson said. "And we are investigating."

"There weren't any," Donnie said.

Another reporter asked if they were pursuing charges against the Lipschitzes. Donnie got up. Disco jumped off the sofa and followed him back to the dining room table.

He and Keely checked YouTube. "Flip Disco" was up to four thousand hits.

CHAPTER FORTY-NINE
MOVING THE MARKET

KEELY LEFT AT NINE, FOLLOWED ALL THE WAY HOME BY news vans, which were stopped at the entrance to her house by Van Van Metre. His prominence as a developer extended even to Milwaukee. Standing in front of the reporters' microphones, he said, "Yes, my daughter, Keely, who is a champion dressage rider by the way, is Donnie Waits' girlfriend and knew the deceased. All I can say is that Donnie is an outstanding young man and we support him. Please come watch my daughter Keely compete at the Dressage Spring Regionals in Chetwynd, Indiana, in May."

"Oh Daddeeee!" Keely wailed when she saw it on the ten o'clock news.

In a spare bedroom that had belonged to Frank's son, Peter, now a lawyer in Milwaukee, Donnie slept until nine. He would have slept longer, but Disco swabbed his face, causing him to jerk upright.

"Have you been eating shit?" he demanded, sniffing. "You have! You've been eating shit! Who let you in here?"

Donnie went into the bathroom and took a shower. It

was nine thirty by the time he made it to the living room, where Kate had set up shop in front of the television tuned to Fox Business news, her open laptop at her side.

"Ma! What's going on?"

"Werner's stock is trading at an all-time high. Frank went to the plant. Every media organization in the world wants to talk to you. For now, all the requests are going through Lon Hargreaves. He wants to set up a conference call with you for eleven."

"Jeeez," Donnie said. "What's going on?"

"It's that video you posted last night. Want some breakfast?"

"Sure. Got any bacon?"

Kate rose like smoke from the sofa, wearing jeans and a man's shirt with the sleeves rolled up. "Does Woodman's Grocery have wine?"

After breakfast they watched the news. School would reopen on Thursday. The Gunderson School District was bringing in counselors. The earnest young Hispanic news reader said, "Authorities are pursuing criminal negligence charges against the boy's father, Irving Lipschitz." There was footage of Lipschitz angrily slamming the door of his home, besieged by journalists.

"And in a bizarre turn of events, a video posted by young hero Donnie Waits has gone viral and may have enormous and positive effects on the local economy. That video when we return."

Kate turned to Donnie. "What video?"

"I guess they're going to show it."

They waited for the commercials to end. The news reader returned. "Last night Keely Van Metre, a student at Gunderson High, posted a video of Donnie Waits and his dog Disco training for the World Disc Dog Championship. What he had to say at the end has already had a profound effect on the stock market."

They showed the video, including when Donnie turned toward the camera and said, "Disco eats Werner's franks! Flip, Disco!"

Kate squealed and hugged him. "My boy is a genius!"

Her phone chimed. "It's Frank," she said, holding it to her ear and winking.

Donnie got up and headed for the patio, Disco at his heels. Kate put a hand up.

"Hold on. Frank wants to talk to you."

Donnie took the phone. "Hey, Frank."

"Donnie, we'd like to meet with you at two o'clock. I'd like to discuss a licensing deal with you and Disco. Bring Disco."

"All right! You bet!" He handed the phone back to Kate and listened to the rest of the conversation. Finally, she turned it off.

"What?"

"Don't you think we'd better get our own lawyer, Ma?"

"Y'know, kiddo, Frank and I are getting married. I don't think he'd enter into a contract that was deleterious to his own stepson."

"You ever watch *Judge Judy*?"

"You're a smart kid. We'll run it by someone not connected to Frank."

"What's the press conference for?"

"Well I guess it's to announce the licensing deal with you and Disco. By the way, I talked to your homeroom teacher, Mrs. Brautigan, this morning and she thinks you need counseling. I agree."

"For what?"

"Yesterday your best friend was gunned down not ten

feet from where you stood! You'll need help dealing with that."

"I don't feel like I need counseling."

"Well I'm your mother and I say it wouldn't hurt for you to at least talk to an expert. Will you do that for me?"

"Alllll right."

"And be ready to leave by noon, and dress nice for a change. No torn T-shirts."

"Jeez. We ain't even entered a contest yet. Come on, you mutt! Let's flip." Donnie opened the door, and he and Disco went out.

Kate went online and looked at the YouTube video. It was up to four hundred thousand hits.

CHAPTER FIFTY
AN EXCLUSIVE

DONNIE WORE A CRISP WERNER'S WIENERS T-SHIRT THAT had sat in a box for thirty years and featured a retro design of the Weenie Wagon as drawn by Ed Roth, with a bug-eyed monster sprouting through the roof, hand on a hot dog–shaped shift stick, enormous rear wheels and headers.

Donnie and Kate ran a gauntlet of news crews at the entrance, and when they entered the foyer, people stood and applauded. On the fifth floor, green bottles of champagne covered the board table, along with a sideboard loaded with cut-up sausage, ham and freshly nuked bacon, artisanal breads, artichoke and cheese dips, vegetable platters and other accoutrements of an office party.

Frank embraced Kate and Donnie, then stooped to hug the dog. "Werner's stock is trading at a twelve-year high," he announced as executives and regular workers, including Paco and Roddy, congratulated him. So many people slipped Disco treats, Donnie had to scoop her up.

"She'll get fat!"

Forty-five minutes of back slapping later, Frank shooed everyone out of the room except for Donnie, Disco, Kate, Vice President for Marketing Harlan Schuh and company counsel Lon Hargreaves. Frank sat at the head of the table.

"We've prepared a licensing agreement for you that of course we encourage you to take to your own lawyer and review thoroughly before you sign anything. It will grant Werner's an exclusive, five-year lease on Disco's likeness and name and will require you to participate in a certain number of publicity events. Werner's will underwrite all your expenses for training and participating in events related to the World Disc Dog Championship. Lon?"

Hargreaves was a slight balding man with a fringe of gray hair and the look of a startled hedgehog. "We're establishing a ten-thousand-dollar line of credit for expenses. We will insure Donnie and Disco for a million dollars each. You will be required to participate in six events a year, with others to be negotiated. We will pay you five thousand dollars per appearance." He went on for ten minutes.

Frank smiled. "What do you think?"

Kate shook her head in wonder. "It sounds too good to be true."

"Donnie?"

"I'd like you to establish a college scholarship fund in honor of Malcolm Lipschitz."

Frank and Hargreaves looked at each other.

"Uh," Hargreaves said, "we'll have to hold off on that for the time being until we have an opportunity to study the situation. Deepest condolences on your friend, but it does appear as if he had murder in mind."

"I don't believe it!" Donnie said.

"It would be more appropriate to establish a scholarship in your name," Hargreaves said.

"No way! I haven't done anything to deserve it."

"Others might disagree," Frank said. "You have single-handedly saved the company."

"Y'know, Keely deserves all the credit. It was her idea to shoot the video and put it up."

"We will of course negotiate with Miss Van Metre for the rights to use her video," Hargreaves said. "We will also have a crew following you around as you compete this summer."

"I'd like to bring Keely onboard as consultant," Donnie said. "After all, this is mostly because of her."

"I don't see a problem," Frank said. "I hope that we can sign an agreement sometime next week. Is that amenable?"

"Let's see," Kate said. "We're going to have to run this by our own attorney."

"I understand," Frank said.

"And of course none of this can be allowed to interfere with Donnie's education."

"Such as it is," Donnie said.

Crinkling and snorting sounds emanated from the sideboard, where Disco was working her way down the platters.

Donnie sprang from his seat. "Disco!" He scooped her up and sat at the table, holding her firmly on his lap as everyone laughed.

"Dogs will be dogs," Frank said. "So I think those are the major points. Donnie, I understand you got your driver's license. Congratulations."

"Thanks, Mr. Werner. There is one more thing I'd like you to put in the contract."

"What's that, Donnie?"

"I want you to refurbish the Weenie Wagon and make it Disco's transportation."

CHAPTER FIFTY-ONE
ASSEMBLY

ON THURSDAY, KATE DROVE DONNIE TO SCHOOL, WHICH had been closed since Monday. Despite a light rain, students and teachers waited on the steps for his arrival and mobbed him like a rock star. Coach Pagel said he'd asked the school to change the team name from the Gunderson Gremlins to the Gunderson Disc Dogs. In homeroom Keely blew kisses at him.

Mrs. Brautigan slapped her ruler on the desk. "Listen up! There will be a general assembly in the auditorium at one for all students. Principal Price will address the recent tragedy. Now I realize this has been traumatic for everyone. Never in a million years did I think we would experience the type of terror that we did on Monday. If it's true that Malcolm was bullied, each and every one of you must ask yourself if you had anything to do with it. You see what bullying leads to. How would you like it if you were the target of hateful comments and emails? Sarah, I see you texting. Put it in your desk."

The girl sheepishly slipped her smart phone beneath the desk.

"Don't let this terrible event interfere with your development as a student and as a person. As I have said on numerous occasions, the purpose of school is to help prepare you for life as an adult. We're all here to learn how to be better persons, myself included. With that in mind, please pray for Malcolm's family and be very serious about your time here."

"You can't say 'pray,'" said Billy Clanagan.

"Feel free to report me, Billy."

In the cafeteria, Mr. Haskins told Donnie that the school was ditching the federal school lunch guidelines and entering into an exclusive agreement with Werner's Meats.

"We must each ask ourselves, what would Disco eat?" Donnie said.

"Exactly," Mr. Haskins said.

At one the student body, approximately twelve hundred students, gathered in the auditorium. Molly Price was a diminutive woman with an almost mannish haircut, who stood on a stool to see over the podium.

"Good afternoon, students and faculty of Gunderson High. I never thought we would meet under such tragic circumstances. You hear about these shootings from time to time but you think, 'Not here. It can't happen here.' And because of the bravery of one young man and the quick response from our police, a greater tragedy was averted."

Donnie rolled his eyes as Keely squeezed his hand.

"I did not know Malcolm Lipschitz well. I wish now I had taken the time to get to know him better. Malcolm's death is just as great a tragedy as that of any other child who dies too early. Like a lot of you, he felt alienated, an outsider, picked upon. I'm aware of allegations of bullying and I take them very seriously. Bullying is something we cannot and will not allow. Of course bullying is not an excuse for murder. We don't know what Malcolm's intentions were, but our policy on bringing weapons to school is clear. We all need to ask ourselves if there's anything we could have done to avert this tragedy. If you knew Malcolm, did you make disparaging remarks about his appearance? Did you call him names, thinking it was funny? Put yourself in his shoes. Each student who enters Gunderson High feels like an outsider to some extent. It's just part of growing up. I think the Golden Rule applies here: treat others as you would like to be treated.

"We are bringing in some grief counselors to help those students who feel they need it. They will be here tomorrow, and if you want to see one, please tell your homeroom teacher. These meetings will be kept confidential.

"I also understand that the Lipschitz family is having difficulty paying for Malcolm's funeral, so we have set up a box in the front office for those who wish to make donations. Malcolm's funeral will be held Sunday at the Klein Funeral Home at one o'clock. Now Coach Pagel would like to say a few words."

Principal Price ceded to the coach as Keely pulled out her phone and texted. Donnie pulled out his own phone and visited several disc dog sites, making mental notes. Thirty minutes later the assembly ended with the singing of the school song, "Go Gunderson," and the national anthem. Several students refused to stand and sing. Teachers dismissed the students by rows to avoid a pileup. On the way to his sixth-period class, Donnie was intercepted by Mr. Haskins.

"Donnie, the principal and I would like you to go see Dr. Denison in the school counselor's office."

"Do I gotta?"

"I think it's a good idea."

"All right," Donnie said with an air of resignation.

CHAPTER FIFTY-TWO
HOW DO YOU FEEL?

DR. NIKI DENISON WAS A PRIM, TIGHT-LIPPED thirtysomething with glasses and her hair done up in a bun so dense, it looked like it might explode. She stood, smiled and offered her hand. "Hello, Donnie. I'm Dr. Denison. Please have a seat."

Donnie sat while Dr. Denison looked through Donnie's file.

"That was a very brave thing you did the other day. You should be proud of yourself."

"I don't think it was brave, ma'am. I was just trying to stop a friend from making a fool of himself. I don't think he would have used that gun."

"Yes, well you never know. Kids do shoot other kids."

"I know that."

"So tell me how you feel."

"Honestly?" Donnie said.

"Of course."

"Is this confidential?"

Dr. Denison's mouth formed a razor slit. "All right.

Yes. I promise not to reveal anything you say to me to anyone else."

"Are you recording this?"

The razor slit. Dr. Denison reached in front of her to the open desk drawer, picked up a small recording device, shut it off and placed it in front of Donnie. "Not anymore."

"Well I feel that if those kids hadn't constantly bullied him, he wouldn't have done it. I'm angry."

"What kids?"

"I already spoke to the police about them."

Dr. Denison made notes in the file. "Are you having difficulty sleeping?"

"No."

"Have you experienced a loss of appetite, feelings of guilt, anxiety and helplessness, anything like that?"

"No more than any other adolescent."

Notes. "It's normal for a person in your situation to experience those feelings. It's nothing to be ashamed of."

"I'm sorry, ma'am. I just feel sad about the whole thing. Why would I feel guilty? I haven't done anything."

"Because you're alive and your friend is dead."

"I didn't shoot him."

"I see in your files you don't participate in any extracurricular activities although you posted the fastest six-hundred-yard time in school history. Why is that?"

Donnie shifted around to get comfortable. "It's not like I don't have anything going on. I work after school and weekends, I'm training my dog to participate in the World Disc Dog Championship and I've got a girlfriend."

"Really." Notes. "They didn't tell me that. What kind of job?"

"Stock clerk at Piggly Wiggly."

"And what's this about a dog? I never heard of the World Disc Dog Championship. What is that?"

Donnie told her, with sidebars about Cactus Jack.

"And what kind of dog is this?"

Donnie brought up a picture on his phone and showed it to her.

"Oh, he's so cute! I have four cats. What kind of dog is he?"

"She's a purebred Wisenheimer."

"I've never heard of such a breed."

Donnie stared at her, and all of a sudden she did a little hop in her chair. "Oh. That's funny. How's the training coming?"

"She's very smart. I think she'll be ready for the first event in May. I'm working with her as much as I can."

"Tell me about your girlfriend."

Donnie felt uncomfortable. "She's just a girl. We're there for each other."

"Does she go to this school?"

Donnie wanted the interview to be over. "Maybe."

Notes. "I see you live with your mother. Is your father a factor in your life?"

"I never knew him. He took off before I was born."

Scribbling like Bob Cratchit. "That must have been rough."

Donnie shrugged.

"Does your mother date?"

"Excuse me, ma'am, what does this have to do with my feelings regarding Malcolm?"

She looked up. "I'm just trying to get a more complete picture of where you are as a person. I'm trying to understand your circumstances."

"Do you have any kids, Dr. Denison?"

The slit. "No."

"Are you seeing anyone?"

"This isn't about me, Donnie. I'm only trying to help you."

"Well let's just stick to my feelings."

"Right now you appear to feel hostile."

Donnie was getting steamed. He wondered what would happen if he just got up and walked out.

"All right," Dr. Denison said. "Are you and your girl-friend having sex?"

Donnie gaped like a grouper. "Are you kidding me?"

"Just answer the question."

Donnie stood. "Forget about it! This is bullshit!" He walked out.

Dr. Denison stood and came out from behind her desk. "Wait! Do you have any guns at home?"

CHAPTER FIFTY-THREE
MONGOLIAN BOOMERANG

AFTER SCHOOL, KEELY GAVE DONNIE A RIDE TO THE Piggly Wiggly. "I have to race home. That foal is due any second."

Donnie kissed her in the car. "Want to do something tomorrow night?"

"Like what?"

"We could see that new Pixar flick. I'll call you."

"Okay."

Donnie worked for ninety minutes before the first news crew arrived. He saw the van with the letters and the antenna pull up in front and park in a handicap spot, and went directly to Mr. Burke.

"Sir, I'm very sorry to have to tell you this, but these newspeople keep following me around. They're parked outside in a handicap spot."

"No problem," Burke said, reaching for his phone.

Before the news babe had finished applying her makeup, a policeman arrived and began writing a ticket. Mr. Burke filmed the news van in the handicap zone and didn't have to say a thing. Either they left or he would release the footage to a rival news network.

Burke drove Donnie home under a leaden sky. Kate had returned home with Disco, who went off like an air raid siren when she saw Donnie.

"Oh, I'm glad you're home," Kate said. "It's supposed to snow. How did the counseling go?"

"Fine."

"Well tell me about it. Who was your counselor? Do you think it helped?"

"My counselor was a Dr. Denison. She was a lot of help, Ma."

"That's good to know. I don't want you worrying about what happened on Monday."

"I'm not worrying about it, Ma. I just wish everybody would stop worrying about me worrying about it."

"I know, baby, I know. It's because we care about you."

Donnie worked with Disco on new tricks, including getting Disco to jump on his back while he was on hands and knees. He'd seen it in videos online and deemed it a useful addition to their arsenal. He thought about the routine almost as much as he thought about Keely. Which was a lot. He had to fill two and a half minutes with a dazzling display of canine athleticism.

He used a spiral pad to list the tricks: backward flip, Mongolian Boomerang, Watusi Sidestep, Foaming Pipesnake and Paddling Blowfish. The Mongolian Boomerang consisted of tossing the Frisbee in a parabola, Disco leaping onto Donnie's shoulders over the head, and Donnie standing abruptly to launch Disco into the air, where she snagged the disc on its return. It was an extremely difficult trick, not something he could practice in the house, and had never been successfully completed. It was the holy grail of disc dog tricks.

They worked on the butterfly catch, wherein Donnie flipped the disc end over end and Disco caught it. Snow began to fall. By nine it had settled on the sills and the balcony, covering the earth in white as far as the eye could see.

Donnie was getting into bed when his phone rang. It was Keely.

"She foaled! We're naming him Malcolm!"

"That's great! See you tomorrow."

"Here's a kiss for you." Smack. "And here's one for Disco." Smack.

Donnie got under the covers and held them for Disco, who went under, circled three times and settled in next to Donnie's ribs. He thought about Keely, and that kept him up for an hour. He thought about the evil Barnes brothers and hoped they'd been killed in a shoot-out. He thought about the Waits/Werner wedding and what that would look like.

He thought about Malcolm.

He thought about Nate.

There was nothing he could do for Malcolm, but Nate was still there. Donnie hadn't spoken with Nate since he'd gotten his driver's license. He vowed to speak to Nate tomorrow, and stop by if he was able.

CHAPTER FIFTY-FOUR
HOME BY MIDNIGHT

THERE WAS TWO FEET OF SNOW ON THE GROUND IN THE morning, and school was canceled for the day. Frank cruised by in his Jeep Grand Cherokee at nine and picked Kate up for work, leaving Donnie and Disco alone for the day. Donnie took Disco out to play in the snow, the little dog forging a trail through the drifts like an icebreaker, backing off and leaping on the snow, flattening it with her belly. She scooped snow up with her nose and tossed it in the air, yelping.

They worked their routines in the pole barn and returned to the apartment around noon. Donnie heated a can of vegetable-beef soup for lunch and, when he was done, set the bowl on the floor for cleaning.

He phoned Nate. It rang six times before going to Nate's voicemail.

"Hey, man, it's Donnie! Give me a call."

He felt something on his nose and looked in the mirror. Zit! He popped that sucker and watched it bounce off the mirror. That left the rest of the day. He went into Kate's room and went online. Both Cactus

Jack and Lily Carruthers had FB pages. Both were filled to capacity and both linked to videos of Jack and Lily performing. Lily looked like a forties-era movie star, with a statuesque body and hair fixed like a head of broccoli. Cactus Jack hugged the earth like a low-rider until it was time to act, and then he exploded. Donnie watched in awe and with a sinking feeling as Lily and Cactus Jack rocked the Frisbees to the Beach Boys' "Dance, Dance, Dance."

Donnie created a Facebook page for Disco and linked it to the YouTube video.

"Disco is a purebred Wisenheimer, one of only twelve in the continental United States. Help Disco in her quest to win the World Disc Dog Championship! Tell your friends about Disco and come cheer her as she competes with the world's best!" He uploaded pictures of Disco flipping, flying and lying on her back with her paws in the air.

Malcolm's page was still up, filled with heartfelt remembrances from people who hadn't given a shit when he was alive. There was a picture of Malcolm the foal on Keely's page. Donnie thought about Keely and masturbated three times to get it out of his system. He phoned her.

"We still on for tonight?"

"Sure. I'll pick you up at six. We'll get something to eat and then we'll go see that movie."

County snow plows worked all day, and by early evening the streets were again passable. Kate got home at five.

"What do you want for dinner, kid? We've got frozen lasagna, pizza and Salisbury steak."

"Keely's picking me up, Ma. We're going to grab something and see a movie."

"What movie?"

"*The Littlest Wombat.*"

"Be home by midnight. Aren't you working tomorrow?"

"Yes, Ma."

He showered, sprayed himself with Axe body spray, put on clean jeans and a yoked Western shirt with mother-of-pearl buttons. Donnie watched for Keely through the window, and when her tires crunched up to the front entrance he was ready. He popped into the passenger seat, leaned over and gave her a kiss.

"Mmm," she said. "You smell delicious."

"I'm trying to smell less like a dog."

They had dinner at the A&W. Donnie picked up the bill.

Once in the car he said, "You don't really want to see that movie, do you?"

Keely smiled. "What did you have in mind?"

"You know."

"Where?"

"Let's go out to Dudley Park. No one will bother us there."

The park was abandoned at that hour. With the seats laid flat, they created a bed. Keely plied herself with spermicide, and Donnie wore a rubber. Afterward Keely said, "Wow! That was so much better! What's the secret to your awesome lovemaking, man of mine?"

"I jerked off earlier. I was thinking of you."

"That's the sweetest thing anyone has ever said to me."

CHAPTER FIFTY-FIVE
A FRIEND OF MINE

MORE THAN TWO HUNDRED PEOPLE ATTENDED MALCOLM'S funeral at the Klein Funeral Home. The family was not religious and so had no affiliation with a synagogue. The Lipschitzes appeared to be in a state of shock throughout. It was left to the funeral director, Robert Blake, to deliver the eulogy, the usual boilerplate about how every life was valuable and that Malcolm would be missed.

When Blake stepped aside, Donnie went to the podium. He wore his only suit—blue, with a white shirt and a black tie. "Malcolm didn't have many friends," he said. "I know how that goes because I didn't have many friends either. He liked comic books,

Grand Theft Auto, heavy metal and guns. Yes, I said guns. I'm sorry but that was one of Malcolm's enthusiasms and it was not unusual. I know a lot of people who like guns. They are, after all, only a tool."

He glanced at Kate, who was wide-eyed with mortification and drew a finger across her neck.

"Sigmund Freud, the father of modern psychiatry, said, 'A fear of weapons is a sign of retarded sexual and emotional maturity.' The story of mankind is the story of war. The peace that we enjoy in the United States is an anomaly. This country was founded in violent revolution, and we have remained free only because of the bravery of those who choose to defend us. I'm not excusing Malcolm's actions. What he did was wrong. The rules are clear. School is no place for weapons, but I still believe he had no intention of shooting anyone other than himself, if it came to that.

"Malcolm was a gentle soul who wouldn't hurt a fly. He had to put up with a lot of grief from bullies. I know about bullies. Bullying is wrong and everybody knows it, yet kids choose to bully. I don't know, something about human nature. I'm sure Dr. Freud would know.

"Anyhow, when I think of Malcolm I think of him digging through his backpack to show me a copy of *Something Wicked This Way Comes* or *The Last Days of Krypton*. Malcolm loved science fiction and turned me on to a lot of good books. Malcolm was a friend of mine and I will miss him."

Someone started to clap but stopped, realizing it was inappropriate.

———

Soon it was Thanksgiving. Donnie and Kate celebrated it with Frank. Days flying by, November slipped into December as Donnie continued to work at the Piggly Wiggly and to train Disco in Keely's horse barn.

Frank scheduled a press conference for December 10 to announce Werner's strategic alliance with Donnie and Disco. In the wake of several homicides, the press had lost interest in Donnie, but the press conference ginned it up again. A correspondent for *Milwaukee* magazine wanted to do a lengthy profile on Donnie.

He demurred, claiming he wasn't old enough to have a lengthy profile. The conference was set for Monday at 5:00 p.m. at the Pfister Hotel in downtown Milwaukee. Keely drove him over with the clothes he'd selected, and he changed in Werner's suite, emerging in a pale blue shirt with a bright blue tie decorated with pigs. Kate brought Disco, Buckaroo Banzai bandanna around her neck. The press conference was to take place in the Grand Ballroom before a backdrop that alternated a stylized Disco catching a Frisbee in flight with the Werner's logo.

Four Milwaukee television stations covered it as well as the *Milwaukee Journal Sentinel*, *USA Today* and *Dog World*. They all waited in a room backstage with a table covered with cold cuts and vegetables. A liveried barman served drinks. Donnie slipped Disco several slices of salami, hoping she wouldn't cut one on camera.

At Frank's signal they filed out to find the ballroom surprisingly busy, at least a hundred journalists and interested parties waiting with recorders, pads and cameras. Donnie and Disco had their seats marked. Kate sat on the other side of the dog. Disco seemed to sense something was up, because she sat and faced the cameras in a dignified manner, snout just above the table.

Frank stood behind the podium that said PFISTER HOTEL. Frank smiled reassuringly, looking like the handsome lead of a daytime soap. "Good afternoon, my friends. I'm Frank Werner, president of Werner's Meats. To my left sits Donnie Waits, the young man who bravely put himself between his classmates and a disturbed friend with a rifle a mere six weeks ago. I've known Donnie longer than that, and he has always been a serious and exceptional young man."

Donnie blushed furiously while Keely blew silent kisses from the seats.

"Donnie has been working with his dog, Disco, for some time, preparing for the World Disc Dog Championship, which takes place July 4 on the mall in Washington. I didn't even know they had a World Disc Dog Championship!"

Pause for laughter.

"It wasn't until Donnie posted a video that became an overnight sensation that I became aware. As you know, these are tough times for business. The truth is, I was just presiding over the decline of the company my grandfather started in 1949. Werner's market share was 37 percent in 1960. Today it is 2 percent. There are many reasons for this, some of them of our own making.

"But I have always believed in our product—the finest in deli meats produced and prepared according to the original German recipes my great-grandfather brought with him when he passed through Ellis Island as a lad of twelve. Ladies and gentlemen, before we proceed I think it behooves us to see the video Donnie posted."

Donnie rolled his eyes at "behooves." The lights dimmed. Donnie appeared against the dark backdrop of the horse barn wearing a Werner's T-shirt with the flying pig.

"Hi, folks! I'm Donnie and this is my dog, Disco!" He fanned three discs, and Disco let fly with that eerie squeak like Jean-Luc Ponty on acid. Over Earth, Wind and Fire's "Sing a Song" played a collage of Disco performing the Foaming Pipesnake, the backward flip and other tricks. When the video ended two and a half minutes later, the audience broke into spontaneous applause.

Frank stood clapping and looking at Donnie. "And now Donnie will say a few words."

WTF?! Gamely he got to his feet and cleared his throat.

"Hi, folks! I'm Donnie and this is my dog, Disco!" Disco got up on the table, walked over and wagged her tail. People laughed and applauded.

"That video was my girlfriend's idea. She put it together and added the music. Keely? Stand up, would you?"

Keely stood and waved as the cameras clicked and followed. She wore a high-necked sleeveless black dress with a priest's collar and a white gardenia in her hair.

"I'd also like to thank my mother, Kate, who has supported me the whole way!"

Kate blushed, stood and bowed.

"Disco and I look forward to seeing you at the state competition in June. You can find all the details on Disco's Facebook page, Disco Waits. Thank you."

He sat down. Disco licked his face.

Frank took the podium. "Within twenty-four hours of that video going viral, we began getting reports of supermarkets and delis selling out of our product. Since then we have been operating at maximum capacity to fill demand, and we are planning on building another packing plant in North Dakota. All this because a little dog likes our wieners.

"Therefore, I would like to unveil our new corporate logo."

The lights dimmed, and a projector cast the soaring Disco grabbing a Frisbee inside a red-and-yellow bull's-eye with WERNER'S MEATS scrolling along the bottom.

"We are also reviving one of Werner's noblest traditions, the Weenie Wagon."

The projector showed an artist's version of a refurbished Weenie Wagon rolling down the road chased by children and dogs.

"We are partnering with Raven Software in Madison to bring out a Werner's Weenie Wagon game."

A new image appeared on the wall, the Weenie Wagon as drawn in the style of Ed "Big Daddy" Roth with a monstrous Donnie sprouting through the roof wearing sunglasses and a backward ball cap, shifting a knob in the shape of a kielbasa, enormous headers sprouting from beneath the Weenie Wagon belching fire.

The lights came on. "I will now take questions," Frank said.

Vicki Dukemajian stood.

VICKI AND HER CAMERAMAN FACED DONNIE. "MR. WAITS, there are allegations that Malcolm Lipschitz was mercilessly bullied at Gunderson High. Are those true?"

Donnie opened his mouth but no sounds came out.

Frank grabbed the mic. "We called this press conference to announce our strategic alliance with Donnie and Disco, and our support for their quest for the World Disc Dog Championship. I will entertain any question dealing with our new direction."

Vicki turned her lamps on Frank. "Mr. Werner, a boy is dead. He may have been intent on killing others. The public wants answers. This is the first opportunity we in journalism have had to ask Mr. Waits about this tragedy."

"No comment!" Donnie said loudly and clearly. There was a momentary lull.

"Would you care to comment on the Barnes brothers' involvement in Malcolm's bullying?"

Donnie shook his head. Disco farted but no one heard it. Frank pointed at a young Hispanic male with exquisite hair.

"You, sir."

"Yes, thank you. Luis Moran from WKLE in Milwaukee. Why are you building your new plant in North Dakota and not here in Wisconsin?"

"When asked why he robbed banks, the great bank robber Willie Sutton replied, 'That's where the money is!'"

"Are you comparing meat packing to bank robbery?" Moran duly asked.

"Come on, Luis! We're building in North Dakota because it is the fastest-growing economy not only in the United States but in the world. The unemployment rate in North Dakota right now is 2.6 percent. It's attracting skilled laborers from all over the world, and North Dakota is one of our premier hog-producing states. Our commitment to Wisconsin is unwavering but we must plan for the future."

"What about the fact that North Dakota is a right-to-work state?" Moran said.

"What's wrong with that?" Frank said.

Several other reporters stood and raised their hands like eager twelfth graders. In a momentary lull, someone in the audience opened a paper bag of potato chips with a crinkling sound. Disco leapt off the table, off the podium and landed in the startled snacker's lap, tail wagging, tongue lolling.

Donnie rose to his feet. "And that, ladies and gentlemen, is the attitude and sheer athleticism that we will ride to the WORLD DISC DOG CHAMPIONSHIP!"

The people dutifully cheered and clapped. Frank shot Donnie a grateful look.

A reporter from the Madison alternative newsweekly *Isthmus* waved her arm. "What will be the function of the Weenie Wagon?"

"It will serve as Donnie and Disco's support vehicle. When they're not competing, the Weenie Wagon will roam the countryside handing out hot dogs."

"Seriously?"

"Seriously," Frank said. "The Weenie Wagon is powered by a blown 426 hemi mill developing six hundred horsepower. It will turn eleven-second quarter miles and top out at over 150 miles per hour."

"Seriously?"

Frank grinned. "Well the part about the engine is true."

The woman with the potato chips raised her hand. She couldn't stand because Disco was in her lap. "Is it all right if I give her some potato chips?"

CHAPTER FIFTY-SEVEN
THE BEHEMOTH

For Christmas, Frank and Kate gave Donnie a 2005 Honda Civic with eighty-three thousand miles on the odometer. It wasn't until January 2 that he remembered he'd never heard from Nate. He called Nate.

"We're sorry, the number you have dialed is no longer in service."Donnie named his first car the Barkmobile, and washed it and waxed it the morning of January 2, even though he could see his breath. When he finished, he drove through sylvan dales, reveling in the freedom you feel only with your first car. He drove toward Nate's Bait. At least the dirt road leading back to the river was packed down.

When Donnie pulled up, he saw that Nate's truck sat out front with six inches of snow on the hood and roof. The last snow had been three days ago. Someone had tramped up and down the wood steps, flattening the snow. Donnie crunched up the steps and opened the front door. There was no one in the little store.

"Nate!" he yelled through cupped hands, seeing his breath. It was no warmer inside the shack than out. Had the furnace gone out? Donnie went straight through to Nate's bedroom and knocked on the closed door. After a while he heard a groan. Pushing against a pile of shoes and clothes, he forced the door open.

Nate lay curled on his bed like a shrimp beneath a couple of threadbare blankets, a dirty white handkerchief spotted with red clutched in his hands. He looked diminished, shrunken. Donnie rushed to him and felt for a pulse in Nate's neck. Donnie had taken a lifesaving class at his previous high school with an eye toward earning money at a public pool.

Nate's pulse beat feebly. There was an empty glass on his nightstand. Donnie went into the bathroom, filled it with water, returned and knelt.

"Nate. Nate. Can you hear me?"

The old man half opened his eyes.

"Drink this." Donnie held the glass while Nate slowly drank half.

"How you, youngblood?" he croaked. "What's goin' on?"

"You tell me. Didn't you get my messages?"

"Nah. You miss one fuckin' payment, they cut off your phone."

"Are you all right?"

"I'm having trouble standing. I get all dizzy and shit."

"Did they cut off the heat, too?"

Nate drifted off. Donnie dialed 911. He heard the siren within fifteen minutes, and shortly after that, the big, square, white-and-red ambulance clawed its way to the front yard. Two EMTs leaped out with a stretcher and ran up the steps to where Donnie held the door.

"In the back."

Minutes later they returned with Nate, put him in the

back of the ambulance and hooked up an IV drip. Donnie looked through the open doors.

"Where are you taking him?"

"County General in Wauwatosa. Follow us."

As soon as the ambulance hit the highway, it turned on the flashers and siren and accelerated to ninety miles per hour. Donnie hung close behind, praying he wouldn't get popped for speeding. Somehow they made it all the way to the hospital without mishap. Donnie followed the ambulance around to the emergency entrance, found a spot in short-term parking and went in.

The techs had passed the security barrier and transferred Nate to a rolling gurney. A uniformed cop stopped Donnie at the metal detector.

"Whoa. May I see some identification?"

Donnie pulled out his driver's license. "I'm a friend of Nate's, that guy they just brought in."

"Please empty your pockets."

Donnie pulled out his cell phone, billfold, pen, loose change and a small pocketknife and put them in a plastic bin. The cop took out the knife.

"You can claim this on your way out. Step through the metal detector."

Donnie did so and retrieved his pocket items. When he tried to follow Nate through the swinging doors, a nurse stopped him.

"You can't go back there, young man. Not until we get a diagnosis. It might be a while."

With a sigh, Donnie resigned himself to waiting room hell, joining a young Hispanic mother with three pre-teens, an old black man in coveralls and two glassy-eyed board punks covered with body piercings and ink. One of them had had a window installed in his jaw so you could see his gum and the roots of his teeth. Probably infected. Donnie sat as far away from them as possible.

He phoned Keely. "I'm at the hospital with Nate. He was semi-comatose when I found him."

"Oh! Do you want me to come down there?"

"No. I just wanted you to know."

"Love you."

"Love you."

Next he phoned Kate.

"Well how long do you intend to stay there?" she asked.

"Ma, I don't know. Nate said he had a daughter somewhere. I'm going to try and get in touch with her."

"Well I don't want you staying there all night."

"Ma, he's got no one else."

The doctor came out, looked around and zeroed in on Donnie. His nametag said CURTIS.

"Gotta go. Doctor's looking for me."

"Call me when you're done."

Donnie stood. "What is it, Doc?"

"Your friend has pneumonia, but we're running some other tests. For now he's stabilized and would like to see you."

Donnie followed the doctor through the swinging doors down a hall to a bed partitioned off from others by hanging curtains. Nate lay against the crisp white sheets like a ginseng root in cotton.

CHAPTER FIFTY-EIGHT
AGENT ORANGE

NATE SPAT AND COUGHED. "THAT FUCKIN' AGENT Orange finally caught up with me," he hacked.

"When's the last time you ate, Nate?" Donnie said.

Nate's lips parted and he stared at the ceiling. "Don't recall."

"Nate. What about your daughter and your ex-wives?"

"Fuck 'em! Ain't heard from any of those bitches in years."

"Dude, this may be your last chance to get straight with 'em."

Nate gazed into a void. Tears came to his eyes. "Last time I talked to Tonya, she told me to eat shit and die. That's my daughter. I guess I fucked that up six ways from Sunday. I don't think...I couldn't bear it if I got in touch with her and she told me to go fuck myself, and sure as shit that's what's going to happen."

Donnie felt bad for Nate. To be that old and not have anyone who cared. He felt himself tearing up and turned away. A man didn't cry in front of others. If Nate died, the hospital would have to notify his next of kin. It was their problem.

"All right. What can I get you? Need anything from home?"

"Where are my pants? They took my goddamn keys."

Donnie looked in the closet, where Nate's soiled dungarees had been neatly folded on a hanger. He fished in the pocket and found the keys on an old Ford fob. "I got 'em."

"Yeah. My dope's inside my nightstand. And there's a book I was reading, *Bones of the Hills* by Conn Iggulden. It's next to my bed. Get that and get me some fresh underwear, clean jeans, my clean Sturgis T and my down-filled parka. I'm outta here in the morning."

"Nate, you've got pneumonia."

A shudder ran through him like an earthquake and he began coughing, whole body spasming. After a minute a nurse came in and shooed Donnie out. Nate wasn't going anywhere. Donnie got home at eight. Disco heard the outside door open and commenced a hysterical ululation until Donnie opened the door, crouched and picked her up.

"I'm happy to see you, too," he said, as Kate came out of her room talking on the phone.

She held up a finger.

"Okay. I'm on it. See you tomorrow." She folded the phone and enfolded Donnie in her arms. "How's my baby?"

"Not so hot, Ma. Nate's sick. He's in the hospital."

Kate put a knuckle to her teeth. "That's terrible! Do they know what's wrong with him?"

"Said it was pneumonia but the doctor also said they were running tests. Nate always said that Agent Orange would get him."

"What's that, dear?"

"It's a chemical they used in Vietnam."

"I made some dinner. It's in the oven."

Donnie looked at a half pizza. He lifted the garbage can lid and saw an empty DiGiorno box.

"He's got no one, Ma. His daughter hates him; his ex-wives hate him."

"Maybe he's not a very nice man."

"Nate's a prince, Ma."

"Well maybe he just doesn't get along with women. There are such people."

"All he's got is me. I gotta be there for him."

"What does that mean?"

"Means I gotta check in with him every day, see if he needs anything. Bring him stuff."

"Oh Donnie, I don't know."

Donnie raised his voice. "What don't you know? He's an old man with no one!"

Kate smiled ruefully. "Kiddo, I love that you're such a kind, generous person. Of course you should be there for him. I'll go see him myself."

"Seriously?"

"Seriously. And when he gets out, we'll look in on him."

Donnie threw his arms around her. "Thanks, Ma!"

Disco saw the whole thing.

CHAPTER FIFTY-NINE
IN THE PACK

DISCO BARELY REMEMBERED THE BAD TIME WHEN SHE WAS kept in a tiny enclosure and couldn't get enough food or water. But she remembered the scent of her tormentors, though she hadn't smelled it in a long time. Things changed so fast. One minute she was in a small, scary enclosure surrounded by malice, the next in free fall, then a hard landing and a man opening the bag and letting in the light.

The man was her pack now, along with his mother and the girl. The man treated her with love and respect, and she was happy because every day there was food, water and play. Especially the play. Disco had two settings: hyper and sleep. Something within the little dog caused her to move constantly in search of things to chew, run around the living room like a tiny Indy 500 and leap onto furniture and laps, eager to make new friends.

She especially loved the happy place where the man threw things for her to catch and she could sniff the German shepherd's butt. Today was such a day! The man and Disco went outside where the cold wet stuff lay. Disco ran through the snow like a freight train, scooping it up with her nose and tossing it in the air until the man called her to get in the car. The man lowered the window so Disco could stick her snout in the air. Never had she felt anything so exhilarating. And the smells!

The closest she'd come to such ecstasy was when they went to the big place with all the lights and people, and the people made a joyous noise with their front paws and hooted, and a lady gave her potato chips.

They drove through the countryside, Disco's snout jutting like the prow of a Viking ship, scooping more scents than there are stars in heaven. As soon as they turned onto the Van Metres' private drive Disco loosed a cannonade of happy yelping! Disco loved life and she loved her pack. She knew what was coming.

Disco couldn't wait for the man to let her out. She followed him out his side, running between his legs straight to the big red barn. It was a sunny day in February, temperature in the mid-thirties. The man let her in through a side door, and Disco zoomed around the big hay-covered space, pausing here and there for rapid barkfire.

Another man, not of her pack but friendly, greeted them and handed her a peanut butter cracker. Then the girl came out and there were more treats. The man removed the flying plastic discs from his backpack and then went to work. The butterfly toss. The backward flip. The Foaming Pipesnake. The girl put on the happy music and they worked the Mongolian Boomerang, but the timing was off and the man kept misjudging the toss so that the disc came back too far away to catch.

They worked on it until the man collapsed beneath Disco, laughing, and she licked his face until he was gasping for breath and the girl scooped her up. They all went inside. The people had soup and the dogs had high-quality chewables.

They went home as the sky was getting dark.

And that was just one day.

"CLASS," MRS. BRAUTIGAN SAID. "WE HAVE A NEW SCHOOL policy. You will turn your cell phones off before the first bell and not turn them on again until after the final bell. I don't have to explain to you why we have instituted this rule."

Immediately several hands shot up.

"Yes, Louella."

A dot-Indian girl with horn-rimmed glasses said, "What if there's a family emergency or something?"

"Your parents can phone the school and we will notify you. Just like in the old days." She looked around. The class was electric with outrage. "Jerry."

A louche in a slouch said, "Isn't that interfering with our rights of free speech?"

"No, Jerry, it is not. The law assigns the school the role of *in loco parentis*, which means that we may reasonably ask you to refrain from certain activities that may be harmful to you or others."

Jerry's phone rang and he turned beet red. He looked at it.

"Turn it off, Jerry."

With a sigh he complied.

"It's his mom checking on whether he brought his strained peas for lunch," the boy next to him said.

Snickers, buzzing, *whack*. Down came the ruler.

"I advise you to use the rest of this hour to study. What the heck. It's school, right? What else would you rather do?"

Mrs. Brautigan turned a deaf ear on the avalanche of wisecracks. "Study, people," she continued. "Or don't. You could end up on welfare buying tattoos and body piercings with your food stamps. Or you could rise to the top of the food chain and live in a magnificent mansion with a view of the Pacific and a pool. The choice is yours."

Groans of resignation accompanied the cracking of spines. Mrs. Brautigan had made her preference for paper products clear. She didn't like iPads or electronic notebooks. "Some of us have pacemakers, people!"

Inspired by Disco's example, Donnie focused on each class. Coach Pagel had resigned himself to the fact that Donnie would never join the track team but encouraged Donnie in his pursuit of the disc dog championship.

"Saw your video, Waits. Good work!"

In English his essay titled "The Economics of Scrooge McDuck" earned an A. Only the feared and reviled algebra resisted his blandishments. Now when he walked down the hall, other students shouted encouragement or bumped fists with him. Suddenly the senior girls took notice, flashing their boobs or twerking when they thought he was looking. Donnie laughed silently. None of them could compare to Keely. She had it all: looks, character and a great sense of humor.

There were songs about her. "God Only Knows."

"She's So Fine." "Brown Eyed Girl." "She's My Girl."
"Cynical Girl." "Cherry Bomb." The list was endless.

People stopped him in the hall to invite him to
parties.

Of Lester Barnes, though, there was nothing. He'd
dropped out. Donnie scanned the *Gunderson Surveyor*,
their weekly newspaper, which dutifully reported all
garage sales, deaths, sporting events and the police blot-
ter. The Barneses had dropped off the face of the earth,
and good riddance.

Police raided the house the two brothers shared and
found the remains of several dogs who had died of dehy-
dration locked in cages. Thinking about it put Donnie in
such a pit of rage and depression, he understood how
Malcolm might have wanted to blast his tormentors to
atoms.

The long school day crawled to the end. Several kids
asked if they could come watch Disco train, and Donnie
always said they had to check with Keely. It was her
house. He walked to the Barkmobile, tossed in his backpack and sank behind the seat, inhaling that peculiar
aroma of old cars: dust, plastic and dog.

He took out his cell phone and turned it back on.
There were several calls, one from Keely, one from Kate
and one unknown. He called Keely.

"When can you come over? I've got some more songs
I want to play you," she said.

"Gotta work this aft but I'm free all day Sunday."

"Great!"

He called Kate.

"I want you to go to the Men's Wearhouse and pick
out a suit."

"Maaaaaaaaaaaaaaaaa!"

"You're not going to look like a slob at the wedding. Be grateful I'm not making you wear a tux."

He called the unknown number.

"This is Dr. Curtis' office."

Donnie's heart rose like a mortar shell. "This is Donnie Waits. I think Dr. Curtis called me."

"Yes. Please hold on."

Minutes later Dr. Curtis came on the line. "Donnie?"

"Yes sir."

"Bad news, son. Mr. Dixon passed away last night at one thirty. We were hoping you could help us get in touch with his next of kin."

Donnie touched the void.

"Donnie?"

"Yes, sir. I know he had a daughter named Tonya. I think she lives in Louisville, Kentucky."

"Can you be any more specific?"

"Sir, I'll go out to his house and see what I can dig up, but I have to work now so it may not be for a day or so."

"Would it be possible for you to do it today? I'll be happy to speak to your employer."

"All right."

THE BARKMOBILE'S TIRES CRUNCHED AS DONNIE PULLED up to Nate's Bait. The trampled dirty snow and open door showed what he'd feared; thieves and vandals had gotten in. Donnie entered the building with trepidation. The store had been cleaned out. Every Red Bull, six-pack of Point, Weasel Peters and Pepsi gone. All the bait and fishing gear gone. Cash register cleaned out. They left the calendar. Someone had spray-painted incomprehensible graffiti all over the wall.

Donnie went into Nate's bedroom. They'd left the sheets on the bed but taken most of his clothes and shoes. They left behind a simple black suit, which Donnie took, as well as an old-fashioned white dress shirt that had somehow escaped notice. They'd even taken his stroke magazines. Donnie found Nate's diary shoved beneath the dresser. As he scooped it up, a letter fell out. It was from Florence Wiggins Dixon-Saunders, dated five years earlier.

Dear Nate: If I had money saved I would

most certainly not lend any of it to you. Need I remind you that you are six months in arrears on your child support and the only reason your ass isn't sitting in jail is because I do not wish to have to explain to your daughter, whom you have not seen in over seven years, why her Christmas and birthday greetings are returned unopened.

I am sorry to hear about your health problems. I don't wish ill health on anybody. I urge you to see a professional, not only for your health problems but for psychological reasons. It is not normal for a man of your age to whine to his ex-wives about his medical bills. You are eligible for veteran's benefits. I urge you to use them.

Please do not contact me again.

DONNIE WISHED he hadn't read the letter. He let it fall to the floor, but he kept the envelope. It had a return address in Louisville, Kentucky. Nate had told him his daughter hated his guts, so why would she send him Christmas and birthday cards? Donnie guessed he would never know. Everybody told themselves lies to help get them through the day.

Feeling sad, he took the suit and shirt out to the car, got in and drove into Wauwatosa and the hospital. He parked in the visitor's lot and asked for Dr. Curtis at the front desk. The receptionist spoke on the phone and told him to go up to the fourth floor.

A nurse's aide on the fourth floor told him that Nate's body had already been delivered to the county coroner. She took the information on Nate's ex and thanked Donnie. The coroner's office was housed in the basement of an old redbrick building on Meier Boulevard with warped wood floors. It smelled of Pine-Sol and formaldehyde. A gray old man who reeked of cigarette smoke watched Donnie approach, holding the suit and shirt on a hanger.

"I'll take that, son. Who's it for?"

"Nate Dixon. I'd like to see him if you don't mind."

"You don't look like next of kin to me."

"Sir, I guess I'm his closest friend, sad though that may be."

The old man looked at Donnie for a minute and motioned him around the partition. They hadn't yet gotten around to installing 24/7 video and metal detectors. The clerk led Donnie through a couple of rubber-tipped swinging doors into a refrigerated room with a concrete floor fitted with drains. Nate lay on a stainless-steel gurney covered with a sheet. The clerk led Donnie back and lifted the sheet.

Nate looked like a wax dummy of himself.

"Needs a tie," Donnie said.

"Who was he?" the old man said.

"He ran a bait shop in Gunderson. He was a Vietnam vet with a couple ex-wives and a daughter."

"And you were his only friend? That's rough, son. Say, he left a few things. I guess you might as well take them."

The clerk went to a series of metal shelves on the wall, took down a cardboard box labeled DIXON with the date on the end in felt marker, and handed it to Donnie.

Inside was Nate's wallet, containing twenty-two dollars; a crumpled pack of American Spirits; a tarnished bronze Zippo with a Vietnam inscription; and Nate's pearl-handled folding knife.

Donnie swallowed a couple of times and turned away. As he headed toward the exit, the old man called after him.

"Know any next of kin?"

"Workin' on it," Donnie managed to choke out.

CHAPTER SIXTY-TWO
RIGHT WITH GOD?

NATE'S FUNERAL WAS HELD AT THE FAITH BAPTIST Church on the last Saturday in February. It was the only black church for miles around and drew parishioners from miles around. The pastor, an old man with a fringe of white hair and bifocals, met them at the door.

"Used to buy bait from Brother Nate on my way to Madison. Lotta folks around here bought bait from him. Asked him when he was comin' back, and he said as soon as he got his head straight with the Lord. I told him, 'You want to get straight with the Lord, you come to church.' Well, here he is."

Aside from Donnie, Keely and Kate, only twelve people showed up for the funeral. They had laid Nate out in his crisp black suit, white shirt and a red tie Donnie had purchased for him at Goodwill.

Whether the hospital succeeded in contacting Florence or Tonya remained a mystery. The bank got into a tiff with the feds over Nate's property, for which he had paid neither mortgage nor taxes. The last time Donnie drove by, it had been condemned.

The pastor spoke movingly of Nate's service. There was no mention of his family. Finishing, he said, "Would anybody else like to say something about our brother Nate?"

Donnie stood and walked to the podium wearing the same outfit he'd worn to Malcolm's funeral, carrying a small boom box. He looked out over the large black congregation. "I never knew my father," Donnie said. "But I knew Nate. When we moved to town, Nate was the first friend I made. He took the time to listen to me; he let me buy sodas on credit. He drove me to my driver's license test and let me use his car. Nate loved his family, regardless of what they felt about him, and I'm sorry not to see any of them here today. Nate loved the blues. He said the blues was nothing but a good man feeling bad. He said if you don't love the blues, you've got a hole in your soul. And he said that if you must choose, let it be the blues. So I think it's appropriate to play this song for Nate. It's Otis Rush singing "Not Enough Coming In.""

He cued the song and a funny thing happened. The entire congregation clapped along in perfect time. When it ended, he shut it off and stepped down from the podium. Everybody there reached for him, clapping him on the back and blessing him.

———

THE FIRST EVENT of the disc dog competition year was the Waunakee Feed and Grain Disc Dog Invitational on May 1, at Fireman's Park in Waunakee. Donnie's greatest concern was whether the Weenie Wagon would roll.

Frank had hired a hot-rodder and airbrush artist named Monte Moore from Colorado to resurrect the

W2. Moore had brought his own engine lift and machine shop and had practically been living in Werner's back warehouse for a month. Donnie was out there whenever he wasn't at school, working or training. Monte was a leathery biker in his forties with long gray hair, a mustache, arms covered with tribal tats and a welding helmet painted like Thanos.

On Friday, April 15, Donnie crouched on a crate behind Monte, who had the valve covers off the hemi. "Whatcha doin' now, Monte?"

"I'm replacing the lifters. They been sitting too long, starting to corrode. Next ahmina replace all the plugs and we'll pump some nitro in this baby and see if we can get it to turn over."

"Nitro? Seriously?"

"No, don't worry. It'll get out of its own way."

"How fast will she turn the quarter mile?"

"This pig weighs fifty-four hundred pounds, but once I hook up the all-wheel drive and we start crankin', should get there in the twelves. Hand me that wrench, wouldja?"

Donnie gave him the wrench and backed up to absorb the glory that was the W2. Monte had repainted the giant wiener the color of a red hot with yellow and purple flames exploding upward from the wheel wells, and he had painted an airborne Disco catching a pizza on each side.

"Will it be finished in time for Waunakee?" Donnie said.

"Should be if I get those transaxles in time."

Monte had gutted the interior, removing the walk-in cooler and replacing it with a doggie grooming station, beds and an airplane-type bathroom.

Donnie looked at his watch. He'd wasted enough time. "Okay I'll see ya," he said.

"Don't let your meat loaf," Monte said.

Donnie got in the Barkmobile and booked. He'd added an after-market CD player that pumped good sound without making the earth shake. He slid in the latest from the Pinecones and cruised home, passing the hardware store, Arby's, McDonald's, Wendy's and Burger King, wondering how they could all survive. Like everyone in town ate fast food. Now that he thought about it, the students of Gunderson High certainly did. Since the new school lunch policy had been instituted, twice as many students now ate in the cafeteria as previously. Students were hungry animals. They craved meat, not raw broccoli, bean sprouts and tofu. Meat, dammit!

Donnie felt great until he turned into the parking lot to his apartment and there, parked across two spaces like an asshole, was Ralph Speece's pickup. He couldn't believe it. What could that worthless lowlife be doing back? Hadn't he gotten the message the first time when Kate gave him the heave-ho? Donnie heard the angry voices even before he was out of his car.

He ran up the steps two at a time and burst into his apartment, where a shit-faced Ralph, who looked like one of *Justified*'s Crow Brothers, was spraying spittle at his mom, who was backed up against the refrigerator, fists on hips. Disco crouched beneath her legs with a Mohawk, growling deep in her throat.

"I want what's mine!" Ralph yelled.

Kate's eyes went to Donnie as soon as he entered.

"Ralph!" Donnie said. "Get the fuck outta here! I just called the cops!"

It was the only thing he could think of.

Ralph turned on him like the bully he was. "You little

pissant, you stole my fuckin' weed, you stole my fuckin' balisong and you stole my fuckin' rodeo belt!"

Donnie was so abashed at the breadth of these accusations that he denied everything. "Fuck you! You're crazy! Get out!"

Ralph grabbed a fistful of Donnie's shirt, and that's when Disco launched herself at Ralph's calf.

"YAHHH!" Ralph said as Disco sank her fangs. Ralph danced a wild Watusi, shaking Disco off. Disco rounded on him; Ralph lashed out and struck the dog in the hip with the toe of his hand-tooled cowboy boots.

Disco yelped.

Sirens sounded.

Ralph looked around with a rictus and mad eyes. "Fuck you! Fuck all of you!" He stormed out, slamming the door behind him.

"Ma!" Donnie said. "Are you all right?"

"He didn't hurt me. Oh. What's wrong with Disco?"

Feeling an ice pick in his heart, Donnie looked at his dog, who limped over to him.

CHAPTER SIXTY-THREE
HYDROTHERAPY

MRS. MCGILLICUDDY HAD CALLED THE COPS WHEN SHE heard the yelling. The cops pulled Ralph over a mile down the road and booked him into the county jail for several outstanding warrants, including two DUIs.

Donnie was frantic. He called Keely.

"What should I do? The Waunakee Invitational's in two weeks!"

"Okay. Calm down. Cully will know what to do. Let me talk to him and call you back."

Sick with worry, Donnie phoned Dr. Morton.

"If you want to bring her over to my house, I'll examine her."

Ten minutes later, Donnie was out the door. He wouldn't permit Disco to walk. He carried her and laid her neatly on a folded-up blanket on the passenger's seat. He could tell she was hurt because she remained seated throughout the drive instead of sticking her snout in the wind.

Dr. Morton lived in a forties-style bungalow on a shaded residential street two blocks off Main. Donnie pulled into her driveway, a twin concrete strip with grassy median, and parked behind her Forester. Dr. Morton had seen him drive up, and opened the door as he approached, cradling Disco in his arms like *The Pietà*.

"Bring her right over here," she said, indicating the sofa. Donnie gently laid Disco down. Dr. Morton sat next to her, and Disco began furiously licking the doc's hand. Dr. Morton cooed softly while her hands felt gently but firmly along the dog's flanks. The vet flexed the limb. Disco yelped.

After some prodding, Dr. Morton said, "No broken bones but she might have a sprain. You'll have to curtail her activity as much as possible for the next several days. I could give you some tranquilizers."

"Doc, we got a competition in two weeks!"

A delta of concern sprouted between Dr. Morton's eyes. "Two weeks? Oh dear. Normally that wouldn't be enough time for her to fully heal."

"What about abnormally?"

"Abnormally too. It was just a figure of speech. I would keep ice on it for now, don't get her excited, don't let her run or jump."

Donnie could only shake his head and go walleyed.

His phone buzzed. It was Keely.

"Cully wants to talk to you," she said.

"What's the problem?" the trainer said.

Donnie told him.

"Oi've had a similar situation with horses. Hydrotherapy seems to work in a lot of those cases. You want to bring 'er out here, we'll give her a burl."

"What do you mean, hydrotherapy?"

"Y'know that swimming pool like we got in the barn?"

"Yeah."

"Well that's what I mean."

For the first time in hours Donnie felt a flame of hope. "I'll be right out," he said, excusing himself, taking his dog and driving to the Van Metres'.

It was seven thirty when he arrived, driving right up to the barn. Disco wanted to jump down, but he kept her pinned in the blanket as he carried her into the barn, where Keely and Cully waited. Horses nickered softly in their stalls. The smell of hay, leather and manure had a calming effect on boy and dog.

The hydrotherapy pool was lit from below and glowed aquamarine. Cully wore baggy surfer's trunks and a tank top and was knee deep on the stairs leading into the water.

"Hand 'er over," he said, arms out like a forklift.

CHAPTER SIXTY-FOUR
"ATOMIC DOG"

DONNIE DIPPED HIS HAND IN THE WATER AND WAS surprised to find it warm. Cully held Disco under the rib cage.

"It's heated to a hundred degrees, the temperature of horse blood. Dogs run a degree or two warmer but this is fine."

As Cully lowered his hands, Disco paddled reflexively. The trainer directed her in a broad circle with himself as the axis. "This is goin' on for a while, if you kids got something to do."

"Come on," Keely said. "Meet Malcolm."

The spotted foal stood on gangly legs following its mother around. Donnie held out a carrot, which Malcolm delicately took. "What are you gonna do with him?"

"Raise him. Train him. Love him. Hey, I got some new tunes for you! Wanna hear?"

"Sure."

"And I got an idea for a commercial. I wrote it down and sent it to Mr. Werner."

They went into the den, aka Keely's trophy room, where she slipped a disc into the big Bose box. "This is George Clinton's "Atomic Dog." I think we should use this for the main routine."

The song shimmied and slunk.

"I like it!" Donnie said.

They mapped out the routine, beginning with a series of backward flips followed by butterfly throws and finishing with the Mongolian Boomerang.

"Has Disco actually done the Mongolian Boomerang?" Keely said.

Donnie grinned. "Well no. But I'm confident she will. I've trained her to leap on my back and catch a ball when I stand up and toss it in the air. Far as I know, nobody has done the Mongolian Boomerang. It's hard to consistently throw that shot. I work at it every day."

"Why do they call it the Mongolian Boomerang?"

"That's what I call it. I invented it. Only it hasn't happened yet."

"Okay, I got some more tunes to play you. And we gotta get more stuff on Facebook. How many friends do you have?"

"I'm at the limit. So's Disco."

"Okay. I made some signs."

Keely brought out two cardboard signs with ropes around them, neatly lettered with fat felt-tipped marker: I LIKE TO LICK! and I LET HER LICK ME.

"Disco wears this one and you wear that one! It's sort of a role reversal."

"I don't lick! Besides, role reversal? Or vole rehearsal?"

Keely stared at him in consternation. "You are so weird."

Two hours later, Cully found them with Disco at his

heels. "She's doin' a lot better, mate! You bring 'er by tomorrow."

"Will she be ready in two weeks? I already registered!"

Cully shrugged. "Who can say? We'll keep up with the therapy until you feel she's ready to train."

Donnie figured he needed at least a week of training to prep Disco for the Waunakee Invitational. That gave her a week to recover from Ralph's kick. The sun was setting by the time Donnie got home, the lonely apartment building shrouded in shadow and solitude. The press had dropped Donnie for the latest news sensation, the kidnapping of an albino buffalo by Indian activists.

"Oh hi!" Kate greeted him. "How'd it go?"

"Cully's working miracles with that therapy pool. We can only pray she'll be ready to go. If not, she'll have plenty of time to recover for the state event."

"Frank and I have chosen a venue, the Raindrop Event Center. It's about twenty miles from here, in the country, very nice. We would like Disco and Chuck to be part of the ceremony."

"Gee I don't know if that's such a good idea, Ma."

"What, are you kidding? Isn't she the best-trained dog in the universe? We just want them to be the ring bearers. Chuck knows all the commands. Sit, come, roll over. We can ask somebody to hold on to them until we call for the rings."

Donnie shrugged. "It's your funeral."

"Very funny. Did you have dinner?"

"Yeah. Mrs. Van Metre made pork chops and collard greens."

"Okay. Gotta go. You and Disco all right by yourselves?"

"You coming back?"

"Not tonight."

Donnie liked it that she didn't sugarcoat it or try to explain. "We're fine, Ma."

She kissed him on the head and left with an overnight bag.

Donnie phoned Chief Robertson. After a short delay, a dispatcher put him through.

"What's up, Donnie?"

"Chief, I just wanted to check if there'd been any action on the Barnes brothers."

"They are the subject of a nationwide manhunt. They will turn up, I promise you. Warrants have been issued for animal cruelty, possession of bomb-building material and possession with intent to distribute."

"Distribute what?"

"We found a meth lab in the basement. Son, you don't have to worry. You'll never see either one of them again."

ONE WEEK AFTER RALPH SPEECE HAD KICKED HER, DISCO was prancing like a pro. The world record for the long-distance Frisbee catch was 285 feet. The farthest Disco had scored was 120, but on Saturday, eight days after she'd been kicked, Disco caught 140 while sailing two feet off the ground in the pasture behind the Van Metres'. Keely recorded the whole thing and came up babbling.

"This is great! We'll put it to Laurie Biagini's 'Rise Up'!"

"I want to hear it first."

"Of course."

"Hey, you wanna go by the plant? The Weenie Wagon's supposed to be done today."

The warehouse doors were wide open, so the sun shone directly on the gleaming Weenie Wagon as a dozen workers rolled it out of its corner so that it faced out. Four monstrous chrome headers with flared openings protruded from each side of the giant sausage. The W2 had three axles; four thirty-six-inch rear mags held enormous bespoke Goodyear tires. Monte Moore crawled all over it like a nervous parent, checking the controls and fluid levels. When Donnie, Keely and Disco entered, he waved them over.

"Get in. Let's see if she'll move."

Inside there were four bucket seats in two rows. Donnie sat in the shotgun seat with Disco in his lap, and Keely sat behind Monte.

Monte fastened his seatbelt. "Strap yourselves in." He looked around, grinning, and turned the key.

The warehouse exploded.

Or so it seemed from the freight train roaring inside their skulls. Speech was impossible. The walls flickered as flame belched from the eight headers. Workers covered their ears and ran for the exits. Monte gripped the wiener-shaped gearshift knob, snicked into first and let out the clutch. They felt the four rear wheels dig in and burn rubber. The massive vehicle poked its snout out the door and lunged forward like a giant dachshund breaking its leash. Over a hundred Werner's employees lined the driveway cheering as the Weenie Wagon turned out onto the highway. Donnie and Keely pressed into their seats with the acceleration.

"IT'S GOT SIX-WHEEL STEERING!" Monte said over the roar. "WAIT'LL I TURN ON THE SOUND SYSTEM!"

Donnie had seen the curved speaker covers integrated into the sleek weenie body. He and Keely had assembled the song list.

"NOBODY CAN HEAR!" Donnie shouted at Monte, two feet away.

"OH YES THEY WILL!" Monte said, then reached out and flipped a switch. Instantly the deafening roar of the exhaust muted. "Electric servos control the baffles."

"Can I drive?"

"Let me get off the highway," Monte said, putting on the turn signal and turning onto County Trunk BN, a two-lane blacktop extending north toward wooded hills and valleys. He stopped the W2 in the middle of the road and switched places with Donnie, who handed Disco to Keely and crunched the gears shifting into first.

"Easy, easy," Monte said. "Rev it to three thou and drop the clutch."

The vehicle lurched forward but Donnie kept it from dying, gave it some gas and shifted into second, then third. They rolled down the winding road at forty-five, descending into a wooded hollow where the trees met fifty feet above the road. They passed the gated entrances to farms and then emerged on a plateau with about a mile of straight road ahead of them.

Donnie made superfluous engine noises in the back of his throat and couldn't stop grinning. Until he looked in the rearview. A car was coming up fast, an orange Camaro. It pulled into the left lane and accelerated so that it was level with Donnie, who looked over to see the driver but was seated too high. There was no one in the shotgun seat. With a surge of power, the Camaro pulled ahead and cut directly in front of the Weenie Wagon, turning on its pounding bass and fishtailing all over the road.

"Call the cops!" Donnie shouted. "It's Travis Barnes!"

"Who?" Monte said, but Keely was already dialing.

She stared at her phone in astonishment. "I don't fucking believe it! They put me on hold!"

Grim-faced and white-knuckled, Donnie stood on the gas, running up behind Barnes so that the W2's front bumper was inches from the Camaro.

"What are you doing, Donnie?" Monte said, gripping the handrail with both hands.

"That's the guy that tried to kill Disco!"

"Well what are you going to do? Run him off the road? You'd better slow down. This vehicle cost over two hundred grand."

With a visible effort, Donnie took his foot off the gas and watched the Camaro pull ahead. There was a minor report, the sound of a tire blowing, and the Camaro shifted abruptly, the tail coming up, forcing the car to roll end over end over end like a child's toy before flipping into the ditch and bursting into flames.

Donnie stopped the W2 in the middle of the road. Monte grabbed a fire extinguisher from the rear bulkhead and ran to the burning car, but it was too hot, a tiny sun by the side of the road. They listened to the driver's screams until they faded away.

CHAPTER SIXTY-SIX
AUTEUR

KEELY'S CALL GOT THROUGH ON HER NEXT TRY, AND SHE told the dispatcher. Monte pulled the W2 ahead, backing it into a farm entrance so that it didn't block the road. It took the police and EMTs twenty minutes to arrive, by which time the Camaro was a smoking wreck.

Donnie felt faint and sat on the W2's running board with his head in his hands, Keely next to him and Disco whining with worry. A county mounty took their statements. As they returned to the packing plant with Monte at the wheel, they saw two county patrol cars speed past them in the opposite direction.

Donnie shook violently with the sudden realization he'd put all of them in danger, including Disco and Keely. Was that any way to be a man? He could practically hear Nate telling him, "A man takes care of his family."

Donnie thought about Nate's daughter, who hated him. And his ex-wives. Nate had been wise and foolish at the same time. They returned the W2 to the warehouse, and as they were getting down from the cab, Frank walked toward them at a clipped pace wearing sunglasses, his tie flowing in the breeze. Disco leaped from Donnie's arms and ran up to Frank, who stooped to pet her.

"Donnie. Disco. I need you to film that commercial. The backflip thing."

"Not today, I hope."

"No. We'd like to shoot it tomorrow in the Van Metres' barn. I've already checked with your dad, Keely. And your script is fabulous. We're securing rights to the song."

"What song?" Donnie said.

"'That's Why (I Love You So)' by the Del Vikings. It's an old song my grandfather used to play, and it's got a line about a back-over flip."

Donnie, Disco and Kate returned at ten on Saturday. As soon as they entered the barn, Disco ran for the therapy pool and leaped in, splashing Cully and a horse he was grooming. Disco swam back and forth in the therapy pool like a collegiate swimmer.

"She's a water dog," Cully said. "You oughta call her Perrier."

"Perrier?" Donnie said.

"Yeah. Not only is she a water dog, she's part pug and part terrier. Perrier."

A woman built like an Abrams tank rolled through the doors wearing denim coveralls, earphones around her neck and those big square wraparound smoked glass Fitovers that old folks wear over their glasses. Frank, wearing creased khakis and a Hawaiian shirt decorated with the Disco image, steered her toward Donnie.

"Donnie, this is our video director, Margot Ross. Margot, Donnie."

She shook his hand with a manly grip. "Love your video. Well done. Have you read the script?"

"Yes, ma'am."

"Any questions?"

"No, ma'am."

"All right, let's walk through it a couple times, soon as my lighting person gets done here. May take a little while. You're gonna have to dry that dog off anyway."

Disco swam around the edge of the pool in a big circle. Cully grabbed an armload of towels and set them next to the steps. Donnie whistled and Disco made a shark line toward him, climbing out and shaking herself off, spraying water in a ten-foot diameter. Donnie and Keely dried the dog off. He was grateful he hadn't yet changed into the clothes he would wear for the video.

"Better go change," Keely said fifteen minutes later. "They've got the lights set up." They walked through it once without the tricks. Margot fitted her earphones to her head and held up her hand.

"We're ready to shoot."

Wearing a crisp new Werner's/Disco T-shirt and cargo shorts, Donnie tossed sliced frankfurters at Disco as she performed backward flips to the music. Following a rapid five-dog toss, Donnie turned to the camera with an "aw shucks" grin and said, "Train like a champion. Eat Werner's meats."

"Great!" the director said. "You can practically smell the hay. We'll edit in a few shots of the horses and a shot of Disco going for the long one. Should be ready to go in five days."

"That's cutting it thin," Frank said. "Waunakee's this weekend."

The director smiled. "You can take it to the bank."

"What if we don't win?" Donnie said.

"Let's not think about that," Frank said.

Kate put her arm through Donnie's and took him aside. "You should read the contract. We have this season and this season only. If Disco fails to win a national championship, Werner's will sever their relationship."

Donnie's stomach clenched. "Then what?"

Kate shrugged with a forced smile. "Your guess is as good as mine, kiddo."

Donnie looked down. Disco barked happily and danced on her hind legs.

TEAM DISCO ARRIVED IN WAUNAKEE ON THE AFTERNOON of Friday, April 30, checking into the pet-friendly Best Western Hotel on Hearn Street, three blocks from Fireman's Park. Team Disco included Disco, Donnie, Kate and Keely. Margot Ross would arrive later to film the event.

On Saturday morning Team Disco drove to Fireman's Park in the Weenie Wagon, parking behind a news van from WMLK in Milwaukee. Within the park, a two-acre greensward had already been marked off for competition, including white chalk lines for the distance event. Spectators had already begun to arrive by eight, setting out lawn chairs, commandeering the picnic tables and brick barbecue pits. Donnie and Disco stood in line with a dozen other teams for their documentation. Competitors' names went into a bingo wheel, from which they would be drawn at random, the results posted on a chalkboard when registration was complete.

Leaving Disco with Keely, Donnie walked around the park, scoping out the competition. There were plenty of

Australian shepherds and border collies, some whippets, dogs that looked like bottle brushes and even some behemoths like German shepherds and golden retrievers. Donnie wondered at the size of their handlers, or if they simply eliminated catches and back launches from their repertoire.

By nine the competition was ready to begin, thirty-five teams listed in order of appearance. Team Disco was thirtieth. Donnie thought he would go crazy with pre-performance jitters. Keely suggested they run back to the hotel for her phone while Disco stayed with Kate. When they got to the hotel room, Donnie said, "How could you forget your phone?"

Keely smirked and took off her T-shirt, braless. "I didn't."

When they returned to the park twenty minutes later, Donnie was much more relaxed. Monte had rigged a platform that could be affixed in the swayback of the W2. Donnie and Keely watched the competition from there in two lawn chairs with a cooler.

"Next up," the PA system boomed, "Frances Marsten and her Australian shepherd mix, Lord Beaverbrook!"

Frances Marsten was a knockabout woman in her fifties with short white hair, in tennis shorts and a T-shirt emblazoned with Lord Beaverbrook's mug. Marsten cued the music, "I Get Around" by the Beach Boys, and dished discs to Beaverbrook like a blackjack dealer. The dog was a spectacular athlete, leaping high to snag discs at head height, leaping into Frances' arms, staggering her and performing with a flourish punctuated by his swishing tail. He dropped only one disc.

At the end of the performance, five judges held up placards with their scores from one to ten. Frances and Beaverbrook finished with a respectable 8.2. The freestyle continued throughout the morning until finally, just before noon, one of the organizers came by with a clipboard.

"You're right after this next team," she said.

The PA system announced Norbert Sykes and his Jack Russell terrier, Jack Russell. Sykes wore a crimson tank top with a black claw emblazoned on the chest, and war paint in the form of two stripes extending from the eyes upward and two extending from beneath the jaw.

Donnie turned in awe to Keely. "That's the Badger."

"Hit it, Zuben!" Sykes said, and the PA system played War's "Low Rider" while Jack Russell and Sykes put on an acrobatic clinic. Sykes did a forward aerial somersault, releasing the disc on the way up, while Jack Russell caught it with a backward flip.

Donnie was slack-jawed and discouraged.

The performance was cut short, however, when a dog howled from the sidelines. Sykes turned and ran toward the complainant followed by a snarling Jack Russell, and they were disqualified. Donnie never did learn what happened, although later it was alleged that a guy had struck a dog and Sykes beat the shit out of him while Jack Russell pissed on his leg.

"Donnie Waits and Disco," the announcer said.

Heart in his mouth, Donnie took to the field with a prancing Disco. The PA system played "Atomic Dog" as Donnie threw five fast butterfly flips while Disco spun in place doing backward somersaults. The audience rose to its feet and cheered.

"Go Disco!" Keely yelled from her perch atop the W2. Others took up the chant. Donnie threw down a garbage can lid with the handle removed and skipped discs off it as if he were skipping stones across the lake. Finally, with twenty seconds left, Donnie signaled for the

Mongolian Boomerang. Disco waited, her little butt in excited motion as Donnie sailed the disc in a broad parabola at forty-five degrees. He waited until it reached apogee and began its homeward journey. He got down on all fours, looked up and said, "Go!"

Disco sprang onto Donnie's back as he straightened abruptly, Disco going high into the air, snagging the disc by the lip and falling into Donnie's arms.

The crowd went wild.

CHAPTER SIXTY-EIGHT
SHANK SHOT

THEIR COMPOSITE SCORE WAS AN UNBELIEVABLE TEN. THE crowd had grown to several hundred, and people stood and cheered and clapped as Donnie and Disco returned to the sidelines. Children surrounded the Weenie Wagon as Keely and Kate handed out rubber keychains. Donnie stopped, jaw on the ground as Vicki Dukemajian zeroed in on him with her cameraman.

"Donnie Waits! You just scored a perfect ten! How do you feel?"

"I'm surprised and delighted, Vicki. We never expected to do this well."

"What is your strategy for the long-distance event?"

"I plan to throw the Frisbee as far as possible and have Disco catch it."

"I'd like to do a sit-down interview with you one of these days if you have time."

"You'd have to ask my manager, Vicki. That's my mom. She's right over there."

Vicki thanked him and turned to Kate, who was looking in a mirror, applying makeup.

They had an hour before the long-distance event. Kate used one of the park's barbecue pits to grill Werner's bratwurst and Polish sausage, which she served on buns with ketchup and relish. She gave a dozen away to kids drawn by the aroma. She gave one to Disco.

Donnie and Disco were twelfth in the long-distance competition. Mike Martens and his dog, McVootie, came to the line. The field was marked with chalk lines and spotters from a hundred feet at ten-foot intervals all the way to two hundred. Line judges stood beyond the two-hundred-foot mark in the unlikely event that someone threw a throw that long. You had ninety seconds to perform, time enough for three throws. Martens's first throw shagged left over the row of parked cars into the street. McVootie calmly watched it go.

The second toss sailed straight and true, and McVootie snagged it three feet off the ground.

"One eighty!" the spotter called.

The competition moved swiftly from that point until two o'clock.

"Donnie Waits and Disco!" the PA blared.

Heart beating, Donnie took the line, Disco at his feet watching his every move. Donnie used an iridescent green eight-and-three-quarter-inch Hyperflite Jawz weighing 145 grams. "You ready?" he whispered. Disco wagged her tail.

Donnie used the backhand grip to fling the disc with maximum rotation perfectly parallel to the earth as he barked, "Go get it!"

Disco zinged down the field, paws barely touching the ground, eyes on the disc as it changed altitude on stray thermals, up a little, down a little, then slowed and hovered just before the drop. Disco leaped! And missed the disc.

"Fetch!" Donnie yelled. Disco grabbed the flying saucer and raced back.

Donnie took his stance. "Ready?" he said. Disco barked.

Donnie flung the disc. "Go get it!"

The disc banked abruptly and struck the earth, rolling off the field at an angle. Disco caught up with it at the feet of a startled little boy and headed back.

Time for one more throw.

Donnie saw Disco in front of him, tongue lolling, panting like the Little Engine That Could. Donnie flung the disc and watched it bank, striking the earth at a right angle, bouncing and landing in the middle of a family of four having a picnic on a blanket. He was so mad at himself, he slammed his hand into his head.

"Dammit!"

Keely ran to him as Disco returned triumphantly with the platter.

"Stop it!" Keely hissed. "People are watching. Act professional."

Donnie got hold of himself. A man didn't throw temper tantrums. He bowed to the audience in three directions and retired from the field to cheers.

Winning the freestyle was no small thing. No one expected a twenty-pound dog to win the distance competition. The awards ceremony and closing ceremony were at four. Donnie and Disco accepted the trophy and the keys to the city from the mayor and posed for pictures, with Keely's arms draped around Donnie's shoulders.

"My hero!"

They loaded up and were back in Gunderson by six, where they held a celebratory dinner at Chef Louis' with Frank, Cully and Monte Moore. Donnie watched in amusement as Kate consumed three martinis and clinked her glass with a spoon.

"Speech!" Cully roared.

"I just want to thank the good Lord that I finally found a man, a real man, and not a boy!"

Frank blushed and smiled.

"And I'm so proud of you, Donnie, I could burst! When he brought that mutt home, I thought it was gonna be trouble."

Frank cleared his throat to save Kate further embarrassment. He lifted his drink. "Folks, I knew you could do it! Never in a million years did I think I would find Werner's salvation in a kid and a dog, but this victory not only vindicates my decision, it's exactly what we need to get this train rolling!

"Here's to even greater success at state!"

Everybody clapped and Disco, who'd been admitted at Frank's insistence, barked.

The company issued a press release.

May 2.

Werner's Meats is pleased to announce that our Werner's-sponsored Disc Dog Team, Donnie Waits and Disco, have won the Waunakee Invitational Disc Dog Freestyle Event with a perfect score of 10. Not only is this the first victory on Disco's march to Disc Dog Supremacy, it is the first disc-dog event they have entered!

Werner's looks forward to the Sky Dogz State Competition, which will take place in Madison on June 1 at Camp Randall Field. Be sure to see Disco's support vehicle, the world-famous Weenie Wagon. We will be handing out keychains, hats, whistles and hot dogs!

Bring the coupon from the June issue of Bark! *for a special premium, and to save on selected Werner's products at your local meat market.*

For further information please contact Kate Waits at: katew@wernersdisco.com.

Werner's—meat from the sky! And pigs. It's also from pigs.

CHAPTER SIXTY-NINE
"I WILL BE GLAD TO KNOW YOU MORE PLEASE?"

A week before the state competition, Donnie was eating dinner in the apartment when there was a knock on the door. Disco howled like an air raid siren. Donnie opened the door to find Mrs. McGillicuddy holding a platter wrapped in cellophane.

"Hello, Donnie. I brought you some cupcakes."

"Come in, Mrs. McGillicuddy."

She ventured in and set the cupcakes down on the dining room table. She was in her seventies with her white hair done in a bun and wearing a matronly dress covered with sequins. "You're the young man with the dog, aren't you?"

Donnie grinned. "That's me. And there's the dog."

"I just want you to know that Mr. Lee and I are very proud of you. I remember when you first moved in and your mother had those terrible fights with her boyfriend. We just thought you were trash. I guess it just goes to show you, you have to get to know people before you judge them."

"Well thank you. Mom's not home right now but

she'd thank you, too. Would you like a glass of lemonade?"

Mrs. McGillicuddy headed for the sofa. "That would be lovely."

"Okay, but I gotta warn you, if you sit she's gonna try and climb into your lap."

Disco leaped into Mrs. McGillicuddy's lap.

"That's all right, dear. I've been thinking of getting a dog myself. It gets lonely."

Donnie opened the fridge, removed a carton of Newman's Own and poured two glasses of lemonade. "Do you have family?"

"My husband died ten years ago. I have a daughter who's a meth addict. The last time I saw her, she stole my jewelry. That was five years ago and I haven't heard from her since."

"I'm sorry."

"Meh! Mr. Lee and I sometimes take dinner together. He's a very nice man."

"The old Chinese guy?"

"Yes. His first name is Henry. He used to be a general in the South Korean Army."

"Seriously?"

Mrs. McGillicuddy drank lemonade and set the glass on the end table. "Oh yes indeed. We both like to garden. I'm raising tomatoes, squash, zucchini and lettuce. I expect I'll have plenty to give away, if you would like some."

"That would be great, Mrs. McGillicuddy!"

Mrs. McGillicuddy finished her lemonade and got up. "Well please tell your mother I stopped by and that I would like to have coffee with her one of these days."

Donnie saw her out, went into Kate's room and went online. Disco's FB page had over thirty thousand likes, and the new commercial featuring footage from Waunakee had gone viral. Donnie's email was filled with solicitations, photos of people's dogs and a bewildering array of offers from young women.

> Greetings To You, My name is miss
>   Cynthia, I come across your profile in
>   face book today and become interested
>   in you, Please i will like to have very
>   good relationship with you, Here is
>   Please contact direct to this not in face
>   book again…

> Hello Dear, my name is Jena David, I am,
>   very happy to contact you, to day
> and i wish to be in good relationship, with
>   you, and i will be very happy if you can
>   reply me through my private Email

> Hello I am sandra good looking girl i am
>   humble and cool i saw your profile at
>   Facebook.com above all i am loving and
>   caring i have gone through your profile
> treuly it is quite intresting to me i will like
>   to have a good relationship with you so
>   kindly get incontact with me through
>   this addres so that i will send you my
>   picture thanks

> I WILL BE GLAD TO KNOW YOU
>   MORE PLEASE? I am Charissa i saw
>   your contact information through Face-
>   book i have something important to

discuss with you write me back, for
more details about me also my pictures
thanks. I WILL BE WAITING FOR
YOUR RESPOND SO THAT

Greetings To You, My name is Vivian, I got
your contact through your Facebook
profile, please contact me through my
private email so that i can write to you
and also send you more pictures of me, i
have very important thing to tell you,

DONNIE POSTED each letter to Facebook and blocked the
senders. How had they gotten his private email? He realized he had achieved fame. Celebrity status. The one
thing young people craved above all else—except, possibly, fulfilling romance.

It wasn't the kind of fame that got him admitted to
clubs, but fame nonetheless. How could he parlay it into
a career? Looking back on the previous nine months, he
realized he'd left a lot of childish dreams behind.

But what did he want to do when he grew up?

Was he doing it?

Was it a career?

CHAPTER SEVENTY

ZERO

DONNIE CHECKED THE SKY DOGZ INVITATIONAL PAGE several times each day for the latest updates and news about competitors. Two days before the event, the page flashed an "important announcement": "Sky Dogz is pleased to announce that Lily Carruthers and Cactus Jack will be competing in the Wisconsin State Eliminations on Saturday, June 1, at Camp Randall in Madison, WI."

Donnie phoned Keely.

"I thought she was in Australia!" Keely said.

"Says she's now based in Madison. Better tell Cully."

"I will. I don't know if I'll be able to see you before the event."

"You're coming, aren't you?"

"Of course."

They had gotten away with this because Keely had shared Kate's hotel room. But this time Kate would share Frank's hotel room. He was bringing a film crew, three board members and a support vehicle for hot dogs and merchandise, including Disco hats and shirts.

Kate, Keely, Donnie and Disco drove up Friday afternoon in Kate's new Altima and checked into the Edgewater, a quarter mile from Camp Randall Field. The Edgewater gave them a ground-floor unit opening onto a green terrace overlooking Lake Mendota. The clerk explained that while they were happy to have Disco and company, they expected Donnie to pick up after his dog as a courtesy to other guests.

After dinner in the hotel restaurant, Donnie and Keely walked Disco on the terrace with several other teams. At seven o'clock on that warm May night, there were five other dogs, including a border collie, a whippet, an Australian shepherd and a Jack Russell terrier, facing Lake Mendota like hood ornaments on a Mack truck, all barking furiously at the ducks. The competitors were a convivial lot.

"You're so young!" gushed Rita Ponds, a fiftysomething with her dog, Rufus, the border collie. "The first time I saw that ad for Werner's, I thought it was a spoof."

"It *is* a spoof!" Donnie said, grinning. He looked over Rita's shoulder to where the Aussie was trying to hump Disco. Frenzied yapping erupted; Disco spun like a vortex and took a chunk out of the Aussie's snout. The Aussie yelped and ran to its owner, a Japanese dude with a shaved skull and a Fu Manchu, and hunkered low with its tail between its legs.

Baldy was the only competitor who hadn't joined in the conversation. He stalked toward Donnie with blood in his eye as Disco stood, hair raised in a Mohawk, growling.

"Hey, dude! Your fucking dog just took a chunk out of my dog's face!"

"Your dog's supposed to be fixed!"

"He is fixed! They didn't do a perfect job. He still gets

boners! He's not capable of impregnating another dog! Your dog came sniffing around my dog! Now my dog's missing a chunk out of his face! What are you going to do about it?"

"Chill, dudes!" Rita said.

Donnie looked over the pool to the sliding glass doors, through which an assistant manager exited.

"Your dog made improper advances. This never would have happened if you'd had your dog fixed right."

Baldy realized Keely had her phone to her eye and rounded on her.

"Give me that!"

He lunged for the phone and before Donnie could think, he'd grabbed Baldy by the back of his collar, shoved his heel into Baldy's right knee and laid him on the ground.

"That's assault!" Baldy cried. "You all saw it! I hope you got that on film!"

The assistant manager reached them out of breath. "Gentlemen! If you don't stop immediately, I will phone the police!"

Baldy sprang up. An older competitor named Hal, with Snord the whippet, tried to console Baldy, who moved in spastic jerks, first one way and then the other, beside himself with fury.

Donnie faced the assistant manager. "Sir, I apologize. This all started when his dog tried to hump mine. Then he got very aggressive. Ask any of these people."

"That's absolutely true," said an older man with a beer-barrel gut wrapped in a Hawaiian shirt decorated with old muscle cars. "My wife and I were on the veranda. We saw the whole thing. Then that guy tried to grab the young lady's phone. That's when the kid stepped in and stopped him."

The assistant manager looked at Donnie with a put-upon expression. "Sir, should I call the police?"

"No. I'm not going to press charges. What he does is up to him."

The manager sighed in relief as if a great weight had been lifted from his shoulders. "Very well. We appreciate your discretion. I'll talk to Mr. Takahari, see if we can't get him moved to another room."

As the manager walked away, Donnie turned to Rita. "Who is that clown?"

"Seaton Takahari, aka Sea-Tak the airport rapper. And his dog Zero."

CHAPTER SEVENTY-ONE
MADISON, DAY ONE

IN HIS ROOM, DONNIE USED HIS NEW LAPTOP TO GOOGLE Sea-Tak. There were thirty-five pages. The son of a B-list cinematographer, Sea-Tak attended Beverly Hills High, where he began rapping. He had two discs out on Damnation Records, including the platinum seller *Stickin It*. His big hit was "If the Love Don't Fit." He had opened for Flo Rida and Pitbull and appeared on *The Tonight Show* and *Good Morning America*.

Donnie tried to listen to "If the Love Don't Fit," but it sounded like glass in a garbage disposal. "Houston" was better. In fact, it was damned good.

> *Gotta fly to Houston, gotta get my juice on.*
> *Standing in line with some motherfuckin'*
>   *muzzies*
> *Lookin' down their robes all I see is Uzis.*
> *Son, they tell me take off your shoes.*
> *Son, they tell me pull up your pants.*
> *Flyin' to Houston, ain't flyin' to France.*

Donnie had to admire Sea-Tak's nerve, but he still couldn't listen to it.

Zero had won the Sky Dogz State Championship twice, including the previous year. Not surprisingly, there was a video of the previous year's award-winning performance set to Sea-Tak's "See Spot Fly." Zero was a doggie Bruce Lee, ribs showing, a flicker in motion grabbing big air. They did a perfect Foaming Pipe Snake. The judges had awarded them a combined score in the freestyle of 19.5. The state Sky Dogz competition differed from the Waunakee Invitational in that it lasted for two days and involved two attempts in each category, similar to the Olympics.

Freestyles took place in the mornings, distance in the afternoon. As there were over three hundred teams, it took the whole day. Donnie and Keely ordered room service and dined in their room watching *Pacific Rim*.

"Don't you think," Donnie said, "if you were going to fight *kaiju*, you'd design something a little more practical than a giant man with a twin brain? Wouldn't it make more sense just to shoot rockets at them?"

"Then there would be no movie," Keely said.

"If I were in charge of stopping the *kaiju*, I'd use a bunker buster that would penetrate deep into the heart of the beast and explode, covering the surrounding countryside with bloody chunks of meat. This could be a boon to world hunger, providing *kaiju* meat is not genetically modified but is, in fact, pure *kaiju* meat. It's quite possible *kaiju* meat contains medicinal properties. Perhaps it shrinks cancerous tumors."

Keely leaned over and put two fingers on his lips and held up a can of spermicide.

Donnie fell asleep around eleven, dreaming of flying dogs crisscrossing the sky. Their wake-up call was for seven. They ate breakfast in the hotel coffee shop and arrived at Camp Randall via taxi by eight thirty. The competition began at nine, and the order had been posted on the huge electronic scoreboard and online.

Donnie and Disco were 125th to compete in the freestyle on Saturday morning. Disco weighed twenty-two at the weigh-in.

The opening ceremony featured the March Fourth Brass Band, twelve kids with a lot of brass and some kettle-drums strutting to a polyrhythmic beat. Then came the parade of contestants, 314 teams representing every state and twenty-four nations. The governor gave a brief address extolling the great state of Wisconsin and the glory that were Sky Dogz. The mayor waxed fat about the sacred bond between person and beast, that it was better to adopt a stray from the pound than pay twelve hundred dollars for a purebred Scots terrier from Texas, and that the Humane Society was among man's noblest institutions.

A priest, a rabbi, a Buddhist monk and a Wiccan blessed the event, and the PA called the first team to the line. "Jack London and White Fang, you're up!"

Donnie and Keely had been too busy getting Disco ready and watching the ceremony to get a good look at their competitors. Now as people sought their places and their seats, he looked around for Lily Carruthers. She ought to be easy to spot. She was a big, broad-shoul-dered but nicely padded woman with coppery hair.

They ascended into the bleachers.

Frank arrived with Cully and guests. Monte had driven up that morning and parked outside the stadium next to a support vehicle selling T-shirts and hats and handing out hot dogs.

Cully sidled up to Donnie. "See her?"

"Nope. But there are a lot of people here. Check the roster."

Cully peered at the scoreboard through a pair of folding binocs. "She's number 128."

Donnie, Keely and Cully sat in the bleachers to watch the action.

"Number-two team," the PA blared. "Abercrombie and Bitch."

Abercrombie and Bitch were a young woman with long blond hair and a greyhound hybrid who worked vaults, taps and the butterfly flip for a score of 8.6. As the morning wore on, kids lined up for free hot dogs and buttons, and Werner's did a brisk business in hats and T-shirts.

Donnie climbed down from the bleachers to sign autographs, mostly on shirts and programs. The side-lines were rife with teams in training, dogs on leashes, makeshift shelters and folding chairs. The Zambians' "Glout hound" proved to be a hyena, and they were disqualified. A team from Taiwan fielded an Akita named Chairman Mo. There were two teams from Alaska, both fielding malamutes. Fyodor Bratislava from Russia looked like Jack Kirby's Hulk. His borzoi, Sonya, weighed a hundred pounds. While Sonya luxuriated supine on a white bear rug, Fyodor worked out with a hundred-pound kettlebell.

Two teams were disqualified for overly aggressive dogs.

At ten twenty the PA called Sea-Tak and Zero. Applause, whistles and gang signals accompanied their perp walk. Sea-Tak cued "If the Love Don't Fit" and began with a series of vaults, Zero leaping off his leg and snagging the disc mid-air, followed by a vault off his back. He finished with Zero catching all five Frisbees in his mouth, one by one.

The judges gave him an 8.9. Zero had dropped one on the last trick.

It was almost noon when they called Donnie and Disco to the field.

CHAPTER SEVENTY-TWO
SHORT THROW

Donnie was aware of the cameras as he and Disco walked out. Not just the television and film crews but the spectators using their smart phones. "Atomic Dog" began as Donnie started with five rapid-fire backward flips followed by a double-disc vault.

The crowd clapped as if in a tent revival, and when the song hit the chorus, several hundred people sang, "Why must I feel like that? Why must I chase the cat? Nothin' but the dog in me."

With Disco barking in delight, Donnie almost lost his concentration. With fifteen seconds remaining, Donnie looked Disco in the eye. "Boomerang!" he said, tossing the disc in a parabola and holding out his hand in the stay command. He watched the spinning disc arc toward the sun and turn the corner. Donnie crouched and said, "Vault!"

Disco sprang at him, leaped on his shoulders as Donnie stood, then flew ten feet in the air and snapped at the returning Frisbee but missed it by an inch. Donnie caught the falling Disco in his arms. The audience groaned with disappointment and then clapped and cheered. Donnie waved to the crowd, put Disco on leash and waited for the results: 8.9. Not in the top ten.

Sea-Tak and Zero were number seven. Tom Knorr, from Cambridge, Wisconsin, with his dog, Rottwang, was number one. Knorr was a powerful mesomorph who tossed his 110-pound rottweiler into the air and caught him on the way down. They belonged on *So You Think You Can Dance*, but their brute physicality and refusal to engage the audience cost them. Knorr never acknowledged the crowd.

The freestyle concluded at 1:00 p.m. The judges announced an hour break before the distance event. Donnie, Keely, Disco, Cully, Kate and Frank ate lunch at a picnic table next to their van. Cully had to get up and discourage a steady stream of fans who wanted Donnie's autograph or to pet Disco.

Donnie stood. "Hey, guys! We're planning plenty of publicity events this summer! Check our websites: WernersMeats.com or WernersDisco.com!"

"Donnie, we love you!" crooned a fifteen-year-old cutie. Keely turned and glared.

Donnie was number sixteen to compete in the distance event. Sea-Tak and Zero were number seventeen. Donnie's nerves drove him to the sidelines, where he threw the disc over and over to Cully, who winged it back, each time a little longer. Donnie didn't kid himself that he was capable of a two-hundred-foot throw, but in order not to penalize smaller dogs, the distance throw was divided into three weight categories: up to twenty pounds, twenty to forty pounds, and over forty pounds. Disco was a "middleweight." No points were awarded for catches under ten yards. From ten to fifteen yards, one point was awarded if one paw touched the ground at the time of the catch, two points if all paws were off the ground. From fifteen to twenty yards, three points were awarded if one paw touched the ground, four if all paws were in the air. Beyond twenty yards, it was five and six.

The current world distance champion, the whippet-poodle mix, Charlemagne, out of Agoura Hills, California, weighed forty-five pounds. Size was not necessarily an advantage in distance.

"Donnie and Disco" blared over the PA.

As Donnie and Disco took their places behind the line, the crowd's roar muted, and Donnie felt like Tiger Woods on the eighth green. As the crowd held its breath, an adenoidal voice piped, "Why must I be like that? Why must I chase the cat?"

Donnie wound up and threw backhand. Disco accelerated like a particle beam after the spinning disc, which sailed straight, hovered and fell on Disco's head.

Time for two more. "Fetch!" Donnie yelled.

Disco was already on the way with the disc. Donnie waited until Disco dropped and told her to sit.

He flung the disc again, shanking it. It hit the ground at an angle and rolled with Disco in hot pursuit. The audience groaned.

"Fetch!"

The third throw was weak. Disco caught it at fifty feet.

Donnie hid his disappointment and waved to the crowd. As Disco returned with the final disc, he stooped and attached her leash and said, "Good girl. Lousy throw."

By the time he joined Keely and Cully in the bleachers, the PA had announced Sea-Tak and Zero. Sea-Tak wore a black muscle shirt showing his yakuza-like tats. Zero hunkered low until Sea-Tak flung his disc overhand with turbine spin. It sailed like a clay pigeon into the sky, Zero keeping pace and snagging it five feet off the ground.

The line judge held up a sign: 212 feet and six points.

The next throw was 214 feet and five.

The final throw was 221 feet and six.

A gang of frat boys wearing Headrush, Dethrone and Tapout paraphernalia drunkenly cheered and high-fived. Sea-Tak waved to the crowd and strutted off the stage.

Donnie looked around for Cully as they were leaving and saw him talking to a statuesque woman with copper hair.

AFTER DINNER, DONNIE, KEELY, KATE AND FRANK SAT ON
the deck with Disco on a leash looking at the stunning
Lake Mendota sunset. Strata of burnt macaroni, blazing
orange and yellow lit the western sky and were reflected
in the water.

Frank and Kate rose.

"Honey, we're going to a club. Don't stay up too late."

"Okay, Ma."

Keely sat with Donnie in a wrought iron white love
seat above the water. "They know," she said.

Panic closed its icy fingers over Donnie's heart. "No
way!"

"Wise up, lover. Your mother's not stupid. Don't you
think she was having sex in high school?"

"I can't contemplate it. I can't hear you!" He clapped
his hands to his ears. "LA LA LA LA LA..."

Keely dragged a hand free. "Okay. Forget I mentioned
it. Doesn't look like we're going to pick up much in the
distance event."

"Nope," Donnie popped. Only the national event

considered scoring to qualify. Anyone could enter the regionals. There was hardly any money involved; it was all done for love of the sport.

Donnie wondered how long that would last. How long before ambition overcame decency and dudes started doping their dogs? Or feeding laxatives to the competition? Look at that Zambian team. A hyena? Seriously? You're really going to go there?

The imp of the perverse suggested that Donnie slip a treat to Zero.

"Hey," Keely said. "Want to go up to the square? They've got free music."

"What kind of music?"

Keely unfolded her copy of *Isthmus*. "Emperors of Wyoming. Butch Vig's new group."

Emperors of Wyoming played gloomy but exhilarating country rock. It was a warm summer eve on Capitol Square, and many of the hundreds of people recognized Donnie and Disco from the news.

They were asleep by ten.

Donnie groaned when he saw the big board on Sunday morning. They were number 219.

"I could have stayed in bed!" he wailed, knowing he couldn't have slept. There was too much going on! Life danced around him. *This must be what it's like to be a dog,* he thought. *It's all good.*

Cully arrived at eleven, wearing sunglasses and dragging ass. "Struth, that woman can drink!" he moaned.

"So, are you and Lily back together?" Keely said.

"Feck no," Cully said. "She's in a committed relationship with a lesbian of color who makes the loveliest dolphin sculptures out of broken glass. Brenda Hollister-Frazier. They run a dog B&B outside of town, but we did have an epic evening, closed out the tavern. She moved here for Cactus Jack to be closer to the competition!"

They were beneath the Werner's tent inside the stadium. Donnie looked up and saw a tall woman with coppery hair heading their way with an Aussie on a leash. She wore a sleeveless white T and blue jeans and had startling blue eyes.

"Lily, Donnie, Keely, Disco."

Lily shook hands. "Heard a lot about you," she said. "Saw your routine yesterday. Liked it."

"Thanks, Lily."

Cactus Jack grinned while Donnie and Keely petted him.

The day dragged on. Donnie didn't watch the other routines, because he didn't want them to affect his performance. Finally, shortly before noon, they were called to the line. Donnie tossed his garbage can to the ground and began with a series of elliptical ricochets, which Disco snagged with an aerial cartwheel.

"Bow wow wow, yippee yo yippee yay, bow wow, yippie yo yippee yay," the crowd sang.

Donnie was going to do the Mongolian Boomerang when they ran out of time. It didn't matter. They scored a 9.5. They spent the lunch break signing autographs at the Werner's tent, and then it was time for the distance event. Donnie sat with Keely and Disco in the bleachers watching through binoculars. Sea-Tak and Zero were number twenty-two. Sea-Tak threw a Peyton Manning long ball that Zero snagged from the air going away, adding five feet and six points to his score of 232.

Unbeatable. Donnie doubted he would even place in the middleweight category. There were too many specialty performers like greyhounds and vizslas. They got the call around three fifteen and took their place at the line. Donnie whipped the disc, all wrist, no arm, and it soared straight with Disco in hot pursuit. She snapped it airborne at 175, and they moved into first among the middleweights.

Keely squealed with delight and threw her arms around Donnie.

"It's not going to last. Janis and Bobby McGee are up."

Janis was Janis Jefferson of Cross Plains, and Bobby McGee was her whippet. Janis and Bobby came out wearing red plastic Devo hats and took them off at the line. Devo's "Working in a Coal Mine" chugged from the speakers as Janis whipped the disc with a sidewinder flick. Bobby McGee was no more than a shadow flying over the turf until she launched herself into the air. Janis and Bobby McGee moved into first with a six-pointer at 190.

It ended at five thirty. Fifteen minutes later, the judges announced the winners. Donnie and Disco came in second in the freestyle and fourth overall, right behind Sea-Tak and Zero. Lily and Cactus Jack placed second, right behind Paul McCarthy and Jet.

CHAPTER SEVENTY-FOUR
REGIONALS, DAY ONE

THEY CELEBRATED AT THE TOP OF THE PARK, LOOKING out on the brightly lit Capitol dome and square. Margot Ross had three Cuba Libres and hauled out her camera.

"Pay no attention," she said over and over. "Pretend I'm not here."

Before dessert, Frank clinked his glass. The dozen people seated in the private dining room all looked up.

"Folks, even if Donnie and Disco don't win another contest, this campaign has been an enormous success!"

Applause and shouts.

"First and foremost, Werner's Meats is not only in the black; our future has never looked brighter. Both Tyson's and Pilgrim's Pride have reached out to us with very generous offers. However, I'm not ready to retire just yet! We've still got a lot to do, new worlds to conquer. We will be introducing new products in the fall, including our chai-infused bologna and truffle-flavored breakfast sausage. Our new marketing program will feature Donnie and Disco, which just goes to show, you don't have to hire outside experts to get things done! Sometimes the best people are right under your nose.

"Donnie, Disco, stand up please."

Donnie stood. "Disco's with Cully at Lily's house, sir. The hotel wouldn't let her up."

The two weeks until the Midwest regionals in Chicago flew by. Donnie quit his job at the Piggly Wiggly with management's blessings, since Werner's now covered all his expenses plus a per diem when he was competing. Donnie spent the time training and serving as an ambassador for Werner's Meats. He and Disco drove to a half dozen store signings in the Upper Midwest, mostly at Woodman's, a huge grocery store chain that was a major Werner's customer.

Good Morning America, *The Tonight Show* and *Huckabee* wanted them, but Donnie turned them down because they required that he and Disco fly to New York or Los Angeles.

With the wedding set for July 1, Kate was in a frenzy. Frank floated above the fray. He had a business to run, and he'd already been married twice. No biggie.

Kate was wise enough to know that no wedding ever went off without a hitch. She just wanted everyone to have a good time. She hired a deejay and a caterer. Their lease was up in August, and then they would move into Frank's house.

Meanwhile, the bank seized Nate's property, razed the shack and sold it to Van Metre Construction to develop into condos.

The Disco bandwagon arrived at Reinhold's Best Western in Evanston on Friday afternoon, the day before the regionals. It wasn't the classiest place in town, but it was pet-friendly and Donnie and Disco scored a ground-floor room opening onto the courtyard, which contained a fenced-off pool and spa.

After dinner, Donnie, Keely and Disco took the air in the courtyard along with other competitors, including Paul McCarthy and Jet, Abercrombie and Bitch, and Sea-Tak and Zero. All dogs were leashed as per hotel rules. Donnie and Keely talked to some of the other players, but Sea-Tak kept his distance. Donnie watched him talk smack about them to some of his pals. They glanced over and sniggered.

The regionals were to be held on a broad greensward at Pops Staples Park, sixteen acres of wooded rolling country. Donnie could hear the music from a block away as he rode over in the Weenie Wagon with Keely and Disco. Pops Staples was a carnival with dozens of vendors selling everything from funnel cakes to time-shares. Gaily decorated kiosks and tents rimmed the great playing field, which included a stage, where a blue-grass band sawed its way through "Rocky Top."

An enormous banner flew above the staging area: MIDWEST SKY DOGZ REGIONALS. Every major pet food manufacturer was there handing out free samples, as well as a dozen beaneries serving up pizza, barbecue and sushi.

As Donnie, Keely and Disco approached the judge's table, Keely held a hand to her mouth. "Don't order the sushi."

"As if!"

More than 250 teams qualified based on their cumulative scores and aesthetics. This included forty-seven tyro teams that had begun competing that year. It had taken five judges weeks to review all the entries.

The band played a fanfare, and an ombudsman called the competition to order. The governor spoke. The mayor spoke. Jim Belushi spoke. They called the first team, but Donnie paid no attention as he and Disco got into the zone. They'd lucked out and drawn number twenty six. At ten fifteen they took the line.

Even before the music began, a hundred people sang, "Why must I be like that? Why must I chase the cat?"

Donnie turned to the audience, raised both arms and played band leader. He signaled the tech, and the music began. Five butterfly throws and a series of vaults left fifteen seconds on the clock. Donnie called the Mongolian Boomerang. He sailed the disc precisely and watched it turn around.

"Disco! Boomerang!"

He got down on hands and knees. "Go!"

Disco sprang off his back as he stood and reached high into the air, snapping her jaws on the disc, hanging for one breathless instant and falling back to earth. Donnie dropped her.

Disco yelped when she hit the turf, and a thousand people groaned in unison.

"Shit." Donnie bit down, careful not to say it loudly. He rushed to Disco, who was up on all fours, tail wagging, holding the disc. He gently probed her haunch as she whined and dropped the disc.

Cursing himself, Donnie carried Disco to the sidelines, oblivious to the score.

CHAPTER SEVENTY-FIVE
IN THE SINK

SHE LIMPED. CULLY FELT HER AND CONFIRMED A MINOR sprain. Disco didn't care. Disco wanted to perform. But Donnie decided to pull her at least for Saturday and see how she felt in the morning. Despite the tumble, they'd scored a 9.1. Since winners were based on adding Friday and Saturday and dividing by two, theoretically they still had a chance.

All they had to do was score a 9.9.

In the history of the Midwest regionals, only fifteen teams had scored a 9.9.

Just before they left, Donnie saw Frank frowning at him. Pilgrim's Pride and Tyson Foods had both sent reps, who'd hung with Frank the previous night and become drinking buddies. Now those two dudes were looking at their drinks.

Disco's performance had no effect whatsoever on the quality of Werner's Meats, but there it was. All these masters of the universe standing around waiting for dog scores in deciding whether to invest in a multi-million-dollar meat-packing operation. Back at the hotel, Cully suggested they take Disco to the pool.

"No dogs allowed," Donnie said. "Says so right next to the gate."

"Well let's not tell anybody, shall we?" Cully said. "Let's just get her out there and see if we can get some work in before they throw us out."

"How are we going to get her into the pool?" Donnie said.

"I'll put her in my beach bag," Keely said, hoisting a canvas feed bin.

Twenty minutes later they exited their ground-floor unit, Keely with a white-knuckle grip on her pendulous beach bag. All wore shades. Disco's black tail protruded like a whip antenna from the end and swayed side to side. Fortunately, there was no lifeguard on duty. They used their key to enter the enclosed area and found three empty chaise lounges at one end in the sun. A half dozen kids and grown-ups splashed and squealed.

As parents played with their kids, Donnie went into the four-foot pool and took Disco from Cully. Cully and Keely quickly entered and formed a human shield as Disco paddled around. All eyes were on Disco, only her snout and bug eyes protruding, like a crocodile. Donnie heard splashing and turned to find a wide-eyed five-year-old girl in a pink one-piece riding a pink inner tube.

"Is that a dog?" she said.

"No," Keely said. "It's my younger sister, Janine. Please don't make fun of her affliction."

"That is a dog," the little girl said. "She looks funny!" She squealed and paddled back.

"Smart girl," Cully said.

Disco cruised around like a big black duck, enjoying herself.

"This may work," Cully said. "Won't know till we get her on land, of course."

Keely looked up. "Uh-oh."

Donnie followed her gaze. A young man in a Best Western blazer and creased tan khakis was headed their way, looking both apologetic and determined. He entered the pool area and came around to where they huddled and crouched.

"Folks, I'm going to have to ask you to take your dog out of the pool area."

"Who squealed?" Donnie said.

Keely overrode him. "Sir, I know this may sound unbelievable, but that's not a dog. That's my younger sister, Janine. She was born deformed and faces many challenges, but she is capable of understanding people. Please don't humiliate her by calling her a dog."

Horizontal lines appeared on the lad's forehead. He was obviously touched, and torn. "Are you serious?" he said in a very low voice, swallowing.

"Yes," Keely said. "She suffers from an extremely rare disease called caninusitis. Literally, 'he who is like a dog.' They're looking for a cure."

The dude crouched and thought about it. Cully slowly winked. The dude grinned.

"You really had me going there. You're with the Sky Dogz thing, right?"

Keely flashed her most dazzling smile. "How did you guess?"

"We're trying hydrotherapy," Donnie said. "She took a spill this morning and sprained her leg."

"Well listen. I can't let you stay. We got a complaint. I

know, I know. But tell you what. We have a really big sink in the laundry room. She could easily fit in there and paddle while you hold her in place."

Keely stuck out her hand. "Deal."

THE SINK WAS ENORMOUS. DONNIE STOOD ON ONE SIDE and Cully on the other, and Disco swam back and forth between them. Every two laps she got a peanut. An hour later, the limp was barely noticeable. Donnie informed the judges they were taking the afternoon off and why. They would have only one chance to score in distance, if they decided to re-enter in the morning.

Everyone took a nap.

At six, a limo picked them up and took them to the Trump Tower downtown on the river, where Tyson Foods had reserved a portion of the terrace. When Donnie, Keely, Disco and Cully arrived, Kate and Frank were already there schmoozing up the Tyson reps. The tables were set with white tablecloths and china, and there were two sterling tureens on the ground: water and choice Werner's meats, which disappeared in minutes. A steward stood by with paper towels and opaque plastic bags.

Donnie and Keely joined Frank, Kate and two guys from Tyson. Lloyd Cantu was young, dark and daytime-soap sinister with a five o'clock shadow and close-shaved black hair.

"Sorry to see that fall. How's she doing?" he said.

"If you'll just lean back a little, she'll show you," Donnie said.

"What?"

"Lean back a little," Keely said.

Smiling self-consciously, Cantu pushed himself back from the table, and Disco leaped into his lap. "Oh!" he yelped in surprise, smiling. He petted her like she might be radioactive, but within ten seconds they were best buddies. Disco turned around and deployed her tongue in Cantu's drink.

"Ixnay!" Donnie barked, standing and moving the glass out of the way. "Put her down, Mr. Cantu. She's being bad."

She jumped into Keely's lap.

The Tyson boys loved the new campaign, loved Disco, loved the new product, were excited about the whole direction. When the food came, Donnie had Disco lie beneath his chair.

Donnie hardly slept, playing the flubbed catch over and over again in his mind. He was sick with guilt and worry. Disco trusted him! He was supposed to catch the dog, not let her plummet to the earth like a bailout.

Even Keely couldn't arouse him, and they slept fitfully with Disco between them.

She seemed fine in the morning. Donnie told the organizers they would compete. When they got to the park, they saw they were number 221. It was going to be a long day. The temperature was in the high eighties, and several parties had brought plastic wading pools to keep their dogs cool. Donnie and Disco stayed cool in the refrigerated Werner's truck until their names were called shortly before noon.

Friends and family had driven down, and as Donnie and Disco walked to the line, several hundred spectators sang, "Why must I be like that? Why must I chase the cat?"

Donnie acknowledged them with a wave, cued the music and did five quick butterfly flips, each one caught with a backward flip. Down went the garbage lid for five skipping launches caught with a backward flip.

With twenty seconds left, someone yelled, "Boomerang!"

Donnie felt the tug. He almost went for it. But it was too soon. Using a jumbo tournament 220-gram Frisbee, he imparted a reverse spin, flipping the disc twenty feet in front of him with enough backspin for it to roll back to him. Disco intercepted on the run and leaped the eight feet into Donnie's arms. He caught her, spun her around to scrub momentum and his beating heart, set her down, told her to stand. The two faced the crowd with outstretched arms and legs.

Score: 9.9. They were still in the chase.

In the distance event, Sea-Tak and Zero scored a 223.

Donnie and Disco scored a 140, putting them in the top ten for middleweights.

CHAPTER SEVENTY-SEVEN
SPAM

WITH THE WEDDING IN A WEEK, KATE WAS IN A FRENZY, shuttling between her PR job and the event. The deejay suddenly had to go to Brussels. Kate turned to Donnie in desperation.

"Donnie, your friends must know a reliable deejay! Ask them! We need someone as soon as possible!"

"Jeez, Ma. I know how to spin sides. Why don't I just do it?"

Kate stared at him in shocked disbelief that morphed into enlightenment.

"Do you really think you could?"

"Of course! Keely will help."

"None of this rap, now. And it can't all be this new-agey garbage or whatever. Dance music. You know, like the Bee Gees, J.Lo, Madonna, stuff like that."

"Maybe some Benny Goodman and Duke Ellington?" Donnie suggested.

Kate made a thumb's-up. "Nothing screechy. No Ramones!"

"What about country?"

"That would be fine, too. The horsey set likes country. Do you have all your stuff packed and ready to move?"

They planned to move the day before the wedding. Donnie told Kate not to worry about it, he would take care of everything. The living room was filled with cardboard boxes, most of them emblazoned with the Werner's Meats logo, taped and labeled with a felt-tip marker. KITCHEN. KATE'S. DONNIE'S. They lived like monks except for the internet and the television that nobody watched. Donnie was either training Disco or helping Keely with her dressage or reading science fiction. She'd sacrificed her season to be with him, but she still had to take care of her horses.

Malcolm was a spirited brown colt with a white blaze on his nose.

"When he grows up, you can ride him," Keely said.

Donnie regarded the colt dubiously. "Two words: Christopher Reeve."

"Oh come on!" Keely teased. "They're just big dogs!"

"Can he catch a Frisbee in his mouth? Then shut up!"

July 1 was a Friday. Kate spent most of her time either at Werner's or at Frank's, leaving the apartment to Donnie, Disco and Kate. On Wednesday night, Mrs. McGillicuddy invited them to dinner. Her apartment smelled cloyingly of lavender with just the faintest hint of cat piss. An old tabby watched them sedately from a doily-covered chair.

"I should have had you over ages ago!" Mrs. McGillicuddy said, serving them iced tea.

"It's all right, Mrs. McGillicuddy. We must have seemed pretty sketchy," Donnie said.

"What does that mean, dear?"

"It means shady," Keely said.

"Ma had screaming fights with that loser Ralph. I'm surprised you didn't call the police."

"I was about to," Mrs. McGillicuddy confided. "I always wondered how a smart woman like your mother got mixed up with a man like that."

"We wondered too," Donnie said.

He and Keely chewed the leather-like pot roast with enthusiasm and declared it delicious. The peach cobbler was better. Donnie promised to keep in touch after the move. Mrs. McGillicuddy was not online, did not have a cell phone and preferred to hear from those close to her via letter. She had two daughters—one in Florida and the other in Milwaukee—and four grandkids. Out came the photos.

By the time Donnie and Keely made their graceful exit, it was almost dark.

"Poor thing!" Keely declared as soon as they entered the apartment. She threw herself into his arms. "Do you think our home will smell like lavender and cat piss when we're old and gray?"

"It will smell like dogs," Donnie said. Would they even be together in a year? Donnie saw how it was with Kate and her boyfriends. But Keely was nothing like them. She was good and brave and true.

After they made love, Donnie went on Facebook. His page was filled with international accolades, fan letters from Norway and the Philippines, marriage proposals and a dozen messages. One was from Ryan.

"Dude! Coach Pagel can't believe you passed up track to engage in this shit! Heinous! Talk soon."

As he checked his in-box, he noticed the faint "other" notification for messages from people he didn't know.

He flicked it on. Come-ons. Ten messages down was the one that froze his soul.

Lord Vile: "Prepare to die motherfucker for what..."

He clicked on it.

"This message is no longer available because it was identified as abusive or marked as spam."

CHAPTER SEVENTY-EIGHT
FRENZY

WEDDING DAY! A FRENZIED KATE PACKED HER TROUSSEAU and spent numerous minutes in front of the mirror wondering about her complexion.

"Your complexion is fine, Ma!" Donnie assured her.

"This is gonna be my last wedding, swear to God."

"I know it's going to work, Ma. Frank's a good man."

"You like him, don't you, kiddo?"

"What? Are you kidding? I'm crazy about Frank! What's not to like? Didn't he restore the Weenie Wagon for me?"

Donnie had chosen the Weenie Wagon as his turntable. It had the speakers, the bass and the electronics. The caterer, Golden Horde from Elm Grove, had no connection with Werner's Meats. Everybody loved Werner's Meats, but everybody was sick to death of Werner's Meats. The menu included polenta tortillas stuffed with Dungeness crab, pickled asparagus, goat cheese brie, and toasted walnuts, cheese, mushrooms and bacon in a taco shell. Only the bacon was from Werner's.

Donnie had phoned Chief Robertson. Lester Barnes was off the grid. Disappeared. Possibly sneaked into Mexico.

Donnie and Disco showered. By noon they were ready to go. They packed the new-smelling car with their duds, planning to change at the Raindrop, stopping at a Chick-fil-A on the way. The Raindrop was easy to find with the bright orange ass of the Weenie Wagon sticking in the air. At ten feet, it towered over the other parked vehicles.

"If Disco were a dachshund, it would be perfect," Kate said.

"Dachshunds don't do discs, Ma. There'd be no Weenie Wagon."

"I know. I was just thinking—add a snout and droopy ears to that thing and there you are."

The Raindrop consisted of a B&B in an old brick farmhouse, with an enormous outdoor deck bounded on one end by a covered, open-air dance hall, which now held twenty tables and folding chairs, and on the other by a combination kitchen and recreation area. A dozen vehicles sat on the blacktopped parking lot, including a van with GOLDEN HORDE written on the sides.

Keely arrived with Chuck. She let him off the leash, and he and Disco played crouch and bark.

"What if they run off?" Donnie said.

"They won't run off. Chuck won't leave my sight. Besides, the food's here."

The ceremony would begin at four. Normally the bride wouldn't be caught within ten miles of the altar prior to the actual wedding, but Kate was her own girl Friday as well as Frank's, and was there to supervise. She waved Donnie and Keely over.

"If I start acting like one of those women on *Bridezillas*, you let me know, okay?"

"You betcha," Keely said.

Kate handed them a sheet of paper. "Here are the seating arrangements. Please set out the cards."

Keely took the paper. "We're on it!"

The guest list included several Werner's board members as well as the Van Metres and top execs from Pilgrim's Pride and Tyson.

"Wouldn't it be fun if we seated Pilgrim's Pride across from Tyson?" Donnie said.

"I know. But we won't."

They deposited gift packages of Werner's Desiccated Wieners at every seat. Keely provided tiny Batman coin purses to hold the rings and fastened them to Chuck's and Disco's collars. Chuck was a master of sit, stay and come, and Disco went where Chuck went. So that looked good.

Donnie had been programming for days. He had over five hundred songs on his new laptop, which plugged into the W2's sound system that could be detached and placed elsewhere. They had put the speakers behind a small table in the dining area, which featured a dance floor. Cully boosted himself into the cab while Donnie tested the sound system.

"Yer gonna play that Crowded House song, aren'tcha?"

"'Don't Dream It's Over'? You bet! Say, Cully. I wasn't paying attention. Did Lily and Cactus Jack finish in the top ten?"

"Oi you ain't heard? They got first in distance—247 feet. Sea-Tak promised to take it back in Washington."

Donnie looked through the W2's B-25-bomber-like windshield. Kate ran toward the wagon wearing shorts and a T-shirt, her long brunette hair in disarray. Donnie climbed down.

"Ma! What's wrong?"

"I forgot my phone. I can't believe I was so stupid! Would you be a dear and run back to the house and get it for me? I left it on the charger on the kitchen counter. Bring the charger, too."

"No prob."

Donnie thought about asking Keely to join him, but she was busy with the dogs. It would take only about fifty minutes. Plenty of time to be back for the ceremony.

Like she needed her phone.

But of course she needed her phone! How else was she going to post on FB?

He boarded the Barkmobile and booked.

CHAPTER SEVENTY-NINE
ANDRONICUS

THE APARTMENT BUILDING LOOKED FORLORN AND abandoned as Donnie pulled around to the back and parked next to Mrs. McGillicuddy's old Buick. The movers had come and taken virtually everything, leaving behind a nearly empty unit. Donnie went out on the balcony. He picked up Disco's bowls, washed them in the kitchen sink and set them down. He unplugged Kate's phone and put it and the charger in his pocket, grabbed the bowls and headed for the door, pausing one last time to look around the little apartment where so much had happened.

With any luck and the good Lord's approval, they were headed for a permanent home, a real home in a real house with a fenced-in yard. Soon he would get another dog to keep Disco company, maybe a border collie mix, something that could catch Frisbees.

He thought about saying goodbye to Mrs. McGillicuddy but nixed it. He'd stop by sometime later in the summer.

Donnie put the bowls in his car and glanced at the

barn. That's where it had all started. He walked over to gaze around the vast dusty interior, saw the cardboard box where he'd first kept Disco, the old tractor, the riding lawnmower.

A soft noise penetrated his consciousness, the scuff of a shoe on wood. He turned and saw a figure out of a nightmare, the tatted, shaved-skull bulk of what had once been human holding a Bowie knife with a ten-inch blade, backlit against the open door.

"You killed my brother," the thing growled.

Travis Barnes. Dog killer. Thug. Bully. They'd gotten the driver wrong. In that instant, Donnie forgot about the wedding, forgot Disco, Keely and the championship and realized he was in mortal danger. He took an involuntary step back.

"Now I'm gonna fuck you up," Travis rasped, coming toward him.

Instinct took over. Donnie spun and ran for the back door, slamming it open and tearing straight for the waist-high cornfield. There was no place to hide in that corn. He heard Travis' boots thumping the earth behind him as he settled into a runner's rhythm, flying across the hard-packed earth.

This can't be happening to me, not now! Not when I've achieved so much! It isn't fair! I don't deserve it!

Donnie streaked through the corn and plunged into the thin forest fronting the creek, like a deer fleeing hunters. He blasted through the trees heedless of branches whipping across his face and drawing blood.

God, don't let me trip!

Hearing the primal beast thrashing through the forest behind him, Donnie defaulted to reptile brain, no better, no smarter, no stronger than any other creature for whom life was unending terror. He came to the creek, leaped down the two-foot bank and splashed across, water to his knees. On the other side he turned around as Travis leaped into the creek. Travis wore an Affliction wife beater, revealing arms blue with tats.

Donnie fought a sudden surge of nausea, sucked it in and took off through the forest toward the farm. Beyond that was Nate's Bait, but there was nothing there. They'd razed the building and pulled up the pier, and someone had stolen the boat.

Think, Donnie! Think. You know the land better than he. What's there you can use? Weapons? Discarded truck parts? There was a pile of rusting metal in the weeds, if it hadn't been hauled away in the razing of the shack. But what chance did he have against a practiced streetfighter who outweighed him by eighty pounds?

He shoved his hand into his pocket and grabbed Kate's phone, flipped it open, tried to dial 911. No use. He was moving too fast and couldn't get his fingers on the numbers. He stumbled on a root, dropped the phone, almost went down.

Donnie saw strands of barbed wire stretching across daylight twenty feet ahead. He hurdled them with a foot to spare, and then he was pounding across the pasture toward the tree line on the other side, a hundred yards away.

"Fuck!" Travis shouted, cutting himself on the barbed wire.

Good!

Donnie's foot went down a hole. He slammed into the ground like a door shut in anger, the breath knocked out of him.

This was it. This was the end. Travis Barnes was going to gut him like a carp. He rolled over, face smeared with dirt and blood. Travis had slowed to a walk, realizing his triumph. He was twenty yards away, vulpine rictus splayed across his jaw.

"Here it comes, shitbird."

A kettledrum rhythm joined the chorus. No, not kettledrums. The bull Andronicus was bearing down on Travis like a meteor. Travis gasped, dropped the Bowie, turned and tripped on a rock as Andronicus ran over him, catching Travis' side with a hoof. Grunting and panting, Travis struggled to his feet and looked around desperately as the bull stopped and turned. Travis broke into a hobbling run, holding his sides. Andronicus watched for an instant, pawing the ground, then charged, his thundering hooves covering Travis' pathetic squeaks. Andronicus charged like a steam locomotive, forcing Travis up in the air, then gored him as he fell to the ground. As Andronicus withdrew a pink horn, Travis' abdomen pooled blood and his limbs flopped uselessly.

CHAPTER EIGHTY
VOWS

ANDRONICUS UNCEREMONIOUSLY DUMPED TRAVIS ON THE ground and grazed peacefully as if nothing had happened, taking no interest in Donnie, who began retracing his steps. He still had his own phone. He'd call it in, but he couldn't miss the wedding! Chief Robertson would understand.

But why call at all? A dead dude in Andronicus's field. Who's to say Travis hadn't trespassed by himself looking to carve his initials in its horns? Maybe he was high on meth and PCP. Donnie felt as if he were trapped in a Jason Bourne movie. He could call in from a pay phone on the way back to the Raindrop. But they'd trace the call and find it in a direct line between Hallahan's pasture and the Raindrop. It didn't take a genius to put two and two together.

Donnie backtracked toward the apartment building, and when he was in the forest on the other side of the creek, he dialed Kate so he could find her phone. He let himself back into the apartment, took a shower and put on his wedding duds, leaving off the jacket and tie. He phoned Chief Robertson, and the call went straight to voicemail.

"Chief, Donnie Waits. I think there's a dead guy in Hallahan's pasture."

He was parking his car at the Raindrop Retreat when the chief phoned him back.

"This is Chief Robertson. What do you mean there's a dead guy in Hallahan's pasture?"

"Chief, my mother's getting married in an hour. She sent me back to the apartment to get her phone. Travis Barnes was waiting for me. He chased me into Hallahan's pasture, and that bull Andronicus gored him like a shish kebab. Chief, I'll come in as soon as the wedding's over to give a statement, but if I screw up Kate's wedding, well, it won't be pretty."

Donnie heard Robertson thinking over the phone.

"All right. I'll check it out. If it's as you say, I'll come to where you're at and take a statement. Where you at?"

Donnie told him.

"All right. Sit tight. I'll be out."

Heart pounding, Donnie put the phone away, entered the brick B&B and went upstairs to the suite Kate and Frank had rented. By now there were dozens of cars in the parking lot, Frank's friends directing the parking and guests milling about the open bar.

Donnie knocked on the door. Kate's friend Kim, also a bridesmaid, opened it and gave him an appraising glance that ended in dismay.

"What happened to your face?"

"I got in a fight with a tree. Ma! I have your phone!"

Kate emerged from the bedroom in her flowing white wedding gown, face creased in concern when she saw him. "What?"

"Tree branches, Ma. You look radiant. Here's your phone."

She took the phone and tucked it in a tiny handbag. "What tree branches?"

"I was chasing a stray dog."

"You have a dog," Kate said, kissing him on the cheek. "Thank you for being a darling. How you doing?"

"I'm doing fine, Ma. It's not my wedding."

"Are the dogs ready?"

"Everyone is ready."

"Okay. See you out there."

Donnie went outside and found Keely in the dining area fitting Chuck and Disco with bow ties. The caterers had begun setting up, putting out the cold stuff first.

"Who's gonna watch the pups until we need them?" Donnie said.

"One of the caterers will." She looked around, spying a young woman in black slacks and a white shirt. "Diane. Diane, this is my boyfriend, Donnie. It's his mother who's getting married."

They shook hands. "I'm happy to watch the dogs," Diane said. "I have a corgi of my own."

The PA system crackled.

"Dearly beloved," Cully said. "Seats, people. The ceremony is about to begin."

A string quartet played Handel. The bridesmaids and groomsmen lined up on either side of an altar formed by two willow trees bent together and tied with a white ribbon. A hip pastor with a ponytail and a white turtleneck beneath his blue blazer took his place, clutching a King James Bible.

As the string quartet played, Frank walked up the aisle accompanied by his octogenarian mother; he was smiling, tanned and fit. He turned and faced the people, wearing a blue suit, a white shirt and a crimson tie decorated with the Disco logo.

The string quartet played "The Bridal March," and a glowing Kate glided toward him accompanied by Donnie, Keely and Kim. They handed her off and took their places on either side.

The quartet stopped.

"Folks," the pastor said, "I'm Pastor Floyd of Mount Bethel Lutheran, and we are gathered here today to witness the marriage of Frank Werner and Kate Waits. I've known Frank for twenty years, and all I can say is, well, it's about time! A lot of people don't know this about Frank, because of his incredible modesty, but he has donated over a million dollars since we first met to our orphans' fund, which seeks to place kids with foster families. He attends their board meetings, insisting that at least 70 percent of every dollar they collect actually goes toward the upkeep and placement of kids.

"Last year when tornadoes devastated the town of Whitby, Oklahoma, Frank loaded a truck with food and drove it down himself. I don't know Kate as well, but I've seen her handiwork in young Donnie and I think we can all agree Kate's got it going on."

Applause and laughter.

"Will the bride and groom face each other? Frank?"

"Dearest Kate," Frank said. "I never thought I would love again until you came along with your laughter and seventeen essential life hacks. Did you know, for example, you can use a staple remover to open up those spiral key rings? I love the way you keep track of things without becoming compulsive, and I love that you've raised an impressive young man all by yourself. And I love that you make me a better person. I promise to love you forever, laugh at your jokes, eat your cooking, take you to exotic locales whenever possible and support that dog in the style to which she has become accustomed."

Pastor Floyd nodded at Kate. "Kate?"

"Dearest Frank: All my life I've had the worst taste in men. Until I met you. To say you turned my life around would be an understatement. I didn't know someone could be so kind, caring, understanding and sexy at the same time. And I love that you love my boy and his dog. I promise to love you forever, go see those terrible movies you like and make sure there is a mate for every sock."

Pastor Floyd said, "You may exchange the rings."

Kate turned and looked expectantly at Donnie, who glanced toward the dining area.

Shouts and screams shattered the stillness.

CHAPTER EIGHTY-ONE
DOGS' BUFFET

WITH A BOLUS OF DREAD IN HIS GUT, DONNIE RAN toward the dining room, leaped the three steps and stopped cold. Disco was on the buffet, her snout buried in the mushroom cups, while Chuck, on his hind legs, was wolfing down an entire platter of cold cuts.

"CHUCK! DISCO!" Donnie bellowed. Where was Diane?

Diane abruptly appeared out of the kitchen in a state of dismay, both hands to her mouth. "Oh I'm so sorry! I fastened their leashes to that pillar!"

Donnie immediately saw the problem. They'd pulled the pillar loose at the bottom and made for the food. Donnie quickly grabbed their leashes and marched them to the altar, the rings still attached to their collars.

"What was it?" Kate said.

"It's nothing," Donnie said. "Proceed."

Kate and Frank stooped to retrieve the rings. As Frank slipped the wedding ring onto Kate's finger, Chuck cut an enormous fart. As Kate put the ring on

Frank, Disco let loose with her air raid siren. Donnie clamped her mouth shut.

"I now pronounce you man and wife," Pastor Floyd said. "You may kiss the bride."

As the string quartet played "The Wedding March," Donnie headed for the dining area to commence duties. The caterers were in a frenzy cleaning up after the dogs. Soon guests started to file past the buffet table while Donnie played cool jazz to eat by—Brubeck, Wes Montgomery, Jimmy Smith and some reggae.

Keely brought him a plate of food.

"Where are the dogs?" he said.

"They're in that fenced-in area with the gazebo."

A half hour later, Chief Robertson arrived at the back of the dining hall. Donnie left the music on auto and went to meet him. They walked to the parking lot and leaned against the chief's car.

"We identified the body by his driver's license. It's Travis Barnes. Mr. Hallahan is devastated, says he's going to sell that bull. You want to tell me what happened?"

Donnie walked him through it. "So you were never able to identify the body in the Camaro?"

"Burned beyond recognition. Still working on the dental records. But pretty sure that accounts for the Barnes brothers. We're trying to locate next of kin."

It was as if the Barnes brothers had been deposited fully grown by aliens.

"You might ask Ryan Cutler. He was pretty close to them both."

"Like to notify the parents if I could," the chief said, taking notes. "Like you to come by the station Monday and give a statement. Can you do that?"

"Sure thing, Chief. And I really appreciate your not dragging me out of here."

"What the hell, Donnie." The Chief winked. "Your mother only gets married two or three times."

"Hopefully, this is the last."

"Well, you go on back to your party and have a good time. The whole force is rooting for you in the nationals."

"Thank you, sir. Help yourself to the buffet."

The chief cast an eye toward the dining area. "Hmmm."

Donnie went by the gazebo. The dogs were sleeping it off. He returned to his post by the speakers and sat down next to Keely. Frank clinked his glass with a spoon.

"Here come the toasts."

The toasts were long and fulsome as waitstaff whisked away dishes. Werner's vice president, Herbert Woytciwicz, paused in his epic encomium. "Think of it, my friends! Truffle-infused luncheon meat! INFUSED! Think of it!"

Donnie put a finger beneath his right eye and drew the membrane down.

"Bor-ing," Keely said.

"I must act," Donnie said.

Woytciwicz, who was just getting warmed up, paused to sip water and Donnie plunged, cuing the Bee Gees' "Night Fever" and grinning at Keely.

"Let's see them stay seated through this."

Chairs scraped. Keely got up and grabbed Donnie's hand. "Come on!"

The dance floor was soon covered with bodies doing the Frug, the Hullabaloo, the Peppermint Twist and the

Texas two-step. Frank and Kate astonished everyone with their jitterbug moves.

At eight thirty, Donnie and Keely bugged out, taking the dogs with them.

"Come on Eileen" began to play.

CHAPTER EIGHTY-TWO
QUINT

THEY ARRIVED IN THE DISTRICT OF COLUMBIA AT 5:00 p.m. on Friday, July 3, traveling non-stop from Wisconsin in a convoy led by the Weenie Wagon and including a tour bus previously used by Cheap Trick. Donnie, Keely and Cully took turns driving the W2 and sleeping in the bus, while Frank, Kate and Monte Moore spelled one another on the bus.

They checked into the Howard Johnson's on New York Avenue NE, because they took pets. The W2 proved to be an attractive nuisance in the hotel parking lot. A busload of Japanese tourists made an impromptu stop as the passengers all posed in front of the giant hot dog. As usual, the nation's capital was crawling with bureaucrats, lobbyists, tourists and military. There was a rumor that the vice president would kick off the ceremonies Saturday morning and that the Beach Boys would sing. Cully, Monte and Donnie all shared a room, as did Kate and Frank. Only Keely had her own room.

Donnie wondered how he was going to work this.

No way.

Not that he couldn't trust Cully and Monte, but why throw it in his mother's face? He'd just have to control himself until they got back.

Following breakfast in the HoJo coffee shop, they drove to the National Mall, where a space had been reserved for them on the near end of the distance course set up there. Frank had pulled in every favor to get permission from the Parks Department for that parking space. A separate Werner's truck sold hot dogs and merchandise on Seventh Street.

Donnie looked at the towering spire of the Washington Monument and couldn't believe he was actually here. It had all happened so fast! One minute he had been a pariah and the next he was about to perform on the national stage. It was here that Martin Luther King Jr. made his "I Have a Dream" speech. It was here they filmed *Forrest Gump*.

Okay, so it wasn't the Super Bowl. It was his Super Bowl.

Hundreds of participants worked with their hounds while thousands of spectators lined the perimeter. A steady stream of tourists trickled by the Weenie Wagon, posing and taking pictures. A group of Japanese businessmen in suits and ties colonized a nearby picnic table and handled each package of Werner's deli meats with amazement.

It was a hundred yards to the raised dais from which announcers called participants to the line. Donnie hunkered with Disco near the dais underneath a Werner's pop-up tent decorated with the Werner's logo and the flying Disco. The PA system squawked as the organizers took the stage. Donnie had fastened a red bandanna around Disco's neck.

"Good morning, Sky Dogz!" a man boomed. "I'm Paul

Pelletier, president of the International Sky Dogz Association, and I would like to welcome you to the National Mall on this glorious anniversary of our beloved republic!"

Applause, cheers, barking.

"We have a lot of teams signed up, and we will begin at nine. Now please join me in welcoming the vice president of the United States!"

The veep, an éminence grise, took the mic, wearing a gray suit with a red, white and blue tie. "Welcome, my friends, welcome to the National Mall on this glorious celebration of our nation's founding. We are a nation of immigrants! We are a nation of mongrels! As I gaze out at you noble people and your pets, I see many mongrels. To the phrase 'As American as motherhood and apple pie' I would add, 'American as a Labradoodle! As American as a Heinz 57 hound! As American as a cross between a blue heeler and a ward heeler!' America loves dogs!"

Wild applause, hooting and barking.

"There will be no losers here today," the veep continued. "Simply by entering, each and every one of you is a winner! I tried to convince Sky Dogz to stop awarding trophies, but they wouldn't listen to me. I said it's not fair to all those who tried their best and did not win! And do you know what they said to me? Do you know what they had the audacity to say? Competition is good! Competition brings out the best in people and dogs! And you know what? I couldn't disagree.

"I look forward to a tournament of epic proportions!"

The veep left the stage to much applause as Pelletier reappeared. "Please welcome international singing sensation Miss Carrie Underwood, who will sing the National Anthem."

Carrie Underwood wore a red, white and blue pleated skirt, white cowboy shirt and white cowboy hat. She sang a capella, a stupendous version punctuated by the occasional howl.

Pelletier called the first team to the line for the freestyle. As a woman and her border collie took their places to the Kinks' "Sunny Afternoon," Donnie noticed a fracas at the registration table next to the stage.

"Watch Disco," he said, and headed over.

A man with a thatch of wild hair was trying to register a five-legged dog. Donnie stared in amazement at the odd creature, dewclaws intact. It was sleek and gray with black highlights on its muzzle and paws. An extra rear leg descended from its left hip like double wheels on the back of a Ford F-350.

"Look," the man said, leaning over the table, "do you want me to get HHS involved? This is just discrimination against the handicapped."

"Sir," said the official, a middle-aged woman with long brown hair wearing a Sky Dogz T-shirt, "Health and *Human* Services is not concerned with your dog."

"He's my therapy dog. This is discrimination."

"Sir," the woman said without batting an eye, "the fifth leg is not a handicap; it is an unfair advantage. We have no category for mutant dogs."

"Oh, what's the worst that can happen?" Donnie said. "Let 'em compete!" He turned toward the man and stuck out his hand. "Donnie Waits."

"Euglecia Gamburyan, and this is Quint."

Paul Pelletier had observed the exchange. "Sign 'em up."

The woman dutifully registered Euglecia and Quint. "You'll be number 125 in the freestyle."

Donnie and Disco were 124.

CHAPTER EIGHTY-THREE
UPLIFT

SEA-TAK AND ZERO WERE NUMBER NINETY-NINE. THEY began with bouncing wheels, Sea-Tak hurling the disc overhand so that it hit the ground like a wheel and bounced, Zero performing a sideways aerial somersault and seizing the disc upside down at apogee. They got a 9.9.

Donnie's heart sank.

Keely put an arm around him. "Don't worry about it! You're here. That's the important thing."

Finally, it was their turn. They took their place at the line. As Donnie cued the music, several hundred spectators added syncopated hand claps to "Atomic Dog."

"BOW WOW WOW, YIPPIE YO YIPPIE YAY, BOW WOW, YIPPIE YO YIPPIE YAY," the crowd chanted.

Donnie put down his garbage can lid, skipping discs into the sky for Disco to seize while performing aerial somersaults. On the first disc, Disco ran, screaming her rebel yell, composed of high-pitched ululation.

They finished with a 9.8.

Gamburyan and Quint were the last team of the

morning. "Back in the USSR" began to play as Gamburyan led Quint through a series of vaults and hoops, Quint's fifth leg quivering oddly, not touching the ground. As the Beatles sang, "Well the Ukraine girls really knock me out," a squirrel darted past the dais. Perhaps it was insane. Perhaps it was on drugs. Quint took one look and was gone, leaving behind a series of dwindling yelps.

As the freestyle ended beneath a blazing sun, Donnie made the long walk to the air-conditioned Weenie Wagon at the end of the course to consume Werner's hot dogs.

As Pelletier announced the distance competition, a strong breeze swept over the mall, rustling the tree leaves and sweeping paper plates and napkins along. People weighed things down with thermoses and cameras. The shifting wind added an unknown dimension to the distance event, as thermals could lift or plunge a disc.

Teams retained their positions from freestyle, which meant Donnie and Disco would take the field mid-afternoon. Each team had one disc and ninety seconds to make as many throws as they pleased. Each team was entitled to two practice throws with or without the dog. As Donnie had been working on distance all morning on the sidelines, he felt fairly confident of his technique but did not expect to throw more than forty yards.

Sea-Tak and Zero toed the mark at three fifteen. Their first throw caught a thermal and swooped up, Zero in hot pursuit, *Fast & Furious* in fur. Zero leaped as another thermal cut across his snout and the disc abruptly dived, Zero's jaws clicking on air.

The next throw was for 185 feet, good for five points. Zero missed the third throw. The afternoon trudged on.

And on. Donnie thought he'd go insane waiting. Disco napped.

Lily and Cactus Jack scored an aerial 197. Six points. Their combined score on three throws was sixteen.

Keely shook Donnie's arm. He'd dozed off. "What?"

"You're up!"

Dazed, Donnie got to his feet. He looked over to the judges. "Do I have time for two practice throws?"

"Go ahead," Pelletier said.

Donnie took his place at the line and spun the disc while Keely held on to Disco. The disc shanked to the right and bonked on its edge sixty feet away. His second throw was better. It sailed eighty feet. If he threw three short throws and Disco caught them all, that would be six points. That wasn't going to cut it. If Disco caught three throws of over forty-five feet with all four paws off the ground, that would be twelve points. If she caught a throw over a hundred twenty feet with all four paws off the ground, that would be six.

No way was Donnie going to score three throws beyond a hundred twenty.

He glanced at Disco. The little dog could barely contain herself, tail swinging like a metronome. Donnie flipped the disc and said, "Go!" The disc soared, the dog ran. She ran so fast, she caught up with the disc and snagged it out of the air at twenty-five feet. That was good for three.

Disco was back, tail wagging, the disc in her jaws.

"Why must I be like that? Why must I chase the cat?" several hundred people sang.

A sudden breeze caught Donnie's second throw and tilted it into the ground before Disco could reach it.

One throw left.

Please, God, give me a good throw!

I'm sorry, God, I know you have better things to do.

Donnie wrapped up and sought stillness within himself, letting his lizard brain take over. He released the disc as another rogue wind blew across the mall, lifting the Frisbee by increments, higher, higher. Disco was a furry black bullet tearing down the lawn toward the flying saucer, which had started to angle down when another breeze lifted it and it spun on, further, further, black dog in hot pursuit. The disc skimmed the roof of the Weenie Wagon and followed the tail at an ascending angle as Disco leaped onto the Japanese gentlemen's picnic table, scattering dishes and a bottle of 1947 Cheval Blanc. They were over 285 feet from the line.

From there, Disco jumped again and landed on the roof of the Weenie Wagon and scrambled up toward the tail, finding traction where there was none. The little dog leaped off the uppermost part of the Weenie Wagon into history.

From the Author of the Runaway Train series comes Miles in Time, a Thrilling Time-Travel Mystery for Young Detectives.

Solve the mystery, save the future...

14-year-old Miles Hardy spends most of his time as an amateur Sherlock Holmes and running his detective agency with his good friend and loyal assistant, Kevin. However, in sleepy Frontier, Iowa, it's been hard to snag a case bigger than finding some old lady's missing cat—until Miles' genius older brother, Simon the inventor, winds up dead.

Using his knack for uncovering hidden truths, Miles stumbles upon a secret lab where his late brother, Simon, created a groundbreaking time machine. Among the discoveries is a chilling video Simon recorded before his death, revealing his fear of being followed and a dire warning: if anything happens to him, Miles must use the time machine to uncover who is after the invention and stop them. The stakes couldn't be higher—if the device falls into the wrong hands, the future itself could be at risk.

From suspicious classmates to shadowy corporations, no one is above suspicion as Miles races against time to solve his first real case. But one wrong move could change everything—and running into his past self is strictly off-limits.

Can Miles crack the case, save his brother's life, and protect the future? Or will time run out before he uncovers the truth?

AVAILABLE NOW

ABOUT THE AUTHOR

Mike Baron has been creating worlds that explode off the page for decades. He's the mind behind *Nexus* (with artist Steve Rude)—a cosmic avenger story set 500 years in the future—and *Badger*, a series about a martial arts master with multiple personalities, one of whom happens to be a costumed crime fighter. His work has earned him two Eisner Awards (the comic world's version of an Oscar!) and an Inkpot Award for outstanding achievement in writing.

Mike has written everything from *The Punisher* and *The Flash* to *Star Wars* and *Deadman*, plus a library of novels that mix action, dark humor, and supernatural twists.

When he's not writing, Mike's probably out on his motorcycle or hanging out with his dogs in Colorado. You can find him sharing stories and chaos online at *@BloodyRedBaron* on X, *The Comics and Novels of Mike Baron* on Facebook, and mikebaron.substack.com.